To Bill

INCIDENT AT CAT ISLAND

by
Thomas L. Hudgin

Thomas L Hudgin

Hickory Tales Publishing, LLC
Bowling Green, KY

First Edition

Hickory Tales Publishing LLC
841 Newberry St.
Bowling Green, Ky. 42103
www.hickorytales.com

ISBN-10:   0-9709104-9-5
ISBN-13:   978-0-9709104-9-3

Library of Congress Cataloging-in-Publication Data

Hudgin, Thomas L., 1939-
   Incident at Cat Island / by Thomas L. Hudgin.— 1st ed.
      p. cm.
   ISBN 0-9709104-9-5
   1. Cat Island (Bahamas)—Fiction. 2. Counterfeiters—Fiction. I.
Title.
   PS3608.U3256I53 2006
   813'.6—dc22

                                          2006004899

Dedication

This book is dedicated to my wife, Barbara, and my son, Chris, who have flown with me for many years and have given me strength to make this book possible.

Incident at Cat Island

Flight Plan

NORTH CAROLINA

* Wrightsville Beach

SOUTH CAROLINA

* Atlanta

GEORGIA

* Jacksonville

FLORIDA

GRAND BAHAMA

ABACOS

ELEUTHERA

West Palm *

Miami *

BIMINI

Nassau

EXUMAS

CAT ISLAND

SAN SALVADORE

LONG ISLAND

ANDROS

Georgetown ↑

ACKLINS

|.....|.....|

0 25 50 miles

Tom Hudgin

PREFACE

Born with a spirit of adventure in my blood, I've always dreamed of sailing the high seas and exploring tropical islands. People would often tell me that hundreds of books have been written about such dreams ... some of them were mere fairy tales. But ever since I could remember, I'd sit on the beach along the coast of the Carolinas searching the southern horizon for that illusive tropical paradise.

When I completed my college education with degrees in chemistry and mathematics, I received an officer's commission in the U.S. Navy and sailed the Pacific Ocean on tankers and repair ships. Little did I know that the valuable experience gained in deep-water navigation and seamanship skills would be put to use again years later.

Continuing to pursue that spirit of adventure following my tour of active duty, I earned my wings as an instrument-rated, private pilot and bought my first airplane. Every opportunity I had, I'd fly to the tropical islands of the Bahamas and often rent a sailboat to explore the secluded, coconut-lined, white, sandy beaches of the central islands. Abaco, Eleuthera, Exumas, Long Island and Cat Island were some of the most exciting and frequented paradises visited.

But my tenacious passion for the sea continued when I retired from the business world. I purchased a thirty-foot sloop and sailed it up and down the East Coast of the United States and eventually to the islands of the Bahamas for a three month cruise. Itching to do more serious, blue water cruising, I signed on with two others to sail a thirty-six-foot ketch from the islands of the Caribbean to Europe. Despite the fact that this voyage nearly ended in disaster, I still possess a keen fascination for exploring quiet coves, lined with coconut palms along white, sandy beaches in the tropics.

Although this novel is fiction, the places mentioned and flying experiences are real ... the characters and events are not. I have a high degree of respect and love for the folks of the Bahamas. They're proud, honest people and truly live in a paradise unequaled anywhere in the world. This story is not intended to poke fun at their lifestyle or harm anyone whomsoever but is simply a story that could occur anywhere at anytime. Having been to and explored tranquil Cat Island, it seemed to be an intriguing setting for this tale.   Thomas Hudgin

Contents

CHAPTER		PAGE

Tom Hudgin

CHAPTER 1

Flotsam

Tom meandered barefoot along the beach in the twilight hours of a mid-September evening, his toes burrowed deep into the warm sand. The sudden shift and sensation of movement beneath his foot sent his pulse flying. He dropped to his knees and quickly dug through several inches of sand beneath the impression his toe had made until he found the tiny treasure he was looking for. The newly-hatched, loggerhead turtle was ready to emerge from its nest. *Where there's one, there's bound to be more*, Tom thought, and assuming he'd happened upon a nest with other turtles struggling beneath the sand, he carefully dug deeper but found nothing more than a few broken eggshells.

He gently placed the fledgling on the beach and pointed it toward the surf so that it could build up enough stamina to survive its first few moments and beyond in the sea. When the loggerhead was safely in the water, Tom proceeded toward the first row of sand dunes and sat down using the dunes as protection from the wind. From here he could watch for other turtle hatchlings. His mind began to wander as he listened to the symphonic sounds of the whistling wind and the proper pounding of the surf. Before long the soft light of a three-quarters moon flooded the beach and his thoughts gravitated away from the turtles, the surf, the breeze … far away to the most exciting adventure he had ever experienced.

It was late Spring. A few hundred feet ahead something dark

was tumbling in the surf. Born with an insatiable curiosity, Tom hurried along the water's edge to get a closer look before the pounding waves sucked it back out to sea. His senses immediately felt the cool salt water and sea foam flow across his feet as he waded through the ebbing water ... and toward the next mounting wave. He was not alone in his pursuit toward the object, however. A gull with different interest swooped down and plucked at it as it rolled in the surf. Seemingly convinced it was not edible, it flapped its wings, ascended a few feet above the waves and continued its search for food southward.

Now just twenty feet away, Tom could see what appeared to be a three-foot, wooden plank rapidly being pulled into the curl of an approaching, six-foot wall of water. Quickly, he reached under the curl of the wave, grabbed the board, turned his back and started running in waist deep water as fast as he could toward the beach. He managed to cover only three steps when SMACK! A breaker crashed across the back of his head, knocked him flat on his stomach and pushed him forward through the frothing foam like a surfboard. Before the next big wave approached and with the board tightly gripped in his hand, he regained his equilibrium, planted his feet firmly on the sandy bottom and made a second run for dry land. Finally out of reach of the surf, he stood still for a moment to catch his breath. Dripping wet, he felt his senses tune to the rhythmic, fizzing sounds of sea foam as it pushed toward the dunes, the squawking of the sea gulls overhead, the distinctive smell of the salt marshes nearby and the rustling of the sea oats on the dunes as the breeze intertwined its way past each blade.

He held the barnacle-encrusted board tightly and walked toward his beach house one block away. He'd add it to his collection of driftwood in the rock garden in the backyard.

As he hiked along the sandy path among the dunes and the waving sea oats, the origin of the board began to haunt him. *Where'd you come from, huh? What were you a part of? A pirate ship?* Tom smiled wryly at his own foolishness. *How far did you come to land on that little piece of beach? And what story would you tell if your could talk?* He tapped one hand against the soft, wet wood, then shook the fanciful thoughts out of his head as reality came rushing back. *Nah, you're just a piece of flotsam. Driftwood, like all the rest. Nothing more, nothing less.*

Early May brings 90-degree temperatures and scorching hot sands at Wrightsville Beach along the southeastern North Carolina coast, especially the soft, loose sand around the dunes. Today was typical. Even the onshore wind blowing across the 75-degree water had no discernible cooling effect on the sand. When Tom felt the burn on the bottom of his feet, he hopped like a frog in a hot iron skillet. He frantically rushed to the shade of a scrub oak tree nearby and quickly shoved his feet deep into the depths of the cooler sand. It worked.

While the temperature in his feet cooled from near frying point to a tolerable state, he looked at the board again. He noticed that the ends of the board were splintered, as if someone or something had violently ripped it from its source. An orderly pattern of worn indentations appeared on the surface … a hint that something might have been carved in the wood. But the erosive effects of the sun, salt water, marine life and sand had all but obliterated any letters or figures. He couldn't decipher it. The board was rotten.

By the time Tom reached his beach house, his mind was still fixed on the origin of the board. Maybe it was the heat, the sun's glare … any normal person would have dumped this piece of debris in the trash and been done with it. However. his genuine interest in flotsam floating in the sea had been sparked years ago when he had found a bottle rolling in the shallow surf at precisely the same place on the beach. The fact that the bottle was sealed had heightened his interest enough to pick it up and explore what might be inside. Removing the seal and using a stick to pull out the contents, he'd found a note.

To my dearest love, Marie:

I hope this note finds you soon. Even though you left only a few weeks ago, it seems like you've been gone many months. I have cried so much that there are no more tears left, but you are still in

Incident at Cat Island

my heart every day. All of our friends on the island have wished you were back again without the leukemia that took your precious life. Someday, perhaps I'll discover a reason why it had to be you and not someone else, but I know you wanted me to carry on my life and do the best I can raising our son, Stephen, on my own. I have visions of you in my mind constantly, and I can't help feeling that you may still be out there somewhere—maybe at sea, maybe far away in some strange land; maybe you'll see my note. Stephen misses you and asks about you every day. At age six, he tries to understand, but he often walks around in silence hoping he will suddenly find you around the next palm tree or rock. I promise to take care of Stephen and guide him to a successful career. I will love you always and hope you are better now that the horrible disease has finally stopped and left you in peace. I wish you well... and thanks for being my caring wife.

> *Your loving husband always,*
> *Roberto*
> *Deadman's Cay*

Tom had frozen as he'd read it a second time. He'd had trouble catching his breath and swallowed hard to hold back tears. The note triggered a mixture of emotional memories of Sandra, his own wife, whom he had lost in an automobile accident just over one year prior. He could relate to the tragedy and distress that Roberto was going through and the false hope that Marie was still out there somewhere. The discovery of the bottle at the beach haunted his mind for several days until he decided he had to find Roberto. He had to communicate with him somehow. Tom had grabbed a note pad from his desk, crawled into a soft chair on his front porch, stared out to sea briefly and had begun writing.

Dear Roberto,

A most wonderful thing happened to me a few days ago. I found your note in the bottle that you sent to Marie. Perhaps your *wife read it and put it back into the sea for me to find. Who knows why I was the lucky one, but I wanted to write to you. My name is Tom Hannaford, and I stumbled across your note in the surf at Wrightsville Beach a couple of days ago. The reason I think this is so important is because I lost my wife, too, in an automobile accident one year ago. I feel the same as you do. Every day, something reminds me of Sandra, and I relive our wonderful times together. So we have some things in common. I am enclosing some pictures of myself, the beach where I found your note, my house and other things in which I am involved. We were never lucky enough to have our own children, but I want to learn all about your son, Stephen, and how he is coping with the situatio*n.

Tom continued his note to Roberto explaining what he did for a living and promising that they would meet someday. He addressed the letter to Roberto at Deadman's Cay, Long Island, Bahamas, in hopes that someone there would see to it that Roberto received it. A few weeks later Roberto Role wrote back to Tom, and they became fast friends as pen pals.

Because of the experience with the note in the bottle and other objects drifting thousands of miles at sea, Tom felt compelled to try to unravel the mystery of the driftwood. His unanswered questions would not go away. Sometimes he found himself in a state of mind where, the tougher the problem, the more he'd be driven to find a solution. He sat down on the steps of his front porch and meticulously removed the pieces of barnacle shells and other debris one by one with a pocketknife until faint signs of letters engraved in the wood began to appear. Hours passed as he continued to pick away the crustaceans. Finally, he could barely make out something … something that didn't make sense:

NK—BARRINGTON PLA

Since the right edge of the board was broken off rather than cut with a saw, he couldn't tell what letters or information followed "PLA," if anything.... Inspecting the left side of the plank with a

11

magnifying glass, however, he observed that the left edge, though splintered. appeared to be a straight cut very close to the letters "NK." Perhaps this was the left edge of the original board. If there had been something engraved between the letter "N" and the end, most likely only one letter would fit. Being extraordinarily patient and persistent, he spotted a groove cut as a vertical line across each of the splinters on the left edge—a hint of the letter "I." Maybe the first word was "INK." But still the right side gave him no clues as to the meaning of "PLA." This was like a final exam. It became a challenge for him. He had to know more.

The following morning he drove to the university library in Wilmington to seek any known information about "BARRINGTON PLA...." First, he conducted a name search on the computer, which yielded about 2000 references containing the name Barrington. Then he tried "Barrington Pla ..." and left the spelling of the second word or group of letters open for the computer to fill in whatever would come forth. The choices were reduced to 22. However, Barrington Place and Barrington Plantation seemed most intriguing. He knew this was a shot in the dark due to the extremely limited resources the library had available on such subjects, but the sense of mystery drove him on. Even if the computer did identify something concrete, there was a high degree of probability that other information existed elsewhere that might have a more direct bearing on this mystery. And that information most likely would not be at this university. How frustrating! How would he ever know if the information found at this library would show any relevance to the piece of driftwood? He didn't dare discuss his quest with anyone for fear of being accused of being ready for a padded cell. He kept digging in silence.

According to the sparse database, Barrington Place was the name of an inn located in central England. But the second reference seemed more fascinating. It said that Barrington Plantation was an old cotton plantation on Cat Island, one of the out islands in the central Bahamas. A footnote in the text referenced another book on the history of the Bahamas for more information, and he searched the library's listings to see if that historical reference was available.

It was not, but after making a call to the city library, he discovered a copy of the book was there.

Mentally, he pushed every car in front of him as he drove impatiently across town to the city library. He sat down in front of the computer that listed the titles and authors of the books on the shelves and searched for the book's identification number. Quickly finding the reference for the book, he nearly twisted his ankle by rushing to the stacks of shelves on the second floor. Narrowing his search down to one aisle, his eyes raced through the numbers imprinted on the book spines until at last, there it was. He yanked the book off the shelf with such forceful enthusiasm that he almost tore loose the back binding of the book. Turning immediately to the index in the back, he scanned for *Barrington Plantation*, and found it listed on Pages 79-80. His pulse began to rise in anticipation of what he might find, and his hands began shaking. Starting on page 79, the passage read:

In 1783, Lieutenant John Wilson, an emissary for Sir Guy Carleton, found that there were cotton trees growing everywhere on Cat and Exuma Islands in the Bahamas. And even though many of the trees had been neglected, they flourished and yielded great amounts of cotton every year. Cotton had become white gold in the late 1700's, and cotton plantations sprang up throughout the islands. By 1800, however, the chenille worm took its toll on the cotton plants, and the plantations died a slow death, never to recover again. One of the larger and more successful operations during this brief period was Barrington Plantation on Cat Island, but it, too, couldn't survive the destructive forces of the insect and other disastrous economic influences outside of the islands. Another factor to its doomed failure was the growing prosperity of the cotton industry in the United States. The plantation was abandoned in 1802. The ruins lie on the south side of the island near Cutlass Bay.

Tom discovered that Cat Island is forty-eight miles long and approximately four miles wide. It has the highest elevation of all of the Bahamian Islands, 204 feet, but is sparsely settled. By shear coincidence, years ago he had piloted his small, single engine plane from North Carolina to the Cays of Abaco, Exuma and Long Island and chartered sailboats to explore reefs and remote lagoons. Cat Island was never one of his destinations, because he knew the island was remote and the airstrips were few and hazardous. In fact, most airfields on the island were abandoned.

In Tom's wildest imagination, he could picture this weather-beaten, sun-scorched, water-soaked plank being carried by the mid Atlantic-Caribbean currents and trade winds from Barrington Plantation on Cat Island past the northern Bahamas to the coast of Florida. Then the Gulf Stream could have moved it northward along the coast of Florida, Georgia, and South Carolina to the point of its discovery in the surf at Wrightsville Beach. *This all seems plausible enough,* he rationalized ... *but, not realistic. Yet, no one could say with certainty that it would be absolutely impossible. Improbable? Certainly.* The author stated the old cotton plantation had been abandoned since 1802.

Shaking himself from his reverie, he realized that it would be impossible for the board to survive two hundred years at sea. It couldn't have survived on land either—exposed to wind, searing tropical heat, destructive salt water, marine and land creatures and monsoon rains since the early 1800's, when the plantation had been functioning. The board had to come from somewhere else. If the board did endure a long journey from somewhere, it had to be a recent one. Perhaps the board had been buried on an island and was suddenly dislodged and set adrift not long ago during a drenching rain associated with the hurricanes that swept through the islands. *Stupid thoughts! Not a chance. Insects and moisture would have eaten it to oblivion in a short period of time.* Then he rationalized that the board could have possibly come from a crate that fell off a modern ship passing in the night, maybe just off shore from Wrightsville Beach, or drifted from a foreign shore on the eastern side of the Atlantic.

He just couldn't take his mind off it. "PLA ... " could also be placard, planetarium, planography, plant, plateau, plaza, or it could be a company that makes plate glass, plastic, plasterboard, plating, platforms. The possibilities were endless ... and impossible. The word, "INK," didn't make sense and neither did "BARRINGTON." In fact, none of it made sense.

Admittedly he was weaving thin threads of imagination, but Barrington just had to refer to Barrington Plantation as he continued to dream. That old cotton manor lying in ruins on the south end of Cat Island seemed so far away in time and distance. Maybe he was subconsciously searching for an excuse to explore the islands once more and was blocking out any intelligent reasoning. The lure of snorkeling in the warm, clear waters and basking in the sun on a beach lined with coconut palms in the out islands of the Bahamas was tempting him once again ... and most importantly here was a chance to meet Roberto for the first time. Perhaps this was the real drive behind his obsession with the board.

On his drive home from Wilmington, his thoughts turned to planning a flying vacation to the Bahamas in his single engine, four-seater plane, so the following day he called Chris Holland, a friend and flying partner and asked him to come to his house to talk about something important. If he were to mention to Chris that he wanted his opinion on a piece of driftwood he found, Chris would have immediately responded with "You're wacky!" and hung up. In one of Chris' weaker moments, however, Tom managed to persuade Chris to come over without revealing the reason.

Chris was in his early 30's, single and a seasoned sailor. He worked for Abernathy Tool Manufacturing as Inventory Control Manager. They had met at the University of North Carolina at Wilmington when they were sophomores twelve years ago and had remained friends ever since. They had common interests—flying, sailing and a high spirit for adventure, to name a few. Chris studied business while in school. Whereas, Tom pursued a degree in chemistry and landed a job as Regulatory Affairs Manager for Carter Pharmaceuticals in town.

Tom and Chris had some differences. Chris was a tinkerer and was very methodical doing problem solving and dealing with mechanical issues. But he had some faults. Perhaps mechanical skills would be stretching it a bit. Some knew him as a buffet of dangers. Chris was more of a master jury-rigger than a skilled mechanic. Chris' car was a classic example. Tom could always tell when Chris arrived in the neighborhood by the distinctive rumbling, snorting, belching sounds of his rattletrap vehicle. It would be a discredit to the automobile industry to call it a car. Holes in the muffler had been patched with wire and metal from vegetable cans. The left front headlight was held in place inside the fender, not by the normal nuts, bolts and brackets, but by three wooden wedges jammed between the light assembly and the rusted fender body. The light brackets and bolts had rusted off long ago. There was a hole in the floorboard behind the front seat where he had thrust his foot through the rusted body. He had covered the hole inside with a piece of carpeting. The body paint was bubbling and peeling from bumper to bumper. To his credit, Chris made no claim that his car was a thing of beauty. It did get him where he wanted to go ... most of the time. Chris danced a fine line between being a public nuisance with his car and a genius at making things work.

Tom, instead, loved to deal with complex challenges. His job with Carter Pharmaceuticals dealt with strategic planning and motivating fellow employees to put forth their best efforts in their specific job assignments. But more than anything, Tom enjoyed pursuing his own extraordinary, free-time adventures. His work involved travel, and he loved exploring new places and learning how others lived in different parts of the world. He enjoyed sharing these adventures with Chris, but sometimes he questioned Chris' judgment about things.

A week ago Tom had asked Chris to help him out with a computer problem. After twenty minutes of fiddling around with Tom's computer, he announced, "Aha, I found your problem. There is a faulty connection between the seat and the keyboard."

"Okay. In other words, the problem is me, right?" Tom said.

"You got it," Chris answered. "Actually, what you do have here is a computer virus, and I just removed it for you, so your computer should be fine now. If you had run the anti-virus program, you could've fixed it yourself."

Chris was quite clever and innovative in keeping not only

computers running but also whatever was at hand. But at other times, he did things as if his head were filled with sawdust. Tom remembered when they were riding in Chris' car recently, they had heard a loud pop. The car suddenly felt like they were bumping across railroad ties. Chris pulled over to the side of the road and stopped. When they got out, they discovered the right rear tire was flat. Chris scratched his head and said, "Well, thank goodness it's only flat on one side."

"What? When a tire is flat, it's flat … all around," Tom said in disbelief. "I'll pretend you didn't say that."

"So 'tis, so 'tis," Chris acknowledged. He replaced the "one-sided" flat tire with the spare tire. When they got back into the car, Chris said, "Hey, this reminds me when we were taking final exams at UNCW at the end of spring semester in our junior year. It was one of life's lessons drilled into our heads the hard way. We decided to party instead of studying. Next day was our biggest exam in physics. We showed up on the day of the exam and told our professor that our car broke down the night before due to a very flat tire, and we needed a bit more time to study. The professor granted our wish, and he gave us one more day. Remember that time, Tom? We showed up and were told to go to two separate classrooms to take the test. And do you remember the directions we were given on the exam?"

"Yeah, sort of," Tom replied.

Chris continued, "For 5 points, explain the contents of the atom. For 95 points, tell me which tire was flat." We blew it, man. You said it was the right rear. I said it was the left front tire. We were darn lucky that the professor had a good sense of humor and allowed us to take a makeup exam several days later after you and I stewed awhile."

"I remember that situation. The moral is no more flat tires. Right?" Tom said.

"Forget it," Chris shouted.

Chris was a good friend, and he did truly love to fly with Tom. Both had a ravenous appetite for adventure, but Tom wanted to test Chris' reaction to his theories on the source of the piece of driftwood … even at the risk of being humiliated. He imagined such responses as, "I can't believe you called me over here to talk about a dumb piece of driftwood" or "You're goofier than I thought."

They met that evening. Tom started the conversation by praising Chris for his recent achievements and pretended he was interested in Chris' activities. He had to butter him up before he mentioned the piece of driftwood. Finally, he said, "Oh, by the way, Chris, I've got something to show you. Wait here a minute. I'll go get it." Tom left the room, went to the closet in his bedroom and picked up the piece of driftwood. When he returned to the living room, Chris was in the kitchen with his head inside the refrigerator door.

"What are you doing?" Tom asked.

"Uh, well.... I was looking for a beer," he responded in a tone like it was really none of Tom's business. Tom started to tell him that he didn't have any beer, but then he figured Chris might be more receptive to his ideas about the driftwood if he loosened him up a bit.

"The beer is in the cooler downstairs in the storage room. Help yourself."

He left without noticing what Tom had in his hand. When he returned a minute later, Tom let him pick up the conversation first. Still not noticing the board or asking why he had invited him over to visit, Chris started right in by talking about his car.

"Tom, I have to tell you about this new gadget I found at the auto parts store. It's a compass that sticks on the inside of the car windshield and doesn't need compensating for the car's metal body. It has a dial that tells you the outside temperature, as well. Man, it's great. I haven't installed it yet, but ..." Having the attention span of a gnat, Chris thrust his chin toward Tom. "What's that rotten board doing in your lap?"

"Oh, it's just a piece of driftwood I found on the beach," Tom explained. "I was going to add it to the other pieces of driftwood in my garden."

"So, why are you holding it in your lap?" asked Chris, looking vaguely suspicious. His face had a "what-in-the-world-is-that" frown as he continued to stare at the board.

"All right, maybe it's not just an ordinary piece of drift-wood," Tom confessed. "I found it in the surf yesterday. There's something about it that intrigues me."

He told him what he knew so far. Ignoring what Tom said, Chris continued to examine the board in silence. Tom could tell by the look in Chris' eyes and expression on his face that he already was half-doubting his sanity.

"Are you listening?" Tom asked impatiently.

"Uh … yes, yes of course," he responded unconvincingly.

"Well, what do you think?" Tom asked.

"I think you're crazy," Chris said in a soft, sing-song voice. "This whole thing is stupid, but I'll tell you what I'll do. I promise not to tell anyone so they won't haul you away."

"What!" Tom laughed. "You know that I'm not crazy. I'm just curious about where this came from. Everything that washes ashore has a story. I'd like to know what tale this board can tell. Call me stupid if you want."

Chris continued, "You don't know anything about that old piece of wood, just that you found it floating in the surf there at Wrightsville Beach on Friday afternoon ... period. Big deal! What a waste of time! If you really want to pursue this, you're going to have to do a lot better than that. You need facts, man, I mean real facts, not frigments of your imagination," Chris replied arrogantly.

"That's figments, not frigments," Tom interjected. "Now who is being stupid?"

Chris kept on with his attack, "If you want to start with the ridiculous assumption that the board came from Barrington Plan-tation, I suggest you find out if there's anyone living there now. It's possible someone has restored it as a private residence or a resort or a business … or even an ink factory! But I can't believe you're wast-ing your time on this garbage. It's ridiculous!" Chris repeated. He seemed to be enjoying goading Tom, and now that he'd started, he was on a roll. "If someone were living on the plantation, maybe a shipment of supplies was delivered on the island in wooden crates marked *ink*, but the contents of the crates may actually have been something else. This could go in a thousand directions."

He leaned forward and rested his elbows on his knees and, with a look of great self-satisfaction, said, "Come on, Tom, enough of this nonsense. Why did you really ask me to come tonight? I can't believe you got me here just for this. You have nothing here but beach trash. It's just a piece of rotten wood. It could have come from anywhere. Barrington Plantation on Cat Island is not likely one of them. You admitted yourself the plantation was abandoned so long ago that nothing exists there but perhaps a few, old concrete foundations buried in tropical jungle undergrowth on a sparsely populated island." Chris was really fired up now.

Tom threw up his hands. "Okay, maybe you're right."

But Chris continued, "You're acting as if this board carries a deep secret, as if something mysterious were connected with it, perhaps something illegal. Wake up! You have a real hang-up about this whole thing!" He slammed the board down on the table.

"Will you shut up!" Tom finally snapped. "I've had enough. I know there's little to go on, but at least I'd like to check it out further."

Tom got up and paced the small room, always coming back to look at the board.

"I just have a gut feeling this board has some connection with Cat Island. But you're right. I can't justify my reasons. It's just a hunch. Humor me for a while until I can do more research. And by the way, when are you going to get rid of that belching junk heap in my driveway? I can hear you coming five blocks away, and if I look out the window, I can see your smoke trail on the horizon all the way here. Take it to the salvage yard. It's a piece of beach trash itself!"

"Whatever!" Chris laughed. "At least I know you have some sense in your head. And you're right about my little cream puff out there," he said jerking a thumb toward the yard. "I guess it's time to get rid of it. Oh, and do keep me posted about the driftwood," he added with a snort as he walked out the door.

Tom sat down and stared at the board. *Maybe this whole thing really is stupid,* he thought.

The following morning Tom decided to telephone a local travel agency to find out if a resort or inn called Barrington Plantation currently existed on Cat Island. Nothing was listed in their travel directories, but the agent mentioned that many years ago there was a small, secluded inn overlooking Cutlass Bay on the southern tip of the island. Like many of the out island resorts thriving in the 1950's, 1960's and 1970's, however, it had gone out of business and was abandoned. A small landing strip near Cutlass Bay was marked on the aeronautical charts as "unattended." The small airport most likely was left to the destructive forces of nature when the inn closed. He had learned that when airports in the Bahamas are abandoned, they're likely to be left in disrepair and dangerous.

Perhaps if he hunted through his collection of old charts, maps and resort brochures that he had collected over the years of vacation trips to the out islands, he might find a telephone number for the George Town airport. Years ago when he'd flown his plane to Stella Maris, a small village on the northern tip of Long Island, he had stopped en route at the George Town airport on Great Exuma Island for fuel. Cat Island was just 46 nautical miles north-northeast of the airport, but the island had not been his destination on that trip. He knew nothing about the place, except what was printed on an old aeronautical chart. At that time he gave Cat Island no further thought. Maybe someone at the George Town airport could give him some information about the abandoned Barrington Plantation on Cat Island. As he searched through dusty boxes in the attic, he found his aviation chart of the Bahamas Islands. Luck was with him. The telephone number of the George Town airport base operations was listed on the chart.

He started to dial the number; although, halfway through, he got cold feet and hung up. "Maybe Chris was right. This is ridiculous," he muttered to himself. "Why should I spend my money calling George Town about a piece of driftwood?" He gave himself a mental shake, and after a few moments of settling his nerves and unscrambling his thoughts, he fetched a piece of scratch paper and wrote down some questions to ask. He dialed again.

Incident at Cat Island

"Helloo," a voice said with clearly a Bahamian accent.

"Hi. Is this the George Town Airport?"

"Aye. Dat it is fo' true. Who's calling, chap?"

"This is Tom Hannaford from Wrightsville Beach, North Carolina. I'm calling to get some information about Cat Island. Have you heard of a place called Barrington Plantation?"

There was silence on the other end of the line.

"Hello … HELLO? Are you still there?" Tom asked.

"Aye, yes, Mon. Repeat what you say, please. Somethin' musta happened to the telephone circuitry."

"I want to know if there is a place known as Barrington Plantation on Cat Island?" Tom repeated.

"Yes, Mon, me thinks long time ago" he replied. "I maybe remember someone tellin' there's such a settlement on Cat Island once. But that was so long ago, Mon. No one wolk there. Nothin' there now. Gone … just ruins. Uh, why you ask, Mr. Hannyfore?"

Just in case Chris was right and his driftwood story was pure imagination, Tom decided not to mention it. He answered, "Well, I was just curious. I recently read in a book about the history of the Bahamas that from the late 1700's until the early 1800's a cotton plantation existed on Cat Island near Cutlass Bay called Barrington Plantation. I wondered if the site is still in use, has been restored, has been turned into a resort or what."

Another long pause transpired.

"Mr. Hannyfore, the settlement is gone! There's nothin' there. It's grown up with thick weeds, impossible to reach. Why you wanna know 'bout Barrington?" he repeated. The pitch in his voice jumped up a notch when he asked the question. He sounded a bit anxious.

"It's really not important," Tom replied. "I was doing some research, and I just wanted to check out some information about Barrington. I'm a private pilot and flew to George Town several times in the past few years. You probably don't remember me since it has been two years since my last trip, but I have a blue and white Cessna Cardinal with the call sign N33223."

There was another long pause on the other end of the line.

"No, Mon, I'm afraid I don't 'member you. Lots of planes flying in and out of airport. Plenty things happenin' here. It's hard to 'member everybody, you understand?"

"Oh, I understand that, Sir. I'm considering flying back to George Town next month for a little vacation of sailing and snorkeling and may go over to Cat Island to do some sightseeing. And besides, I love exploring historical sites," Tom explained stretching the truth a bit. "Oh, yes. I want to see a friend of mine who lives nearby."

"I see. You says you from Whysville Beach and your plane is Cessna Cardinal N22233?"

"That's close. It's 33223," Tom responded.

"Ah, yes, I thinks I 'member you, Mr. Hannyfore. Yes, I thinks I remember you," he repeated. "Say again when you comin' to George Town?"

"Oh, perhaps in a month. But no definite plans. Thanks for the information. Bye." Tom started to hang up.

"Wait, don't go, Mr. Hannafore," he said with urgency. "I knows where you can get information 'bout Barrington settlement. Manager of the Conch Harbour Inn in George Town could help you. Gie me your telephone number, I have 'em call you."

"Oh, that's okay. I don't mind calling him. What's his number?" Tom asked.

He gave Tom the hotel telephone number and hung up. Tom sat and thought about what he had learned so far—nothing, except how to generate a large telephone bill. He considered his offer to call the hotel.

However, he needed a little more time to think this through. He went into the kitchen and fixed some lunch and looked over the Bahamas aeronautical charts again. As he sat there at the table, his mind began to drift back to one of his trips to the islands. His enthusiasm grew as he recounted the events of island hopping, snorkeling, sailing, and exploring. He focused on one event several years ago when he flew to Long Island near Stella Maris for a few days. He remembered returning to his plane to fly back to the States and discovering someone had drained the fuel from his plane's tanks. The airport was unattended, so in desperation he went back to the general store in the village and started asking questions. He met the local clerk at the store.

"Excuse me, Ma'am," Tom had said. "I'm just visiting the island here, but I discovered someone stole gas from my airplane at the airport. Is there some place on the island where I can get more fuel?"

She shook her head in a negative way and smiled, "No, dis happens a plenty, Mon. You see, no one here at airport. People come, people go … only when plane come. Maybe three times a week. From Nassau. Don't know when, in the mornin', I think."

"I understand, but is there any place I can get fuel?" he asked again.

"No, Mon, not here, sorry," she said and smiled again. "No where on island, Mon. You must wait til plane comes here. Ask de pilot to sell you some fuel. Only way. Happ'n many times. So sorry, Mon."

"If it happens that often, why can't they catch the thieves," Tom asked.

"Not possible," she said. "Drug runners, you see. They fly late when it's dark from somewhere—South America maybe—on way to States. They look fuh little planes parked at airports up the island chain. When they sees one, they land and steal the gas. Jes like dat. They use no lights. Then they jes bust out. No one tries to catch them. Too dangerous. Have guns. Lock your gas tank caps; only way to stop them."

This was the first time he had been caught up in drug running operations, so he had to find out when the next flight from Nassau was due to arrive. Obviously no one at the store knew. He found a little restaurant down the dusty road and made an attempt to get more information. With some luck he noticed a yellowed and torn piece of paper tacked to the wall that said *Nassau Flights*. Handwritten below in pencil were some times that looked like some sort of schedule. Reading further, it said, *Flight from Nassau arrives Tuesday, Thursday and Saturday mornings*. That was it. He asked the waitress, "What time does the flight from Nassau arrive these days."

"Oh, I don't know really. Could be anytime in da mornin'," she said. "The capt'n circles 'round da island twice to tell da passengers to come to airport to get on plane. You just hafta be ready all mornin'."

It was Monday; he had to wait one more day. The next morning he was at the airport at daybreak to wait for the flight from Nassau. Sure enough, around 10:15 A.M. a twin engine prop plane came into view, circled the island twice and made an approach to the airport. As the pilot guided the plane on final approach to the runway, two cars drove into the sandy parking lot. Four people got out, pulled some suitcases from the trunks and walked over to the "boarding lounge" ... a park bench under a palm tree next to the plane parking ramp. Tom waited a few more minutes as the plane pulled along side the bench, shut down and the door opened. When he saw the pilot get off to stretch his legs, he came over and introduced himself.

"Hi. I'm Tom Hannaford. I'm the pilot of the Cessna Cardinal parked over there. Apparently, someone recently drained the fuel from my tanks, and I was wondering if I could buy some from you. Just enough to get to Nassau. Maybe twenty gallons?" he asked.

"Sure, Pal. We've done this before. We always carry extra fuel. I've got a siphon hose. Do you have a container?"

Then the horror struck him. He had no container.

"Well," he continued, "Can you bring your plane right up next to mine? Maybe the hose will reach from your wing to my wing. My fuel tanks are higher than yours, so perhaps siphoning will work."

Tom hand-towed his plane over to the commercial plane, and they attached the hose to both fuel tanks. It worked like a charm. Tom estimated when twenty gallons had been transferred and paid him his cost plus a tip for his help. The captain boarded his passengers, closed the door, started up the engines and took off for Nassau.

Sitting at the kitchen table, Tom suddenly realized that he'd been daydreaming again. He stood up and went to the sink to splash cold water on his face and forced himself to come back to reality and start thinking about his next move concerning Cat Island.

When he got up enough courage to call the Couch Harbour Inn, a sweet sounding young lady with a native voice answered, "Good mornin'. Welcome to Conch Harbour. Do you want reservations?"

"Hi. No, I'm calling to get some information about a place on Cat Island."

"Dis ain't Cat Island, Sir," she promptly replied. "Dis George Town, Exumas. Do you want reservations?"

He repeated, "No, thank you. Please, I know you're in George Town, but I've got a question about Cat Island. Can you help me?"

"Oh, don't know about dat. I don't lives on Cat Island. I lives in George Town. But maybe I can help you. Who's dis calling, Sir?"

"My name is Tom Hannaford. My home is in Wrightsville Beach, North Carolina."

"What do ya want to know 'bout Cat Island, Mr. Hannyfore?" she asked impatiently.

"I've flown to George Town in the past, and I'm curious about the history of the old Barrington Plantation on the nearby island. Do you know anything about it? Is it still abandoned, or has someone developed a resort there?" Tom asked.

After a moment's hesitation she replied, "Sorry, Sir, I live in George Town settlement. I knows nothin' 'bout Barryman Place. One moment, Mr. Hannyfore. Don't hang up phone, please. You speak to manager." Her tone of voice suddenly changed from that of a pleasant receptionist to that of one who was nervous and uncertain. Before Tom could say anything more, she left the phone for several minutes.

"I say, how may I assist you, old chap?" a deep, base voice said with a distinctive English accent.

"Yes, Sir. This is Tom Hannaford from North Carolina. I'm trying to get some information about Cat Island. Do you know anything about an old, abandoned plantation near Cutlass Bay called

Barrington?"

"Uh, why do you ask? What do you want to know?" he asked sternly. He seemed bothered that Tom had interrupted him from whatever he was doing.

"I'm just doing some research on the history of some of the out islands, and I recently came across the name Barrington, which I understand was once a cotton plantation near Cutlass Bay. My question is whether or not the plantation is still abandoned or has the site been taken over and turned into a ..."

"It's abandoned," he interrupted. "There's no one there."

"Is the site accessible for exploring?" Tom asked.

"No. Absolutely not. It's private property and closed. Too dangerous. There are no buildings, and the old, open dry wells are hidden beneath the thick vegetation...."

"What about the airport?" Tom broke in. "According to my aeronautical chart, there's a small grass strip near Cutlass Bay. Is it usable?"

"No. The airport is abandoned, too. It's full of holes, washouts, large rocks ...very dangerous," he said emphatically.

That was the end of the conversation. Tom finally conceded that the old plantation site was abandoned, and he reluctantly had to admit that Chris was right. He had reached a dead end on the mystery of the driftwood.

That evening, the telephone rang. When Tom picked up the receiver, he could hear a faint hissing on the line like the call was coming from a long distance away. "Hello ... hello ... hello?" Tom queried, but there was no immediate response.

Finally, a voice spoke, "Is this Tom Hannaford ... in Wrights-ville Beach?"

"Yes. Who's this?" The line went dead.

CHAPTER 2

The Intruder

Chris was having second thoughts about his car after Tom's browbeating and the growing complaints from his neighbors. They protested that the choking smoke screen Chris' junker was leaving along the streets had reached a level where the atmosphere had literally become toxic. Finally succumbing to social pressures, Chris called a junk dealer.

"Hello. I've got a 1967 VW, which is, well, uh … more or less in fairly good shape, and I was wondering how much you would give me for it? It has 145,222 miles. You could use it for parts, perhaps," Chris said enthusiastically.

The voice on the other end was bored and unenthusiastic. "Look, it doesn't matter how many miles it has or the condition of the car. We pay $25 for all vehicles ... provided you drive it to our lot. If we have to pick it up, we don't pay anything, but we'd charge for the pickup."

"Okay, let me think it over. Thanks." Chris hung up.

He called a mechanic friend and mentioned the offer from the junk dealer. His friend suggested he run an ad in the paper and see what happened. He told Chris some people would pay up to $200 for anything that runs, regardless of the condition.

The next day the ad read:

67 VW for sale. $199 or best offer. Runs. Call 555-8980.

That evening Chris received two calls. One was from a man named Jim, and the other was from Frank. Both seemed interested and wanted to see the car that night, so Chris agreed that they could come to his house as long as they came before 10:00 P.M. An hour later, a motorcyclist pulled into Chris' driveway, dismounted, walked to his front door and rang the doorbell. He was removing his helmet when Chris greeted him.

"Hi, are you the guy who has the VW for sale?" he asked.

"Yep, that's it in the driveway," Chris pointed to the car.

"I'm Jim. I called a little while ago," he said.

"Hi. Okay. Let's go look at the car."

As they walked around to the side of the house, Chris explained there were a few things that needed fixing, but that the car did run. At that moment, another person with a friend pulled into the driveway. The motorcyclist obviously became a little anxious, sensing that he was faced with some competition, so he immediately offered $199 for the car. Chris suggested that he take it for a spin around the block to confirm that it did run, but Jim declined. Before Chris had a chance to agree to the deal, however, the new arrival, overhearing the offer, ran up and interrupted.

"Just a minute, Sir," he said hastily. Then he turned to Chris and said, "Excuse me, I'm Frank. I called earlier about your VW and mentioned that I wanted to see it this evening. Are you Chris?" he asked.

"Yes, I'm Chris."

"You said best offer in your ad, right?" Frank continued with a determined look in his eyes.

"That's true … best offer," Chris said.

"I like the car. It's just what I'm looking for. I'll give you $225," Frank said.

"Well, it's certainly better than $199," Chris said. "I guess the car is yours.

Jim became incensed and raised the bid to $250. He insisted that he get it, because he didn't have time to look for another one. Frank countered with $275. Chris was dumbfounded. How long was this going to escalate? He started sweating. It was a little nerve-wracking. He sure didn't want the buyers to come to blows.

Jim turned to Chris with fire in his eyes and yelled, "You set me up. If I had known you were going to force me to bid on this car, I would never have come. You lied to me."

Chris tried to settle him down by denying his accusations, but it was no use.

"I'll give you $285 … that's final," Jim said in a fit of anger.

"That's fine, I'll raise it to $300," Frank calmly countered.

Jim immediately climbed on his bike, cursed, made an obscene gesture to Frank and fled the scene. For the next few seconds Frank and Chris stared at each other.

"Well, your last offer was $300. It's yours for $300," Chris said.

"Will you take a personal check?" he asked.

"Sure."

He handed Chris the check. Chris signed over the certificate of title, gave him the keys, and Frank drove away with his friend. The following day Chris went to a used car lot and bought another old wreck.

A week later Chris and Tom met for lunch. Tom noticed Chris was driving a different car. It wasn't smoking, and it wasn't making irritating noises. It wasn't even bad looking.

"Whose car is that?" Tom asked.

"I placed an ad in the newspaper and sold my VW for $300 a few days ago. Then I bought this little dream from a used car lot. What do you think of it?" Chris asked.

"You got $300 for your old bucket of rusty bolts?" he exclaimed.

"Yep."

"Who in his ever-loving, right mind would give you $300 for that old car?" Tom questioned.

"You don't want to know. Let's just say that the ad was quite effective."

Over their drinks, Tom recounted his conversations with the George Town airport staff and the Conch Harbour Inn desk clerk.

Chris finally remarked, "So, that settles it. I told you the plantation was abandoned. There is no Barrington Plantation."

"Okay, okay. That's the end of it," Tom conceded.

"Did you tell them about your stinking, rotten, little plank?"

Tom Hudgin

Chris asked sarcastically, trying to pour salt in the wound.

"No, I didn't! Besides, you said yourself that I didn't have anything worth mentioning ... just a piece of water-soaked wood," Tom replied.

"And what about your crazy *ink* idea?"

"I said that's the end of it," Tom insisted. "I threw the piece of wood on top of my driftwood pile in the garden."

Tom shifted in his chair and raised his glass to take a drink, then said, "Let's change the subject. Listen, I must admit that this recent scurry of activity has renewed my interest in flying back to the Bahamas for a vacation ... to do some fun stuff like sailing, snorkeling and beachcombing. And, for the past six months, I've been getting cabin fever. Working at Carter Pharmaceuticals has been tiring, and I'd like to get away for a week for a rest. I feel brainwashed. Besides, another reason I want to go to the Bahamas is to see Roberto. You know about him. He lives at Deadman's Cay on Long Island near George Town. Want to come along and maybe share expenses?"

"You want to go to George Town or Deadman's Cay?" Chris asked with renewed interest.

"Well, why not George Town? The water in the Exuma Islands is extraordinarily clear. I've snorkeled among the reefs there with visibility 200 feet or better. There are lots of isolated coves lined with coconut palms and white, sandy beaches. Since we like to sail, perhaps we could rent a small sailboat and explore those many isolated coves. Deadman's Cay is only a few miles away from George Town. Surely Roberto could come to George Town and meet us there," Tom explained. It didn't take much arm twisting over lunch to convince Chris to go. They decided to depart in four weeks on June 15th.

As soon as Chris left, Tom drove home and quickly sat down and wrote Roberto a letter explaining their plans to be in George Town the next month. He invited Roberto to join them. He knew Roberto worked at the marina in Deadman's Cay, and hopefully, he could take a couple of days off to come to George Town.

A few days later, Tom meandered down to the Marina to

find Chris so that they could go over some details of their trip. Chris' pride and joy was his 37-foot sailboat, Mystique, which surprisingly, he maintained in pristine condition. The boat was tied up in slip 32. Tom figured he was on board when he saw a bucket of soapy water, a sponge and a mop laying on the deck. He was obviously doing some cleaning, but he was nowhere in sight. Tom climbed on board and went below. When he heard water running in the shower stall, he walked forward in the cabin toward the head and hollered, "Hey, Chris, it's me, Tom. Are you in there?"

Chris didn't hear him, so Tom crept slowly to the shower stall where he saw a head wearing a baseball cap just above the shower curtain.

"Chris, it's me," he shouted again. He could see Chris' outline through the shower curtain and was shocked to see him taking a shower fully dressed—with hat on and all. Chris was startled when he heard Tom's voice. Chris shut the shower off and stepped out of the stall in soaking wet clothes, obviously embarrassed.

"Wait, I can explain," he protested.

Tom didn't let him finish his sentence, as he joked "My friend, you've gotta be out of your mind! Who but an idiot would take a shower in his clothes?"

"Just give me a chance to explain, will you?" Chris said in desperation. "I was cleaning the outside hull of the boat when I lost my hand hold and fell into the water. I swam around to the stern and climbed back on board. I figured I'd go below, strip, dry off and put on clean clothes, but I wanted to get the salt water out of my clothes. So I just decided to take a shower with my clothes on. Doesn't that make sense? Then you walked in. My timing was a little off, I'd say."

"No, that still makes no sense. I would never do anything that stupid. You've done some wild things, but taking a shower with your clothes on! That takes the cake! Have you seen your doctor lately?" Tom said, laughing and poking at Chris in the ribs.

"Don't get cute. I told you exactly what happened," Chris insisted.

Tom was momentarily lost for words as he sat down in the

main cabin waiting for Chris to get some dry clothes on. A few minutes later, Chris emerged looking as if nothing had happened. He simply shrugged his shoulders and went over to the galley to get a drink. Tom observed him carefully, half-expecting him to do something else bizarre. But he was disappointed. Chris seemed normal, so Tom changed the subject.

"Hey, speaking of sailing, why don't we take the boat out this afternoon for a short sail in the ocean? Unless you have something more special to do this afternoon … than taking showers with your clothes on?" Tom teased.

"Nooooo. That sounds good to me," Chris replied.

Tom went over some details with him about their flight to the Bahamas, and then they began rigging the sails. Chris started up the diesel engine to let it warm up while Tom got out the seat cushions and charts. Soon, they were ready to release the dock lines to get underway. They steered Mystique southward down Banks Channel to the Masonboro Inlet. There was a wind from the southeast about 10 knots … perfect for a comfortable sail offshore. Chris raised the mainsail and jib while Tom guided the boat toward the inlet, and in a few minutes, they were under full sail.

Tom loved the sound of water rushing past the bow, the wind whistling through the rigging and the occasional sea gull squawking as it flew overhead. They turned 90 degrees left and headed out the Masonboro Inlet to the sea. Enduring a gentle, three-foot swell buffeting them from the south, they soon spotted two dolphins approaching from astern. Then there were two more. Each time the dolphins surfaced for air, they gained ground on the Mystique. Suddenly, they came up out of the water a foot away from the starboard rail. If Tom and Chris had been closer to the railing, they could've touched them, but by the time they leaned over the hull, the mammals were just below the water line. The dolphins maintained the same speed as their boat for at least five minutes as Tom and Chris stood watching them; then the dolphins darted ahead of the bow. Brief moments like these made these two good buddies feel that they themselves had some interspecies connection with the dolphins' lives. Tom looked at the knot log and noticed they were making a good five knots through the water. Chris engaged the autohelm, went below and fetched some drinks and pretzels to munch on while they cruised up the North Carolina coast.

"I'm glad you asked me to go with you to the Bahamas," Chris said. "I just wish we could sail my boat there."

"You can," Tom replied. "But this year we're flying."

"I know. By the way, what'll be our route? Will we fly straight from Wilmington to George Town, or what?" Chris asked.

"I haven't plotted it out, but I envision flying from here to Jacksonville for fuel and a rest break. Then we'll go on down the Florida coast to Ft. Lauderdale or West Palm Beach. There we'll file an international flight plan and fill out customs papers and other documentation to be presented at our first landing site in the Bahamas. There're a number of international port-of-entry airports in the Bahamas. I haven't decided which one we'll use. After we clear Bahamian Customs, we'll head over to the Eleuthera Islands and then down to Exuma and George Town. That's basically it. We should be able to make the flight in one day."

After a couple of hours sailing northeast along the coastline, they came about and headed back to the inlet. The two of them were alone at sea with a gentle breeze and an occasional sea gull flying overhead. It was peaceful except for the wind singing through the rigging and the bow splashing through the water. The wind had not changed, so they were able to make good speed back to the channel. As a precautionary measure with a following sea, Chris started up the engine and engaged the propeller even though they were still under sail as they entered the inlet. The swells pushed the boat 30 degrees to the left and then to the right as they literally surfed through the inlet into the harbor. Chris had to use the power of the engine to help maintain steerage through the breaking waves. They turned north again and headed up Banks Channel to the marina. Tom took over the helm while Chris lowered the sails and stowed them below. Soon, they eased into the slip at the dock and shut down the engine. It was a perfect sail on an equally perfect afternoon—one more adventure as a prelude to their trip south.

Tom Hudgin

The next day, Tom began updating his aeronautical charts, buying ocean navigational charts of the Exumas and surrounding out islands and searching for land maps of the islands. He found brochures on charter sailboat operations as well as places to stay. Still two weeks before their departure, he had the plane inspected by an aviation mechanic to make sure all operating systems were in good condition. The required FAA annual inspection wasn't due for another seven months, but he was willing to pay for an interim check, since they'd be putting a lot of hours on the plane over remote and unforgiving areas.

There were a couple of small items that he knew needed attention. One of the navigational radio receivers operated only intermittently, and he had discovered on his last flight that the brakes were starting to make a grinding sound when he rolled to a stop on the runway. Probably new brake pads or disks were wise. The plane had several types of navigational receivers for tracking radio beacons on the ground for a hundred miles or more. A lot of redundancy existed on board in terms of radio, vacuum driven and electrical instruments, for safety reasons. Some of the critical gyroscopic flight control instruments were operated from a vacuum power source, while backup instruments were operated from an electrical source. It would be unlikely both systems would ever fail at the same time. Similarly, there was dual radio communication and navigational equipment on board.

Tom had one leg in his car to drive to the airport to meet with the mechanics, when Chris crunched up the driveway in his new car.

"Thought I'd stop by and show you my latest toy," Chris enthused. He opened the trunk and pulled out a metal detector. "It's the latest state-of-the art device. I wanted to try it out here at the beach. It'll be a lot of fun exploring with it in the Bahamas. Here, watch this." Chris threw a handful of coins in the sand in the front yard of Tom's beach house and turned on the detector. It emitted a squawking sound. But even when the detector wasn't near the coins, it kept screaming. Over and over Chris made adjustments to try to shut it off, but without success.

Incident at Cat Island

Tom watched him for a few moments, then suggested, "I have a suspicion what's wrong."

"I know what I am doing," Chris muttered and continued tinkering with the machine. A few minutes later, Chris said, "Okay, what's wrong?"

"You're standing right over the main water pipes to the house. But the real issue is that this is too big to take with us in the plane. Sorry, but it has to stay home for this trip," Tom said.

"Aw, shoot!" Chris poked out his lip. "I was afraid you might say that."

After a few minutes of good-natured ribbing, Chris hopped in Tom's car, and they drove to the airport to meet the avionics technician and mechanic to go over the repairs. Fortunately, business was slow for the fixed-base operator, so full attention could be devoted to Tom's plane right away. After discussing the repairs and checks needed, they left the two maintenance men at the plane to work out their schedules while Tom and Chris ambled over to the hangar at the far end of the aircraft ramp. Ducking under and skirting around an assortment of Piper and Cessna aircraft tails, wings and fuselages, they threaded their way through the maze of planes to the pilot lounge located along the back wall of the hangar.

The old, wooden door of the lounge stood open against the wall when they entered the room. Mechanics, Sam Burkholder and Cary Smith, were sitting at a table in the center of the room with Jim McDonald, a fellow pilot. On the right side of the lounge was a table with an almost-empty coffee pot. The last few inches of liquid remaining were so black that Tom suspected a spoon could nearly have stood upright in the center of the tarry mass. Along the wall on the right side of the room were a telephone that linked directly to Flight Service for pilot weather briefings and flight plan filings, a pad of blank flight plan forms, some empty ceramic coffee cups, some sugar packets, plastic spoons, paper napkins and a jar of non-dairy creamer.

In the back corner, sitting in a green leather chair, a girl was reading a newspaper. Tom had never seen her before. His eyes automatically focused on her as she glanced up from the newspaper she was reading, especially when she looked like she tried not to notice them coming into the lounge. She had blue, wide-set eyes and her nose was a bit long for her face. But her long, black hair flowed freely across her shoulders and down to her waist, making her strikingly beautiful in an unconventional way.

Tom figured she was a transient pilot, either waiting for improved weather conditions or for repair work on her plane. Or she might be waiting to meet someone, perhaps another pilot. He found it difficult to ignore her the first few minutes he was in the pilot lounge, but he tried not to stare. He turned his attention to his friends sitting at the center table and greeted them.

"As soon as we get a cup of coffee, we'll join you," he said to the table crew.

Tom reached in his pocket for some change and placed a few coins in the donation jar for the coffee fund.

"Yuk!" Chris exclaimed. "Used crankcase oil is better than this swill!"

Everyone in the room nodded in agreement. Chris rooted around for a coffee filter. "I'll make a fresh pot. Go join the guys. Be there in a minute."

Tom pulled out a chair and sat with Sam, Cary and Jim at the table and waited impatiently for just the right opportunity to interrupt them with the news about their upcoming trip to the Bahamas. Finally, Jim gave him the chance. "What have you been up to lately?" he asked.

"Thought you'd never ask." Tom grinned. "I came to get some work done on my plane for a trip to the Bahamas next month."

"The Bahamas! Yeah? Where in the Bahamas are you going?" Jim asked.

"Well, Chris and I thought we'd head down to George Town, Exumas—for a little fun and sun."

A slight movement caught Tom's attention when he mentioned George Town, and he saw the girl lower the newspaper just enough so that her blue eyes peeped up over the edge. But when she caught him watching her, the paper was quickly snapped back upright, hiding those remarkable eyes again behind its pages.

Incident at Cat Island

Chris returned with two fresh cups of coffee and sat down between the two mechanics.

"There. At least this batch won't eat through the bottom of your coffee cup. However, I contaminated your coffee with artificial sweetener and powdered creamer," he said, shoving one ceramic cup toward Tom.

"Thanks. That's perfect. Just the way I like it … as muddy as you can make it."

Tom took a careful sip of his hot coffee, then continued, "We could fly there in one day. And since I have my instrument rating, we won't likely be delayed by weather. We're planning to leave on June 15th and stay for a week. Just to add a little spice to the trip, we might rent a sailboat for a day or two to snorkel and explore the beaches and coves. We might even go to nearby Cat Island. That's one island I've never visited. I've heard there were some old cotton plantations near Cutlass Bay, and we thought ..."

Tom glanced over at the girl in the corner for a second and noticed that this time she was staring at him over the top of her newspaper. He turned his attention back to his group and went on with his plans. Just at that moment, he heard liquid spill on the floor. The girl had managed to knock over her half-filled coffee cup, and a stream of warm coffee was flowing across the floor toward their table. Instinctively, Tom got up and offered to help clean up the mess.

"Are you okay, Ma'am?" he asked as he approached her.

She seemed embarrassed, but she quickly regained her composure. "Uh … yes. I'm okay. It must have just slipped out of my hand. I'm so sorry. I'll clean it up."

But Sam immediately got up and fetched some paper towels from the restroom. "Here, Ma'am, I'll take care of it. There's no harm done. These things happen. Let me get you another cup of coffee. Even got a fresh pot."

"Oh, no thank you," she responded. "I've had quite enough already."

Sam seized this opportunity to talk with her and invited her to join them at the table. But looking at her watch, she declined and explained she had to leave for an appointment.

Determined, Sam made another attempt to find out who she was, "Where are you from, Ma'am?"

"Miami," she replied.

"Miami. Ah, I've been there once. Didn't like it much. It's too big. Took me hours to get out of town. And it seems most people speak Spanish. Nothing wrong with Spanish, you see, but I don't speak it, and I got lost in a Cuban neighborhood. Don't get me wrong. The people were nice, but I couldn't understand their directions or what they were telling me. I like the smaller coastal towns. I'm Sam Burkholder," he said. He wiped one of his greasy hands on his overalls and thrust it toward her.

"Hello," she replied, with a wiggle of her fingers instead of a handshake. "I happen to like Miami."

"Wha'd you say your name is?" Sam persisted.

"I didn't say," she retorted.

"Ah, yes. You didn't say. I guess you're the mystery lady of the day," Sam said, his face turning a dull red. "So what do we call you, *Miss Sterious*?" By now it was obvious that Sam didn't care what she thought. As far as he was concerned, she was a pain.

"My *friends* call me Sheila," she said in a tone that made it clear that Sam could not count himself in that company. Then she turned to Tom and said quietly, "Excuse me, but I couldn't help overhearing your conversation. Your trip to Cutlass Bay—it sounds interesting. I'd like to hear more about it."

"We're looking forward to it. What do you want to know? Have you ever been there?"

The expression on her face could only be described as bemused. She seemed to be searching for just the right way to answer.

"Well, yes … I mean, sort of. I was in George Town about three years ago on vacation. I remember a dinner one evening at a local restaurant where an old, wrinkled-faced man with a white beard was sitting at a table next to me. He was telling stories to a striking native girl about Cat Island and Cutlass Bay. She had dark eyes and beautiful, long, silky, black hair and spoke with a heavy

Incident at Cat Island

English-Bahamian accent."

At this point, Sheila stopped speaking for a moment and gathered her own long, black hair with both hands and pushed it back over her shoulders. Tom didn't know when the last time was that he'd seen prettier hair. He had to give himself a mental shake when Sheila started talking again.

"I thought the old gentleman was trying to seduce her for the evening. But a blond-haired man, perhaps in his early 30's, sitting nearby, had apparently overheard their conversation and began to take interest in her as well. He got up, came over to the couple and introduced himself. He had an American accent, so I assumed he was from the States. They started talking in a whisper, and I could hear only bits and pieces of the conversation after that.

"At that point the older man excused himself and disappeared among the party patrons milling around the pool at the hotel next door. I admit I was intrigued by the old man and his stories. I wanted to hear more, so I wandered over to the pool myself and listened in on more of his conversation with his buddies. He continued with his stories of the old days in Cutlass Bay throughout the remainder of the evening. He claimed the cotton plantations were never very productive, never very large and lasted only a few years before going broke. He talked with authority, as if he had been there himself, almost 200 years ago. He rattled on that all of them were abandoned by 1810 and left to the destructive forces of nature. Now, he said, there was nothing left but memories and crumbling foundations."

"Wow. What a coincidence meeting you here," Tom said. "I recently had some interest in the old plantations on Cat Island myself. The surprising thing to me is why no one, after 200 years, has bought the property and developed a resort or a private estate there by now. It's funny; someone in George Town told me the same story as a matter of fact. Perhaps you...."

She interrupted, "The old man asked me to join him the following evening for dinner. He was the owner and the general manager of a small hotel in George Town ... 'Conch something.' I don't remember the name, it's been so long, and ..." She stopped abruptly and looked at her watch. "Oh, no! I'm late."

She jerked a small, blue backpack off the floor and rushed to the door. Then she paused, caught her breath, turned and looked at Tom as if she had forgotten something. "What did you say your name was?"

"Tom. Tom Hannaford."

"And which plane is yours?"

"It's a blue and white Cessna Cardinal."

"Oh, I'll bet it's a pretty plane. Do you keep it here?" she asked.

"Yes," Tom replied, walking with her to the window. "Come here; you can see it from here. It's the one with N33223 painted on the fuselage … the third plane down in the second row."

She glanced out the window for a few seconds, then explained again that she had to leave and quickly disappeared without saying good-bye. Tom had been tempted to tell her about the piece of driftwood he found. But … oh well. He had no proof of anything.

"Well, she was an interesting person, even if she was a bit flighty. It was fascinating to hear her stories about George Town since I've been there myself," Tom concluded.

"Just interesting? Have you gone nuts!" Chris exclaimed. He pounded his fist on the table in frustration. "Wow! She was a real knockout! I'd go out with her. I wish I knew where she's staying, but she was in too big a hurry." His shoulders slumped. "Oh well, win some, lose some."

Chris and Tom finished their coffee and headed for home.

Just as Tom reached the porch stairs at his house after his walk on the beach the next morning, the telephone rang. He loped up the steps, hoping it was the mechanic from the airport with some good news that they had finished with the plane, and it was ready to go.

"Hey, you got the airplane fixed?" he said into the phone's receiver.

"Good morning. May I speak to Tom Hannaford, please?" She had a pleasant, soothing, sing-song voice—one with a southern accent.

Incident at Cat Island

"S-speaking," he stuttered, only a little embarrassed.

"Mr. Hannaford, we haven't met. My name is Renee. I heard you were planning a flying trip to the Exumas in your plane. I've always wanted to go there, and ... well, I was wondering if you'd be willing to take another passenger along? I have a dear friend in the islands I haven't seen in a while. I'm willing to pay my share of the expenses."

"What? Wait a minute. Back up there. This is Renee who?" he asked.

"Renee Wilshire," she said.

"Where are you calling from? And how did you know I'm flying to the out islands?" he asked.

"I'm calling from Atlanta. I've got friends all over, but it's not really important about how I knew. I guess the word about great adventures gets around, and I really am very interested in flying with you."

"But I'm curious. Was it someone here in Wilmington that told you about our plans?" Tom asked.

"No," she said. "I just love unusual adventures. Would it please be okay?"

"Who are you? What do you do? Why are you so fascinated with the Exumas?" Tom paced the small kitchen while he listened to her bubbly voice on the other end. His brow furrowed in deep lines as she continued.

"I'm between jobs at the moment and have some spare time. I want to get away on vacation. Something different like flying in a private plane to the Bahamas appeals to me. It just seems that the timing is right now. The beach and tropics have always interested me. And I want to see my old friend in the islands. When I heard about you, I thought, *Here's my chance.* So, can I meet you in Wilmington? What do you say? Am I in?"

Tom stopped pacing and ran a hand through his hair. "You sure caught me by surprise. I can't answer right now. I have to talk it over with my partner. I admit that the thought of having someone else share expenses does sound attractive. But there may be a problem. We're planning to leave on the 15th, only a week away ...

and you're in Atlanta. We're not flying through Atlanta."

Without hesitation, she replied, "I'm ready to come to you. I can be in Wilmington before the 15th."

"Let me talk it over with Chris, my partner. What's your telephone number? I'll call you tonight and let you know."

"Thank you, Mr. Hannaford. I really do want to go. You don't have to call me. I'll call you. What time should I call?" she asked. From the tone and excitement in her voice, she didn't need to convince him that she was anxious to fly with them.

"Anytime after 7:00 is fine."

"Oh, thank you very much, Mr. Hannaford." Then after a pause, "May I call you Tom?"

"Yeah, sure. That's fine. I'll talk to you tonight."

Tom hung up with mixed feelings about taking a stranger with them. And he really wanted to know, *Who in Wilmington had told her about the trip? Who was this Renee?* Since he couldn't come up with answers to those questions, Tom called his friends at the airport and talked to the avionics specialist. The radios had been fixed and would be reinstalled in the airplane by the end of the day. Before they said good-bye, however, Tom asked if he knew a Renee Wilshire. He didn't. Tom asked the mechanic and his friend, Jim, but they had not heard of Renee either.

Later that afternoon, Tom talked it over with Chris.

"Cool! What luck!" Chris exclaimed. "She just might make this trip a little more interesting, and I'm game for some real entertainment."

"Wait a minute, Chris. You don't understand. We don't know this woman. It bothers me that she knew we were going to the Bahamas in a private plane … next week, no less! Aren't you even a little bit curious how she found this out?"

"Nope. Don't care. 'Sides, she may be cute. Tell her it's okay. I see this as an opportunity to meet someone new, someone who has a spirit for adventure, has some free time and is single."

"Whoa! You don't know she's single," Tom rolled his eyes.

"I can dream, can't I? It's simple, deductive thinking" Chris continued. "If she were married, she wouldn't be so willing to undertake such an adventure, particularly with two complete strangers. How many husbands would let her do that? None that I know. No way, man. Remember, she called us—which tells me she has a strong desire to go. This is cool, man."

"Or maybe she might have some other ulterior motive!" Tom added sarcastically.

"A what? Motive? Like what, Sherlock Holmes? Maybe she's a spy. Wooooo!" Chris waggled his fingers in Tom's face, then laughed, "Who cares! Life's a gamble anyway. Let's go for it, buddy!"

The idea of splitting flying expenses three ways, instead of two, was enticing to Tom, but he still felt uneasy about sharing their vacation with a stranger.

A few minutes after 7:00 o'clock that evening, Tom's phone rang right on schedule.

"Hi, Tom. This is Renee. Did you talk to your friend? When do you want me to meet you in Wilmington?"

"I still want to know how you knew that we were flying to the Bahamas, and how did you get my telephone number?" he asked.

"An aviation friend told me. You know how those guys talk," she responded calmly. "I really do want to go. It's very important to me."

Tom chewed the inside of his cheek for a moment. She was right, there was constant chatter at the airport, even over the telephones.

"All right, you can join us. I figure your share in the plane costs will be roughly $200. Is that okay?"

"Yes."

"And understand that as soon as we get to the Exumas, you're on your own. My friend and I want to spend our vacation together doing our own thing. I don't know how long you plan to stay in the Bahamas, but if you want a ride back, you'll have to comply with our schedule. We plan to return in a week. That's June 22nd," he explained.

"Oh, that's alright. I won't need a ride back. My friend in

George Town will arrange for me to get back to the States," she said.

"There are some other things you need to know. We're leaving early in the morning June 15th from the Wilmington Airport. Because we're flying a small plane, we have to pay close attention to the weight and balance of the plane. That means there are weight restrictions. Each person will be limited to 50 pounds of luggage. This includes all your personal belongings like purses, cameras, snorkeling gear—anything carried on board. Also, I don't mean to be personal, but for safety reasons I must know how much you weigh—your honest weight, please? This is important to do the weight and balance calculations for the plane to make certain we aren't overloaded."

"I weigh 117 pounds," she replied.

"Great. Thanks," he said.

"It all sounds good to me, Tom," Renee responded.

"Could you come meet us in Wilmington a day or two early to get acquainted and do some last minute planning."

"Sure. I could be there by the 14th," she replied. "I'll get a room at a motel and just meet you at the airport around noon. Would that be okay?"

"Yes, that would seem to work. But how are you going to get to Wilmington?"

"Don't you worry about that," she replied. "I'll be there. You can count on it."

"Okay. Call me when you get in town. We'll see you next week," he said. "Oh, don't hang up yet. I just thought of one more thing. Do you happen to know a lady named Sheila from Miami?"

"Sheila who?" she asked.

"I don't know her last name," he said.

"Sorry. I can't help you there. I don't know anyone from Miami. Why?"

"Oh, just a long shot. Never mind," he said.

He telephoned Chris again and told him they had a partner for their adventure.

"Hot dog!" he yelped. "This'll be more fun than I thought."

Incident at Cat Island

"You're gonna be shocked if we discover she's an old hag," Tom responded.

"Hey! I'll take my chances."

"By the way, since we're thinking about renting a place in George Town with a stove and refrigerator so we can save money on meals, we need to talk about food. Buying food in the Bahamas is expensive because of the high import taxes, and because the thin soil on the islands makes it difficult growing crops. So, we have to leave room for groceries in the plane. I told Renee we'd be limited to 50 pounds of personal gear each. It will still be a tight fit."

The following morning Tom drove to the airport to check on the progress of the plane. Sam Burkholder was putting the cowling panels back on the engine compartment, and he mentioned that he had replaced the disc brakes, changed the oil, had done a compression check on the cylinders and had performed a routine 100-hour inspection on all of the operating systems. Everything was in good working order. Tom called Chris from the airport and asked if he'd like to join him around noon for a check ride in the Cardinal, just to make sure all electronic and mechanical systems were working properly.

While he waited for Chris on the airport ramp, he completed the preflight ground checks for all the systems outside the plane, climbed into the cockpit and turned on the radios. He tuned in the automatic terminal information service to get the current airport weather conditions and the runway in use. The sky was clear with light winds from the southwest. It was an ideal day for flying. The runway in use was number 24.

Chris parked his car next to the plane, and Tom waved to him to climb aboard. Tom gave him the checklist. After they buckled up and shut the door, Chris read through the start up checklist while Tom performed the functions. Everything ran smoothly. Tom called ground control for clearance to taxi to the active runway and advised the tower that their intentions were to depart the airport on an easterly heading and climb to an altitude of 2500 feet.

After they taxied to the end of runway 24, the tower cleared them for take-off. They climbed to 2500 feet and banked eastward toward the coast. Once they cleared the airport control area, they flew along the coastline and checked out all of the navigational equipment onboard. All of the flight instruments and flight controls worked perfectly. All systems were go. After listening to the radio again to get the latest airport information, Tom contacted the control tower and requested clearance to land.

They were cleared for a straight-in approach to runway 24, and the landing was so smooth that Chris joked, after the wheels touched the pavement, "Tell me when we've landed."

"Okay, Chris. As soon as I shut off the engine at the ramp and open the door, we'll be on the ground," Tom retorted.

"Cardinal 33223, bear right next intersection," the tower operator said as Tom applied the brakes to slow down on the runway.

Chris immediately picked up the microphone and replied, "Roger, we have him in sight."

Tom jerked the microphone away from Chris and said to him in a stern voice, "You can't say things like that to the tower."

"But, he said there was a bear on the right at the next intersection," Chris laughed.

"Oh, good grief!" Tom snorted.

The tower cleared them to the parking ramp.

"Well, now we're ready!" Tom said excitely to Chris. "The plane is performing beautifully. By the way, we need to take three life jackets with us. Can you remember to bring them from your boat to the airport next week?"

Chris responded, "Done."

Chris helped with securing the plane, then left for home while Tom stopped by the base operation's office to request that the fuel tanks be topped off before nightfall.

CHAPTER 3

The Freighter

A stolen panel truck, with its sides crudely painted over to hide the original company logo, raced through the back streets of Miami. Two well-tanned men, unshaven and wearing baseball caps, sat in the front seat. It was a few minutes before midnight.

"I sure hope those fools are going to be at the dock on time tonight. I get scared driving this cargo around these dark streets. It's a bad neighborhood. It's prime time for the bums roaming around here to be doing their funny business," Carlos remarked.

"Yeah, I get your drift, man. I'm not keen on this job either, but at least we're getting paid good money," Jack said.

"Look up ahead, at the corner. Those two guys, standing in the shadows next to the curb, don't look good to me," Carlos said as he lifted his cap to rub his hand through his hair.

"Yeah, I see them. Just keep your speed up. Ignore the stop sign. Just plow on through," Jack insisted. The truck roared through the intersection as the two guys stood there staring at them and giving them a finger gesture as they speeded by.

"See what I mean. This is doomsville, man. Only about a mile to go, Jack."

"Yeah."

The whole neighborhood was dominated by abandoned store fronts and warehouses. Vandals had destroyed the street lights some time ago with gunshots and rocks, and the area was left in darkness. The humidity was nearly 100 percent from the tropical breeze blowing off the south Florida coast, and sweat dripped down their faces as they waited at a traffic light. Carlos and Jack continued to scan the corners for activity, ready to step on the accelerator to run traffic lights, if necessary. So far, the streets were quiet.

Just as the traffic light turned green, a police car pulled up to the intersection and waited. Jack and Carlos accelerated gently through the intersection and proceeded at a slower speed down the block. When the light turned green for the policeman, he turned the corner and followed them until he caught up with the truck at the next red light. For a moment, the policeman sat in his cruiser and stared at the back of the truck. When the light turned green again and Jack and Carlos eased through the corner, the policeman turned on his flashing red light and siren.

"Oh, rats!" shouted Jack in disgust. "What does he want? We ain't done nothing wrong."

"I got no idea. We sure don't need this garbage tonight."

Jack slowed down, pulled the truck over to the curb and came to a stop.

"Don't you get out, Carlos. Make that scoundrel come to us," Jack mumbled.

The policeman walked to the driver's side of the truck, held out his badge and demanded, "I need to see your driver's license, please."

Jack reached in his back pocket, pulled out his wallet and showed him his license. The policeman looked at it for a minute with his flashlight and handed it back to Jack.

"This is a routine check. Where are you two headed at this hour of the morning?" the policeman asked.

"Making a delivery, Sir," Jack responded.

"What do you have in the back of the truck?" he asked.

"Some supplies for a print shop," Jack said.

"Mind if I have a look?" the policeman requested.

"Carlos, get out and open the back door so he can see what's inside," Jack ordered.

Carlos jumped out the door, walked around to the back of the truck and met the policeman there.

"And your name is?" the policeman asked.

"Carlos," he said.

"Carlos who? Oh, never mind. Just open up the back and let me see what you have."

Incident at Cat Island

Carlos unlocked the door and opened it. The policeman started to climb up into the back to get a better look but changed his mind when he saw the step was too high for easy access.

"Okay, you guys. You can go. Be careful out here. This is a bad neighborhood," he cautioned. "Oh, one more thing. Don't most shops take deliveries during daylight hours when they're open?" he questioned Carlos.

Jack butted in, "Yeah, you're right ... usually. But this place has a rush job. They're working all night, poor slobs. And now so are we."

"Okay. Have a good night," the policeman said.

As the police car disappeared around the next block, Jack wiped his face with his handkerchief and remarked, "Whew. I'm glad he didn't check those containers too closely. I didn't want him to follow us to the warehouse and dock. That would've been a sticky business."

Only a few blocks away from the dock, Carlos breathed a sigh of relief.

"Almost there, my friend."

"Yeah" Jack said.

They turned into a narrow, dark alley between some old, unoccupied warehouses and proceeded to the dock where two men were sitting at the water's edge waiting for them.

"Hey, we made it. I hope we didn't keep you guys up past your bedtime," Carlos yelled out the truck window.

A Cuban dockworker got up and walked over to the truck to greet them. "About time you jerks got here. Where you been? Out playing hop scotch with your grandmother?" he chided arrogantly.

"Shut up, you worthless trash," Jack shouted as he quickly pulled the truck door handle, intending to give him a smack in the face. But Carlos reached across the seat, grabbed Jack by his shirt and pulled him back into the truck.

"Listen, Jack, don't let that arrogant idiot get to you. It's not worth it. Just cool it. He's not your boss. Let it go.... Please!" Carlos pleaded.

"Hey, where you want this stuff?" Carlos asked the Cuban.

"Just stay right there and open up the back. I'll get the lift," the Cuban said. Jack went around to the back of the truck and slid open the paneled doors. The Cuban drove his forklift to the back while Jack and Carlos slid ten wooden pallets of cargo to the edge of the back door. For the next hour, the Cuban maneuvered the fork-lift and transferred the ten pallets to the ground. Then he pulled hard on the lead line attached to the freighter's crane cable to lower the hook over the cardboard boxes sitting on the pallets. He looked up at the crane operator on the freighter and signaled him to move the hook more to the right so he could snare the metal straps wrapped around the pallets and boxes. By 1:00 A.M. black puffs of smoke belched from the freighter's stack as the operator revved up the engine to hoist the heavy boxes on board. When the cargo was amidship, the Cuban signaled the operator to lower the crates into the hold. There was a loud thud when the pallets hit the metal deck below. The loading operations continued on until 3:30 A.M.

The lights of downtown Miami a mile away lit up the black sky in stark contrast to the dark, abandoned warehouses along the narrow Miami River where the rusty freighter was moored. Most of the dock pilings had long been the victim of sea parasites, salt water and weather and were either missing or broken. A single light on a wooden post at the east end of the dock faintly illuminated the loading dock.

Nearly 4:00 in the morning, a bearded, heavy-set man exited from a cab in the alley adjacent to the warehouse and walked to the rusting coastal freighter docked at the far end of the building. His face was weather-beaten and wrinkled from spending most of his life at sea. As he approached the side of the ship, he waved to a crewmember standing in the pilothouse door to alert him that he was coming aboard. Acknowledging the captain, the sailor left the pilothouse, climbed down the ship's ladder to the main deck and lowered the gangway.

"Good morn', Capt'n," he said with a sly, distrustful, toothless smile. "Cargo's on board. We're ready to set sail, Sir."

Incident at Cat Island

"Good, Jones. You're a top notch seaman and cargo master," praised the captain. "Looks like the weather will be fair for the next several days. Winds are from the south at 10-15 knots. Should be good sailing to the islands."

"Aye, Capt'n. I've made certain the heaviest wooden crates were loaded midship for good ballast, and we stowed the 20 cartons marked *Keep Dry* that we loaded yesterday in the bow holds for protection from water damage. And, oh yeah, the rest of the cargo holds are filled with our usual load of lumber. But the special crates and dry cartons are surrounded by stacks of lumber to keep the cargo from shifting at sea ... and hidden. Things are all in order, Sir."

"What about the paper work, the manifest? Let me see the papers, Jones," the captain insisted.

"Aye, Sir. Come with me to your cabin. They're on your chart table," Jones replied.

The two of them threaded their way among strapped lumber on the deck until they came to the ladder leading to the second level where the captain's quarters was located. Jones led the way up the ladder. Just before they entered the hatch to the interior of the ship, they heard a small boat coming up the river. At first they paid little attention to it until a spotlight from the boat streaked across the freighter's decks. They ducked behind the hatch door and watched. The boat slowed down, and the spotlight continued scanning the deck from the bow to the stern. As the boat slowly drifted by, the light at the end of the dock illuminated the craft enough so they could read *Miami Harbor Police* painted in large black letters on the starboard side. Seemingly satisfied that nothing suspicious was going on, the marine police turned off the searchlight and then continued cruising up the river.

"Wonder what they were looking for?" Jones remarked, relieved that they didn't stop and come aboard.

"Who knows? Probably they were doing routine checks," the captain said. "I want to see the papers."

They proceeded to the busy chart table. Jones picked up the manifest and handed it to the captain.

"Let's see. Manifest ... lumber ... Bahamas, ah yes. Well done, Jones. Get the crew together, and let's get underway. I want to be off shore before daybreak," the captain ordered.

At 4:36 in the morning, the Cuban dockworker loosened the bow and midship dock lines from the pilings and tossed them on board. The helmsman turned the wheel hard to starboard and signaled the engineer in the boiler room to put the starboard engine in reverse and the port engine ahead to swing the bow of the ship away from the dock. When the freighter reached a 45-degree angle with the dock, the Cuban untied the stern line and tossed it on board. The captain ordered both engines ahead one-third, and the rusty hulk began to plow slowly east down the Miami River toward Biscayne Bay. As the ship faded into the darkness of the Miami River, the corroded stern reflected in the water briefly from the waning dock light. There were six crewmen on board: a Cuban engineer, a Chinese navigator-cook, the Cuban dockworker, the cargo master-helmsman, one American deckhand and the captain. The name on the vessel's hull read *Southwind*, but the vessel's registration number was fictitious.

Catapulting under the last drawbridge into Biscayne Bay, a boat sped directly toward them from astern. Miami is a large city that never sleeps and boat traffic is common in Biscayne Bay all hours of the morning; consequently, the freighter crew didn't pay attention to the craft at first. In five minutes, however, the small boat was along the port side of the freighter and slowed to match the freighter's speed. It was the Miami Harbor Police boat again.

One of the officers stood up with a megaphone and bellowed, "Permission to come aboard, Sir? Harbor Police. We want to do a brief inspection."

The captain knew he had no other option but to accept the police request.

"Aye, we'll lower a ladder over the side." The captain signaled to the engineer below to reduce speed to idle and alerted all hands that his ship was about to be boarded by the police. Jones lowered the ladder and secured it to the ship's railing. Two officers climbed aboard and shook hands with Jones, who was waiting at the top of the ladder on the main deck.

"I'm Inspector Harrison, and this is my partner, Inspector Garner," he said as they presented their identification badges. "We want to see the captain."

"Okay. Follow me, I'll take you to him," Jones replied. They walked across the main deck to amidship to climb the ladder leading to the second level where the captain's cabin was located. The captain was standing just outside his door waiting to greet them.

"Capt'n, these men are inspectors from the Harbor Police," Jones said.

"Greetings, Gentlemen. I'm Captain Garth."

"Fine, Sir. This is my partner, Inspector Garner, and I'm Harrison. Here are our identification tags. First, tell us what you're carrying on board, Captain?" Harrison asked.

"Raw lumber," Garth replied.

"What is your next port of entry?"

"The Bahamas."

"Yes, but where in the Bahamas?" Harrison asked.

"Cat Island," the captain said.

"We would like to check the cargo holds, if you don't mind, Captain."

"Be my guest. Jones, escort these gentlemen to any part of the ship they want to see," Garth ordered.

"Aye, Captain." The three men left the main deck and went below to the cargo holds. Ten minutes later they returned. The officers seemed satisfied.

"Captain, may we look at the ship's manifest and documentation papers?"

"Sure. They're in my cabin. Come with me, gentlemen."

They climbed the ship's ladder again to the second deck and went into the captain's quarters. On the table lay the papers. The officers spent a few minutes looking over the documents.

Not realizing the registration number and paperwork entries were false, Harrison stated, "Everything seems to be in order. Thank you, Captain, for your time. Smooth sailing." The harbor police left the ship and sped back to the Port of Miami.

At the same time, Captain Garth signaled the freighter's engineer, "All engines ahead two-thirds," and they resumed their course to the islands.

The coastal freighter passed the last landmark in Biscayne Bay and headed for the open sea. Captain Garth peered through his binoculars at the distant sea buoys and ordered the helmsman to steer a course of 135 degrees for the South Riding Rock Light, 64 miles from Miami. Far off on the eastern horizon, a faint glow lit up the sky, hinting the first signs of sunrise. There was no ship traffic in sight, and the sea was calm. Soon the lights of the Miami coastline were no longer visible. The captain left the pilothouse, climbed down the ladder to the main deck and walked forward to the bow. When he reached the head of the freighter, he stopped, dug down in his coat pocket, got out a pipe, added some tobacco from a bag stowed in his outer coat pocket and lit the aromatic mixture in his pipe bowl. He leaned onto the bow railing and looked out to sea ahead of the path of the coastal freighter. He was dreaming of the next day's events at Cat Island.

Twenty-six miles south of Bimini, there's a small break in the barrier reef that guards the edge of the Great Bahama Bank. With 25-feet water depth through the narrow cut, the captain was confident he could safely navigate his freighter around the coral heads and steer a 079-degree heading to Northwest Channel Light to circumnavigate the north end of Andros Island. Even though the location of the first reef passage was marked with a lighted marker, the charted day buoys marking the actual channel through the reef were long gone, wiped out by a hurricane many years ago. Fortunately, it was daylight, so the crew could visually spot the coral heads and reefs from the bow of the ship to navigate safely through. Using the lighted marker, the freighter headed south-southeast along the eastern shores of Andros Island into an area called the Tongue of the Ocean where the depths reached more than a thousand fathoms.

CHAPTER 4

Renee

At 11:00 o'clock Chris and Tom drove to the airport to meet Renee. It was the day before their departure, and she had agreed to meet them at noon in the pilot lounge. Tom was already dreaming that by this time tomorrow they'd be somewhere in southern Florida. When they arrived in the parking lot, Tom suggested they check out the plane one more time. He rolled down the window, inserted the plastic gate-pass card into the electronic gate lock and drove to the general aviation ramp and directly to the plane.

Chris jumped out of the car the second Tom put on the brakes, and before he could shut off the engine, Chris made a record-setting dash around the plane, jumped back into the car and pronounced, "Everything looks okay. Let's go meet Renee."

Tom had hardly set foot on the pavement. "Ha! I wish it were that simple," he said. "I want to go through the ground pre-flight check anyway. It will only take a few minutes."

He methodically went through the checklist as he walked around the starboard wing to the nose of the plane. He opened the inspection ports to the engine compartment, and he checked the oil and other mechanical parts to see if anything was obviously out of sorts. Everything seemed to be in order.

As he was closing the cowling doors, Chris said, "Wait! Let me look at something in there again." Chris reached inside the engine compartment and pulled on a large wiring harness.

"Hey, Tom, look at this. There's a big hole in the insulating sleeve for these wires. Doesn't look right to me. We should wrap this up with tape. The heat and vibrations from the engine might harm the wires inside the harness."

Tom was impressed with Chris' observations. Or to be more

accurate, he was amazed that he knew enough about the plane to catch this anomaly.

"Let me see that," Tom said. He felt the wires for any wear or cuts. To his dismay, he discovered two broken wires in the bundle. They were the largest ones in the harness. "This doesn't make any sense," he muttered. "The plane was fine last week."

Tom rushed back to the hangar and promptly summoned the mechanic. Fortunately, Sam Burkholder was available, and they hustled back to the plane. "I thought you had just completed a 100-hour inspection of the plane and had found everything okay last week," Tom said.

"I did. We even did a run up test on the ramp. Everything ran fine. Trust me, I know how to do my job. Let me look at that wiring," Sam insisted. When he examined the broken wires closely, he remarked, "No way! I don't believe this. These wires have been cut. Sam pulled the wires further out to show Tom and pointed to the sharp ends. This is not due to normal wear. Someone has cut the magneto wires since I did my inspection. I can tell it's a fresh cut since no oxidation has built up on the ends."

"Come on. You're joking, right?" Tom hoped. "But who? Why?"

"I haven't got a clue," Sam shrugged. "But one thing is for certain. Whoever did this knows something about aircraft engines. These are the only two wires in this harness that would prevent you from starting the engine, the magneto wires. Pulling a plug wire or cutting the fuel line would have been more obvious. This was real subtle. Chris, I've got to hand it to you. You've got sharp eyes."

Tom kept questioning, "Why would anyone want to do this? Nobody has a grudge against us. As far as I know, I don't have any enemies here at the airport. It must have been done by some random vandals, just for meanness. Sam, should we report this to the FAA and the local police?" he asked. "This looks like sabotage."

Sam suggested they wait. He said he wanted to discuss it with his boss, the owner of the fixed-base operations, and with his staff. He gathered his crew into the maintenance hangar and told them what they had found. Each face registered the same concern.

No one spoke. Sam questioned whether anyone had noticed any strangers in the area recently. Unanimous response was negative.

Sam explained to Tom that he could notify the FAA and other authorities, but that would definitely mean a delay in their departure. Most likely the FAA or police would impound the plane for the duration of the investigation if they made a big deal out of the cut wires.

Tom thrust his hands deep into his pockets. He was too anxious to head south to jeopardize their departure date now. "Forget it," he told the mechanic. "How soon can you fix it?"

Fortunately, Sam had the wiring cables in stock and agreed to have it replaced and the engine log book brought up to date in about two hours. Tom glanced at his watch. It was already 12:30. They were thirty minutes late for their appointment with Renee in the pilot lounge. He hurriedly gave Sam the authorization to make the repairs and trotted off to the lounge. Chris skipped in front of Tom like a kid playing sidewalk games.

A young, blond-haired, blue-eyed girl, wearing tight jeans and a red-and-white-striped jersey, was sitting on a couch in a corner of the pilot lounge. She was reading a magazine and didn't seem to notice them as they entered the room.

Tom looked from her to Chris just in time to see his eyes widen. In fact he seemed to slip into a trance. Tom nudged him in the stomach with his elbow to bring him back to earth.

"Excuse me, Miss. Are you Renee?" Tom asked tentatively.

The girl looked up and jumped to her feet.

"Yes. And you must be Tom Hannaford?" she said, stepping toward them.

"Yes, and this is my friend Chris," he added.

"Hi. Nice to meet you both. I'm so excited about this trip, and I can't thank you enough for letting me come along. Are we all set for tomorrow?"

"Yes, I believe so. I did a quick check of the plane just a few minutes ago, and everything seems about ready," he said stretching the truth a bit.

Chris continued standing there, just staring at her with his mouth open. Tom had to nudge him once to bring him back to reality.

"H ... hi," Chris stammered. "I'm glad you're joining us, too. We're going to have fun."

"I hope so!" Renee beamed. "Well, now that we've all met, maybe you can show me your plane. Is it here? Do you have a few minutes to show me around?"

Tom agreed, and the three of them walked out to the ramp where Sam had already removed the rest of the engine cowling to have better access to the wiring terminals. Tom casually mentioned that the mechanic was making a minor repair, but that everything would be in perfect running order by the end of the day. He asked her if she had ever flown in a small plane, and she said she had, about fifteen years ago. She couldn't remember the make of the plane except that the wing was on the top of the plane. He suggested that it probably was a Cessna. She shrugged her shoulders like she didn't really know... or care.

Tom asked her again how she learned about them going to the Bahamas. And again she gave a vague answer. "Through a close friend," she said.

"Hey! Was her name Sheila?" Chris asked suddenly.

"Sheila who? I don't know a Sheila," Renee insisted and turned to Tom. "Tom, you already asked me that question once before."

Chris looked vaguely suspicious. "How was your trip from Atlanta?" he asked.

"Okay, Chris, leave her alone," Tom butted in. "You're asking too many questions. You're making her uncomfortable. Let's talk about our trip to the islands."

But she continued, "My trip from Atlanta was fine. A friend drove me here. He had business to take care of in Wilmington and offered me a ride."

"What a coincidence. What kind of business?" Tom asked.

But Chris interrupted, "Hey, Renee, where are you staying tonight?"

"The Beach Inn. That reminds me. I could use a ride there."

Incident at Cat Island

She looked up at Tom's eyes and laid one small hand on his arm. "Are you going in that direction after we're done here?"

Over her shoulder, Tom almost laughed out loud when he saw the suspicious look on Chris' face suddenly turn to rejection. He agreed to give her a ride.

"Is your friend staying with you at the Beach Inn tonight?" Tom asked.

"No. He had a quick job to do. Then he's returning to Atlanta this afternoon. I'm on my own now," she explained.

Chris and Tom gave her a brief tour of the Cessna Cardinal, and they tried to impress her with some aircraft performance statistics. They talked about the flight plan for tomorrow. Tom told her that if they left on time at 6:00 o'clock in the morning, they should arrive in George Town, Exumas, by late afternoon. They'd make fuel stops in Jacksonville, West Palm Beach and Nassau, and they'd clear customs and immigration in Nassau. Then they'd fly southeast for 130 nautical miles along the Exuma Island chain to George Town on Great Exuma Island. She seemed enthusiastic about the flight.

"Why did you choose Exumas for a vacation when there are other islands just as beautiful in the Bahamas?" she asked.

"Well, there are many reasons. I had been there years ago and fell in love with the place. It's the prettiest island chain in the Bahamas in my opinion. Also, Chris is a seasoned sailor, and we love to snorkel. George Town seems like the perfect place to do both. Another reason has to do with Roberto, a friend who lives on Deadman's Cay, Long Island. We've been writing to each other for several years but have never met. I'm anxious to meet him while we're in the area. And there's another reason. It has to do with an island not far from George Town that's aroused my curiosity. I thought while we're in the vicinity we might have the chance to explore it by sailboat."

"What island is that?" she asked with heightened curiosity?"

"Cat Island. Have you ever been there?"

"No. Sounds interesting though," she replied.

"Do snorkeling or sailing interest you?" Tom asked her.

She replied she had never done those things but that she was willing to try. Chris immediately volunteered to teach her all the basics.

"Well, guys, I'm ready to head over to the motel. You did say you would take me there, right?" she asked Tom.

"Of course," Tom replied. Already rejected, Chris yawned and asked to be dropped off first at his house before they went to the motel, saying he still had a lot of packing to do, some phone calls to make and some errands to run before he hit the sack for the evening. They drove across town to Chris' place and let him off. He agreed to meet them at the airport at 6:00 A.M. sharp for departure. Renee and Tom continued on to the motel.

"Say, Tom, how about you joining me for dinner tonight?" Renee said in a soft, persuasive voice.

"Oh, thanks for the invitation, but no thanks. I've got a lot to do, too, before our flight tomorrow morning," he said.

"Like what? You still have to eat, don't you? I'd love to have dinner with you tonight. Okay?"

"Thanks for asking, but really, I do have a lot of things to do tonight," he repeated.

"Oh, come on. I insist," she said.

"You're being so very kind … and I don't want to hurt your feelings, but I shouldn't," he said.

Renee trailed one brightly polished nail along Tom's leg. "You disappoint me, Tom. I came all the way from Atlanta. I was looking forward to spending this evening with you, before we leave on our trip tomorrow. It would be a nice chance to get to know each other better. How about it? Let's have dinner together."

Tom blew out a nervous sigh and said, "All right, but I can't make this an all-evening event. Just dinner, and then I have to go. Okay?" he said.

Renee clapped her small hands. "That's wonderful. I'm excited. How about picking me up at the motel at 6:00. You choose the restaurant."

A few minutes later they arrived at the Beach Inn and got out of the car. Tom opened the trunk and carried her luggage into the lobby. Renee grabbed his hand, squeezed it for a moment and whispered in a sweet voice, "I'll see you at 6:00."

Tom left the Beach Inn and headed back to the airport to see how Sam and his crew were coming along with the repairs on the Cardinal. Arriving fifteen minutes later, he jumped out of his car, walked into the hanger and found Sam filling out the required maintenance repair information in the plane's engine logbooks.

"Everything's all fixed. You're ready to go. I've already done a full run up check on the engine. It's running smoothly now," Sam explained.

"What a relief. Thanks, guys," Tom said.

At 6:00 sharp, Tom showed up at the Beach Inn to pick up Renee. She was standing in the lobby waiting for him when he walked in the door. Wearing a bright blue, low-cut dress, her only accessories were dangling gold earrings, heavy perfume and those too-blue-to be-true eyes that she batted so effectively as she held out her hand to greet him.

"Hi, Tom. Ready for an exciting evening?" she asked in a honey-soft southern drawl.

"Hi. Uh … yeah. You look nice," he responded.

"Thank you. Where are we going for dinner?" she asked.

"It's a surprise," he said.

They walked out to the car, and he opened the door to let her in. When she sat down in the front seat, she caught his full attention when she hiked her dress up to just above her knees.

"These long dresses may look nice, but they're a pain in the rear when you're getting into cars and other tight situations," she said smiling. "I don't want to get the bottom of my dress dirty on the car floor. You understand, don't you?"

"Right," he acknowledged.

They drove to the River View Restaurant located on the Cape Fear River. It was a small, intimate place with a formal atmosphere. When they met the hostess inside, they were told a table would be ready for them in a few minutes. It was an elegant restaurant. Tables were set with white tablecloths and illuminated with candles. While they were waiting to be seated, a man walked in wearing worn boots, dirty and ripped jeans, a red T-shirt and with tattoos on both arms. He approached the hostess and said, "Hey, sweetheart, where's ya john?"

"Follow the hallway and turn left at the end. When you come to the sign that says *Gentlemen*, just ignore it and go inside," she replied, looking like she'd smelled something unpleasant.

Overhearing the conversation, Renee laughed and congratulated the hostess for handling the situation the way she did. Tom just shook his head.

"My friend here told me this is an elegant restaurant. You just proved him right," Renee said to the hostess.

"Thanks. We have to deal with all kinds of people here," she said in defense of her actions.

They were shown to a table for two next to the window overlooking the river. The waiter followed behind the hostess, gave them menus and asked if they wanted anything from the bar.

"Yes, I'll have a gin and tonic, please," Renee said.

"And you, Sir?"

"Oh, I'll just have black coffee," Tom said.

"Do you want cream with that?" the waiter asked.

"No, just black," he repeated.

"Ah, come on, Tom, have a drink. We have a long evening ahead."

"No thanks. I have to drive home and do some flight planning tonight. I want to be able to think straight," he said.

The waiter wrote down the order and left them alone.

"Would you believe that? You said black coffee, and he asked you if you wanted cream. That's funny," Renee laughed.

They paused and looked over the menu. The waiter returned to their table with their drinks and asked, "Have you decided what you would like?"

Tom gazed at Renee with a blank look, and she returned the same expression to him.

"No, Sir, we need a few more minutes, please. We haven't decided yet," he said.

"Very good, Sir, I'll return shortly. No hurry. Take your time," he responded.

"What do you recommend?" she asked Tom.

"I've had the pork roast here. It was excellent. That's what I'm thinking about getting."

"That sounds good to me. I'll have the same."

He gave their orders to the waiter; then they sat and smiled at each other for a moment before the conversation resumed.

"Tom, I've been thinking."

"About what?" he asked.

"Well, I've been reading lately about Long Island, one of the out islands just southeast of George Town. It seems fascinating, much more exciting than George Town. The reefs and coconut-lined coves appear absolutely magnificent according to the pictures I saw. And I heard you can charter a sailboat out of Stella Maris for unbelievable snorkeling adventures and ..."

"Wait," he interrupted. "What are you trying to say? We're going to George Town, not Long Island."

"I know, but I was wondering if you might reconsider and go to Long Island. It sounds a lot more fun than a week in George Town. How about it?"

"But it's too late. You see, we've already made our plans for George Town," He said.

"It's not too late to change, Tom. Do you have reservations for any place to stay in George Town?"

"Well, no, not exactly reservations, but that's where we're supposed to meet Roberto...."

"See, we can go to Long Island. You can meet Roberto there. Let's do that instead, okay?" she wheeled.

"I can't make that decision now. I have to talk to Chris first."

"So, go call him while we wait for dinner to be served," Renee insisted.

Tom pushed back from the table and folded his arms across his chest. "Renee, you are really pushing for Long Island. Why?" he asked.

"Just because I know Long Island is a treasure trove waiting to be discovered! You seem to be an adventurous soul who loves exploring the secret world. So please go call Chris, now," she said impatiently, fluttering her fingers at him.

Tom considered for a moment then leaned forward. "I'll tell you what. I'll think about it. I want to look at my charts again. I'll admit I've not completed our flight plan for tomorrow yet. When I get home tonight, I'll study the new routing and talk to Chris. At the moment, however, all I can say is *maybe*," he compromised.

"That's fair enough. Just remember, you'd have a much better time…."

"Uh huh," he interrupted. "You've said that already—several times."

The waiter brought them their food, and it looked as sumptuous as it was the last time he'd been there.

The way Renee looked at him over her fork, Tom felt a little bit like he was on the menu. She seemed to be very interested in his lips—at least that's where her eyes seemed to settle, most often. They exchanged small talk between every delicious bite.

When he'd finally wiped his mouth and replaced his napkin in his lap for the last time, he asked, "Well, that was great. Are you ready to go back to the motel now?"

"Sure, I'm done. That was a great dinner. And the restaurant is super. Thanks very much," she answered.

Renee grabbed his hand when they walked out the door and held it as they strolled across the parking lot. They got in the car and drove to the Beach Inn. He opened the door to let her out when she said, "It's still early. Would you like to come to my room? I've got some things I want to show you about our trip."

"Thanks for the offer, but I do have to get home to get ready for tomorrow."

"Oh, don't be silly, Tom. It's only 7:30. The evening is still young. I insist," she said.

"All right. Only for just a minute. Then I must go," he said reluctantly.

They walked down the hallway of the inn until they came to room 132. She reached in her purse, pulled out her key card and inserted it in the lock. When the door opened, Tom noticed that the room was dimly-lit, the bed covers were turned down, Renee's suitcase was wide open, and a nightgown was lying at the foot of the bed. They walked in, and Renee closed the door behind them. It locked automatically.

"Well, what did you want to show me?" he said nervously. She didn't say anything but reached out for his hand and pulled him toward her. He pulled back, but she pulled harder until she could give him a kiss on the cheek.

She looked directly into his eyes and said in a soft voice, "Tom, I had a great time. Dinner was marvelous. And you've been marvelous, too. But now I want a real kiss for a nice evening."

Before he could respond, she wrapped her arms around his neck and planted her lips firmly on his. After a second, he tried to break the embrace, but she held him even tighter. Feeling vaguely embarrassed, Tom reached up and gently disengaged her arms from around his neck and gently set her away from him.

"I really have to go," he said softly. "Do you need me to pick you up at 6:00 to go to the airport?" he asked.

Renee sat down on the edge of the bed and looked up at him with those enormous eyes. "That's okay. I know you have things to do. I'll catch a cab. Come here, at least give me another kiss," she demanded.

She grabbed his arm and yanked him in just the right way that he toppled over on top of her. Blushing to the roots of his hair, he gave her a kiss, said a hurried good night and quickly left her room.

CHAPTER 5

Southbound

Tom rushed home to pack and do his last minute flight planning. He was so excited about the trip that he'd even had trouble concentrating on his driving ... well, between the trip and going over the bizarre dance he and Renee had just done in her motel room. That girl was definitely different! But now it was the night before the trip, and there was still plenty of work to be done.

When he pulled into his driveway, he immediately ran into the house and started piling his swimming trunks, toiletries and the other items he intended to take onto the kitchen table in neat folded piles. Soon he'd gathered everything into one place and organized them into the bags that he would take. When they were packed and placed by the door, he spread his charts out and scanned them for the information that Renee had suggested. Finally, without making a decision about his flight plan, he rose, put the charts away and fell into bed exhausted.

The alarm clock startled him at 5:00 A.M. He jumped out of bed, threw some water on his face, rushed over to the telephone and called the Wilmington Flight Service to get the aviation weather forecast. The latest weather report at Wilmington included a few scattered clouds around 1200 feet with limited visibility in haze. He asked for the en route weather for their flight path from Wilmington, Charleston, Jacksonville, Cape Canaveral and West Palm Beach. The flying conditions were good from Wilmington to Savannah. A stationary front lay on an east-west line in the Jacksonville vicinity and was producing heavy clouds, scattered thunderstorms and poor visibility. Thunderstorm intensity was predicted to increase throughout the afternoon and evening. However, from Daytona Beach southward to West Palm Beach, the forecast conditions were better—just some widely scattered clouds with excellent visibility.

The weather seemed flyable as long as Tom could pay close attention to the potential storm developments in the Jacksonville area. He had an instrument rating, so it looked like the best decision was to file an instrument flight plan for the leg from Wilmington to Jacksonville, getting them above the weather and having the air traffic controllers track them during the route. The Flight Service Agent told him the weather from Florida to the central Bahamas and out islands was expected to remain clear with a few isolated showers popping up briefly around the islands.

Tom did some flight calculations and called Flight Service Agent again to file an instrument flight plan that consisted of a cruising speed of 145 knots at 8000-feet altitude along an airway from Wilmington, North Carolina, to Jacksonville, Florida. He estimated the first leg would take about two hours and forty-five minutes. His flight plan was accepted and placed on hold in the air traffic computer system until it would be activated upon their departure from Wilmington.

He gulped down a quick breakfast and decided he'd better call Chris to make sure he was awake. The telephone rang five times before he answered.

"Yes, I'm up ready to go," he said before Tom could even say hello.

"How did you know it was me?" he asked.

"Are you kidding? Who else would be calling me at 5:15 A.M.? Did you get the weather forecast?" he asked.

"Yes. It's a go. However, when I took Renee to the motel last night, she suggested we fly to Long Island instead of George Town, because she seemed to think that Long Island had more interesting things to see and do. After a long discussion, I told her I'd have to talk it over with you. I personally don't care. It's in the same general vicinity as George Town anyway. What do you think?"

"You were with Renee last night?"

"Uh, yeah. We had dinner. So what do you think?"

"I think that's very interesting…."

"No, idiot! What do you think about going to Long Island instead of George Town?"

Chris laughed. "What about Roberto? Isn't he supposed to meet us in George Town?"

"Yeah, but he lives on Long Island, so we could contact him there as soon as we arrive and just meet him at Deadman's Cay," Tom answered.

"Makes no difference to me. Since she's dying to go to Long Island, let's go to Long Island."

"Okay, I'll work on a flight plan for Long Island. See you at the airport."

"Hey, are you picking up Renee at the Beach Inn?" Chris asked.

"No, she's catching a cab."

"Aha! I'll call her and offer to pick her up, then." Chris sounded eager.

"I don't think that'll be necessary. I offered to pick her up, but she insisted on taking a cab."

"Fine!" Chris growled. "I'll see you shortly."

With his personal belongings, flight gear and charts, snorkeling equipment and camera packed, Tom hopped in the car and headed for the airport. It was 5:30 A.M. No rush hour traffic at this time of the morning. Turning off the main road onto the airport access road, he approached the gate to the tie down ramp, inserted his plastic pass card in the electronic box, opened the gate and drove to the tie down ramp. Two other people were on the ramp preparing their plane for departure, but he didn't know them. They were probably transients. Chris and Renee had not arrived yet, so he decided to proceed with the ground preflight inspection by himself.

He left his baggage in the car for the moment and started following the checklist for the preflight inspection. Beginning with the engine compartment, he checked the oil level, looked for any evidence of leaking hydraulic fluids or frayed wiring, loose cables or anything that didn't appear normal. He even checked for the presence of bird nests. Birds have a nasty habit of building nests in the engine compartments, wing inspection ports, landing gear doors and tail assemblies. He examined the nose gear assembly for fluid leaks and alignment, tire inflation, wear and loose linkages. Moving along the left wing, he checked for possible damage along the leading edge, opened the fuel caps to confirm that the tanks were full, checked the color of the fuel for the correct octane level and drained an ounce of fuel from the tanks to check for presence of water. He continued by inspecting the stall warning indicator, ailerons, main landing gear, static ports and elevator for proper functions.

Chris drove up to the ramp just as he was examining the tail of the plane. He made a mental note of his stopping point and walked over to Chris' car.

"Where's Renee?" Chris asked.

"Not here yet. But it's not quite six o'clock either. She'll be here."

Tom finished the inspection and unloaded everything from his car. Chris pulled the luggage from his own car and set his gear next to Tom's beside the plane.

"Heard from Roberto?" Chris asked. "Is he going to meet us in George Town?"

"No, I haven't heard from him yet, but I assume he got my letter. I'll try to contact him when we get to Long Island. I'll tell him we are near his home on Deadman's Cay instead of George Town," Tom said.

Everything that went on board had to be weighed, including themselves, so they could keep the weight and balance of the aircraft within limits. They knew that their own weight and the 300 pounds of fuel were fixed and the only variable would be the luggage and food. If they exceeded the limits, those would be the items to cut back. Each compartment in the plane had a posted maximum load limit, so placement of the luggage inside the craft was critical.

A taxi stopped outside the gate, and Renee stepped out. She had two luggage items, a medium size suitcase and a small bag. Surprisingly, Chris had more personal belongings than Renee.

Besides their own gear, they had to factor in six bags of groceries. Each grocery bag was marked on the outside with its weight. Tom brought along a portable scale, and Renee volunteered to weigh the luggage while Chris made a written note of its weight and where it was to be stored in the plane. Tom thought about making everyone stand on the scale to verify his and her own weights, but he took their word for it. He made the weight and balance calculations and compared the results with the limits on the aircraft balance chart. The total weight was 30 pounds over the limit. Something had to be left behind. They looked over the itemized list again, but no one was volunteering to leave anything at the airport.

"All right, guys, we can't fly unless we get rid of 30 pounds of weight," Tom insisted. "I'll leave behind my camera, an extra pair of shoes, some books and some canned goods from the grocery bags. How about you, Chris? What can you leave here?"

"Hey, I've got an idea. Let's get some balloons and fill 'em with helium. If we put them inside the cabin, we'll get more lift, and we won't be faced with having to leave thirty pounds behind," Chris joked proudly.

Renee and Tom looked at Chris with matching you're-out-of-your-mind expressions.

"Forget it, Chris. I don't need to tell you why that would not work," he said. "Are you telling me that you're not willing to give up anything for this trip?"

"Okay. Let me think about it for a minute," Chris lamented.

"Renee, you're okay. It's not practical for you to leave anything here," Tom said.

Chris managed to find 17 pounds of items to leave behind: books, diving gear and food. Tom made up the difference of 13 pounds in his stuff. It took about twenty minutes to load the plane.

Chris ducked under the wings and tail and untied the plane while Renee climbed aboard and made herself comfortable in the back seat.

When Chris returned, he cheerfully announced, "Tom, I'm going to ride in the back seat with Renee. That's okay; isn't it?"

"Absolutely not. I need you sitting in the front seat to help balance the plane."

"Actually, guys, I prefer to sit in the back seat by myself anyway. It'll give me room to stretch out and get some sleep." She batted her eyes at Tom, "For some reason I didn't get much sleep last night."

Tom cleared his throat, glanced at her with a wry smile and continued to load the plane.

Tom didn't remember the life jackets until he'd climbed into the pilot's seat. He hadn't seen them on the ramp as they were loading, so he asked Chris if he brought them. "Could they be in the car?" Tom asked.

"Yeah, they're in the trunk. I guess I didn't open it when I unloaded."

Chris loped across the field toward the parking lot to fetch them.

While he was gone, Renee remarked, "I sure had a good time last night. I hope you did, too."

"Yes, but you caught me by surprise. I didn't expect that kind of evening."

"Of course you didn't. It was fun, though, wasn't it?" she smiled.

He smiled back. Chris returned with three life jackets and the scale. He piled them on the scale and read the total weight— twelve pounds.

"Well, we need to dump another 12 pounds out of the plane. Renee, it's your turn," Chris hollered.

"Stop. It's not Renee's turn! She isn't coming back with us to Wilmington. Besides, there's another way to solve this problem. The plane burns 10 gallons of fuel per hour. Each gallon weighs 6 pounds. If we run the engine on the ground for 12-15 minutes, we can burn up 12 pounds of fuel. That's about how long it will take us to get our clearance from the control tower, taxi to the runway and do a run up test before we take off. So we're okay."

They stuffed their carry-on items in every crack and corner they could find in the cabin. By the time they were ready to shut the door and start up the engine, they were crowded in like sardines packed in a can.

After everyone was settled, Tom explained to Renee how the seat belts, the ventilation system and interior lights worked and where the airsick bags were located. He dreaded mentioning the bags because he was convinced that once the subject of motion sickness is brought up to anyone, the thought sticks in his or her mind and makes it more likely to happen. But he also felt it's better to be safe than sorry. He demonstrated the intercom equipment on board, which would allow them to talk to each other above the drone of the engine during the flight.

Tom shut and locked the cabin doors and tuned in the automatic terminal information service on the radio to get the current weather, field conditions and runway and taxiway in use. An overcast sky hung over the area at 3600 feet, but the visibility was good, and the winds were moderate out of the southwest. He told Chris and Renee that his flight plan called for a cruising altitude of 8000 feet, so they should be above the clouds shortly after take-off.

Tom made a couple of notes on his clipboard and handed Chris the start up check list to read back to him as he proceeded with the instrument checks. All of the flight controls were found to be working properly, and Tom made the necessary engine control adjustments to start the engine. The propeller began turning immediately the moment he turned the key and pushed in the throttle. He did a thorough scan of the flight instruments and engine gauges and noted everything was acceptable.

"All systems go," Tom announced over the intercom to Chris and Renee. He contacted the ground controller in the tower and received his clearance to the Jacksonville International Airport. After repeating the clearance back to the controller, he was ready to taxi to the runway.

"Cardinal 33223, you're cleared to runway 24 by way of taxiway Golf, cross runway 35 to taxiway Charlie. Hold short of runway 24. Contact tower when ready for take-off," the tower operator instructed.

Again Tom acknowledged, released the brakes and eased the throttle forward as they slowly pulled away from their tie down spot on the ramp. While monitoring ground control on one radio, he asked Chris to dial in the tower frequency on the other radio and set the transponder code for their flight. When they taxied across runway 35, Renee reached up and opened the vents in the back seat and aimed them at her face. Chris looked at her and suspected that she was already feeling sick.

"Renee, are you okay? Do you want us to turn around and return to the ramp?" Chris asked.

"Huh? Uh, no. I'm fine. It just felt stuffy in the cabin, and I had to have some fresh air."

They finally reached the end of taxiway Charlie and runway 24. Tom turned the plane to face into the wind to do an engine run up check. With the prop spinning at 1800 rpms, he checked all of the flight systems and gauges at high speed. Everything seemed okay. He asked Chris to lower the flaps 10 degrees for take-off and switched to the tower frequency to advise them they were ready to depart for Jacksonville.

"Cardinal 33223, taxi into position and hold. I'll have a release for you in a moment," the tower controller said. Two minutes passed before he called them back and cleared them for take-off. Holding the control column stable with one hand, Tom pushed the throttle forward with the other hand. The plane lunged forward as the prop pulled them down the runway. He kept his eye on the airspeed indicator and turned the control wheel a little to the left to compensate for a left crosswind. At 60 knots, he pulled back slowly on the control column to lift the nose wheel off the pavement. When the airspeed indicator passed 75 knots, the main wheels were free of the runway. They were on their way.

Tom requested Chris to retract the landing gear as the plane's air speed continued to increase. At 100 knots and climbing at 900 feet per minute, he banked the plane to their assigned southwest heading for Jacksonville and continued their climb through the clouds. At 7200 feet the plane broke through the top of the cloud layer into a bright-blue sky. The exhilarating view of the lumpy, white clouds distancing themselves below and the warm sunshine above stimulated everyone's natural adrenaline release as they headed out for the islands.

"Okay, guys, we can talk now. Air traffic controllers will not be talking to us for awhile," Tom said over the intercom.

Chris seized the opportunity first. "So, Renee, what did you do yesterday afternoon? Anything special after we left?" Tom listened carefully to see what she was going to say.

"Well, after y'all dropped me off at the Beach Inn, I put on my bathing suit and walked along the beach. Atlanta doesn't have many beaches," she said jokingly.

"That sounds like great fun," Chris said. "Did you find any unusual shells?"

"Uh huh. But I'm not into shell collecting."

"Did you go swimming? The water temperature should be warm by now. I think it's in the upper 70's."

"I just got my feet wet. That was enough," Renee said.

"Where'd you have dinner last night?" Chris pressed on.

Tom thought, *Will you shut up, Chris!* He swallowed and wondered what Renee was going to say next. He knew Chris would have given his right arm for such an evening with Renee.

There was a long pause. Then Tom said quickly, "Hey look over to your left. That's Myrtle Beach. The river running parallel to the shoreline is the Intracoastal Waterway, and it connects into the Waccamaw River, which flows into Georgetown, South Carolina. Remember sailing down the waterway to Georgetown, Chris?"

"Yeah," Chris said.

"Tell Renee about your adventure to Georgetown," Tom said.

"She doesn't care about my Georgetown trip," Chris stated.

"Yes, I do," she said sweetly.

"Well, it was last summer. Tom and I took my sailboat south along the Intracoastal Waterway for a week. It was uneventful until we had to stop near Myrtle Beach at a marina overnight. Approaching a marina in the south Myrtle Beach area, I called them on the radio to find out if the depth of water in the entrance channel and alongside the docks was at least five feet. The dock master replied, 'Seven feet, Captain.' With that reassuring information we cautiously proceeded off the waterway and into the marina channel.

Mistique promptly ran aground on a sand bar one hundred feet from the dock."

"Oh, my goodness!" Renee squealed.

"Exactly!" Chris continued. "We backed off and made another pass on the left side of the shallow spot, but the water was so black due to its high concentration of tannic acid that it was impossible to detect any hint of shallow water ahead. When the depth sounder again cautioned us not to continue, we backed off a second time. Ultimately, we found a passage into the marina just 4.6-feet deep, exactly 0.1 foot from the bottom of our keel. The reported seven foot channel was nowhere to be found.

"While I eased Mistique against the rickety dock, Tom stood on the bow and tossed a line over the nearest piling. We were dismayed at the marina's state of disrepair. A few of the docks had collapsed into the water, pilings were bent over or missing, the paths around the docks were overgrown with weeds and poison ivy, and rusting boat debris was littering ..."

The air traffic controller called on the radio and gave them new instructions to cross over Charleston. Tom acknowledged.

"Okay, Chris, continue with your story."

Chris went on, "Because daylight was fading, we had no reasonable alternative but to remain there for the night. We eased Mistique between two wobbly pilings and tossed our dock lines around them. I climbed onto the loose planks, walked on shore and across the yard to the marina office and found the dock master sitting on a high stool in a cluttered marina store reading the paper.

"'Are you the person I spoke to on the radio about the depth of the channel?' I asked.

"He acknowledged he was.

"'I'm curious, Sir,' I said. 'Where is the seven-foot channel you said that leads into the marina? We couldn't find it.'

"'It's there,' he said with certainty.

"'Is that at low tide or high tide? And when is the next tide, and how much tide do you have here?' I asked.

"He said, 'I'm not sure what the tide is here. The water depth should be seven feet in the channel and along the docks.'

"Then I said, 'Then I guess I inadvertently hit a ton of fish that just happened to be swimming by when I got stuck.' It was a fruitless discussion, so I walked outta there. Anticipating that there really would be a change in tide level, I adjusted the lines to compensate for a four-foot rise and fall in the water level. While I was working with the mooring lines, Tom decided to explore the marina area before darkness set in. When he returned he warned, 'Watch out for the poison ivy along the docks.'

"Around midnight Tom was quite suddenly awakened by Mistique bumping against the pilings and our dinghy banging against the bow of our boat. The tide had risen to the point where the bow and stern lines were too slack. Realizing that I was not going to get up and remedy the situation, Tom crawled out of bed and stumbled onto the deck without his flashlight. Discovering that the dinghy needed to be tied to the wooden sea wall instead of to the bow of Mistique, he walked along the shaky planks of the dock to the edge of the sea wall, leaned over to pull the dinghy closer to him and promptly fell off the wall into the dinghy. After a few yelps and nursing his sore knees, neck and shoulders, he managed to climb out of the boat onto the sea wall in the darkness, made some adjustments to the lines, returned to the cabin and went back to sleep."

Chris stopped for a moment and looked back at Renee in the back seat. She had her eyes closed and her head against a small pillow next to the window.

"Tom, can you believe it? She's asleep! I bet she didn't hear half of my story!"

Tom breathed a sigh of relief. He didn't blame her, since the story was extraordinarily long, boring and essentially meaningless. Chris liked talking about sailing adventures.

They continued southbound crossing over the city of Charleston and then on to Savannah, Georgia. Clouds were starting to build up ahead, but most were below them so they were unable to see the ground as they approached Savannah. Soon they were between layers of clouds, yet the flight was smooth at this altitude, and Tom continued to monitor the weather on a special radio frequency. Savannah Approach Control advised them of several planes in the area which were coming into and going out of the Savannah airport but mentioned that they were no factor to their route of flight.

Leaving the Savannah control area on the south side, they saw the clouds thicken. Tom knew they were nearing the stationary front just north of Jacksonville. They now were working with Miami Center which controls all aircraft in Florida and parts of southern Georgia, and he asked them for permission to leave the frequency for a minute while he got weather updates. Permission was granted, and he contacted Flight Watch for the latest Jacksonville weather and beyond. He was advised that the weather in Jacksonville was instrument conditions with low ceilings, low visibility due to light rain and was expected to deteriorate over the next several hours. Tom had his instrument charts ready in anticipation of having to make an instrument approach to the airport. So far, there were no reported storms in the area, just fog and light rain. He told Chris this would be good practice for him, and he felt confident he could handle the situation.

CHAPTER 6

Off Course

A moderate trade wind out of the southeast blew off the southern shore of Andros Island. The seven-foot, choppy sea created a rhythmic salt spray across the bow of the freighter as it plowed toward the central Bahamas. Captain Garth stood on the starboard wing of the bridge to shelter himself from the wind as he puffed on his pipe and watched the waves slide from the left side to the right side of the ship. Although the sea looked menacing, the freighter cut smoothly through the water due to the heavy ballast on board.

The navigator walked out of the pilothouse and approached the captain. "We've made a good 12 knots since we passed the Northwest Channel Light three and a half hours ago, Capt'n. We should be due south of Nassau in another hour and a half."

"Okay, Yan. I just listened to the weather broadcast out of Nassau, and we're in for good sailing weather for the next several days. No change from current conditions," the captain responded.

"Aye on that, Sir." There was a pause. Then he said, "Uh, Capt'n. I've been wantin' to ask ya somethin'. Please don't think I'm pokin' my crooked nose where I shouldn't, but I've got a thirsty curiosity. What's this cargo we've got on board? Oh, I knows 'bout the lumber. Everyone uses lumber fer buildin' and stuff. I mean the other cargo. What's it fer? Seems to me that there's no good reason to take this rubbish to such a place like the out islands of the Bahamas. The way I see it, the out islands don't need much, especially a whole shipload of stuff. There ain't no use fer it there. I could see the reason if we dumped it in Nassau or some civil place like that, but ..."

"Enough, Yan. Stick to your navigation duties. You think too much. The ship's cargo is my responsibility. Don't worry about the cargo. You just get us to our port."

"Aye, well said, Sir. I knows you'se the capt'n and every-thing, and I knows you knows best, but I just can't figure it. In all respects to you, Sir, you told me to plot a course to the out islands, but you never said what we we're goin' to do there. I'm sorry, Sir, my mind don't think so good sometimes. I'll stick to my navigatin' and heed to my own business."

Yan turned his back to the captain and returned to the pilot-house. He stared at the charts once more and plotted the next turn toward the east-northeast to navigate through a cut in the reef at Ships Channel Cay on the northern end of the Exuma Islands. After making a few brief calculations, he walked back onto the wing of the bridge and approached the captain again.

"Captn, accordin' to my estimates, we should arrive at Ships Channel Light in three hours and ten minutes. Once we cross the cut in the reef, I recommend we turn to a headin' of 115 degrees which will take us across Exuma Sound in good water."

"Good. You have my permission to do so," the captain acknowledged. Yan then headed for the aft section of the bridge and climbed down the ladder onto the main deck. A spray of salt water smacked his face as he made his way aft to the crew's quarters. When he passed through the hatchway, he closed the watertight door behind him to keep the crew's quarters dry from the blowing mist.

A short while later, Jones, the cargo master, woke up in the crew's quarters and looked at his watch. In thirty minutes he had to take his station on the bridge for his watch duty, so he climbed out of his bunk, went into the head and took a quick shower before he grabbed a bite to eat from the galley. With a few minutes left before his watch began, he decided to take a brief walk about the ship just to make certain everything on board was secure. He went into the cargo hold amidship, walked among the piles of lumber and boxes and pulled on the straps holding them in place. Everything seemed tight. Then he went forward to the bow cargo hold where the dry cartons were stowed. He walked around the stacks of wood which surrounded the boxed cargo and pulled on the metal straps to see if they were loose. He was satisfied all was well here, too.

Just as he was closing the hatch to head back up to the main deck, he thought he heard a noise somewhere behind the boxes. It didn't sound like a piece of lumber had come loose, nor did it sound like a box or drum tipping over. Something light had fallen on the metal deck. He reopened the hatch and peered inside. He could only hear the creaking of the hull against the forces of the waves outside. Nothing seemed to be out of order. But he paused again, because he thought maybe something was loose and he ought to check one more time. He re-entered the cargo hold and walked forward toward the bow. When he looked around one of the boxes under the strapped lumber, he found a pocketknife lying on the deck. Still not suspecting anything out of the ordinary, he leaned over to pick the knife off the deck. At that moment, he caught a glimpse of a pair of shoes from beneath the pallet next to him. Cautiously, Jones inched his way around to the other side of the pallet and found Yan crouched next to the boxes.

"Get up! What are you doing down here?" Jones shouted.

"Uh, nothing, Sir."

"Oh yeah? You expect me to believe that? What's this pocket knife doing here? You think I'm stupid or something?" Jones said.

"No, Sir. I just wanted to get some rest … where it's real quiet. I couldn't sleep with the shenanigans goin' on in the crew's quarters," Yan tried to convince Jones.

"That doesn't explain the knife. Why did I find it lying on the deck? I heard it fall. I still don't believe you," Jones said.

Yan's face was frozen in fear.

Jones looked around the cargo compartment suspiciously, and suddenly he noticed one of the boxes had been cut open. "You did that, didn't you?" Jones pointed to the opened box.

"Okay, so I was a lookin' in one of the boxes. So what! I wasn't goin' to harm nothin'," he said.

"This compartment is off limits. There's no reason for you to be here. I'll give you one more chance. You just stick to your navigation duties. The cargo is none of your business. Now get out! Understand?"

Incident at Cat Island

"Yes, Sir. You're very kind, Sir." Yan left immediately and headed back to the crew's quarters. He crawled in his bunk and drew the sheets up over his head, hoping he would not have to face Jones again right away. Jones secured the hatch door in the bow hold and climbed the ladders to the bridge to assume his watch. He mentioned nothing about the incident to the captain.

Captain Garth reached inside the pocket of his foul weather jacket and pulled out another plug of tobacco and stuffed it into his pipe. Cupping his hands tightly around the pipe bowl to protect it from the wind, he lit the tobacco like an old pro and took several puffs to get the ashes glowing red. The warmth of the pipe bowl felt soothing to his hands. Holding the pipe in his mouth, he stared again out to sea ahead of the bow. *Another twenty hours and our voyage will be finished,* he said to himself as he watched the endless procession of ocean swells slipping silently past the rusting hull.

Jones began his watch duty in the pilothouse as helmsman and lookout. He also was responsible for making sure everything onboard was functioning properly during his stay in the pilothouse. Captain Garth sat in the captain's chair on the starboard wing of the bridge for another thirty minutes, and then he walked into the pilothouse to talk to Jones.

"Everything under control, Jones?" the Captain asked.

"Aye, Sir. I checked around the ship before I took my station here and believe all is well, Sir," Jones said.

"Good. I think I'll head on back to my cabin. Call me if anything urgent comes up, Jones."

"Yes, Sir, Captain."

Garth slipped quietly through the hatch door and walked aft towards the galley and his officer's quarters. When he entered the door to his cabin, he suddenly remembered that he'd forgotten to tell Jones about the inoperative radar. The captain picked up the voice activated ship telephone and called the pilothouse.

"Jones here."

"This is Garth, I meant to tell you that the radar is inoperative at the moment. So, you will have to keep a sharp eye out for ship traffic and any obstacles out there tonight. You know the rules on avoiding collisions, right?" the captain said.

"Yes, Sir, Captain. I'll call you if I have a problem," Jones assured the captain.

"You call me if any ship gets within two miles of us, understand?" he insisted.

"Aye, Sir, within two miles," Jones repeated.

"Goodnight." The captain hung up.

An hour passed and Jones was having difficulty staying awake. He knew the severe consequences of falling asleep while on watch, so he kept moving around the pilothouse to force himself to stay alert, but occasionally he nodded off for a few seconds and almost lost his balance hanging onto the wheel. At one point he thought he saw a faint light far off on the horizon. He rubbed his eyes and looked again thirty degrees off the port bow. The light was not there. He decided his sleepy mind was playing tricks on him, and he headed over to the corner of the pilothouse and fixed himself a strong cup of coffee.

Ten minutes later, he swore he caught a glimpse of a light again, still about thirty degrees off the port bow. He knew just enough about navigation to be able to read a chart, but when he looked at their track plotted by Yan on the chart on the table, he concluded there shouldn't be any land within fifty miles in that area. Jones went out on the bridge and looked in that same direction with binoculars. Again, he could see no light.

He returned to the pilothouse and decided to drink his coffee and tried not to worry about what was out there. Another five minutes passed, and he thought he saw the light again in the same relative position from the ship's bow. He quickly picked up the binoculars and searched the horizon. Sure enough this time he saw the light. He took a bearing on the light with the ship's compass and noted it was twenty-five degrees on the port side of the bow. A few minutes later Jones took another reading from his compass and observed the light was still at twenty-five degrees but closer.

Half an hour passed, and he now saw two white lights and a green light that he estimated at less than five miles away. The compass bearing remained the same. Jones was now fully awake and was concerned how close the other ship was going to come to them. He was taking bearings on the lights now every couple of minutes and the relative position of the ship did not change, except it was obvious now to Jones the ship was closing in on them, a collision course, perhaps. Jones waited until the ship was about three miles away before he turned the wheel hard to the right and changed the freighter's course to the right sixty degrees. He hoped this maneuver would avoid a collison and put them well out of harm's way.

Five minutes after the turn, Jones took another bearing on the lights and made a note of it on a piece of paper. Ten minutes later he repeated the procedure and observed the ship's bearings were changing and moving aft of their course. When the ship was a mile away, he felt relieved and confident they were no longer in danger of a collision at sea.

Jones relaxed a little, locked the wheel on the new course and went to the corner of the pilothouse and refilled his cup with hot, thick coffee. He went out to the starboard wing of the bridge and watched the ship pass by their stern and head away from them. Much later Jones looked across the bow and saw a dim image of a tree lined shore about two miles ahead. He picked up the binoculars and searched ahead with intensity. To his horror, the freighter was heading straight for the beach of some island. In a state of panic, he swung the wheel hard to the left and forced the ship to reverse course. Sweat was beading all around his head and running down his neck. He realized now that he was in trouble and reluctantly called the captain in his cabin.

"Captain, Sir, I am sorry to wake you up, but I need your help on the bridge, Sir."

"What's the problem?" Garth asked.

"Well, Sir, it is hard to explain. I am afraid I got too close to land, and I had to change course, and ..."

"You did what? That's impossible. Yan plotted a safe course for us that cleared all islands and reefs. What are you doing up there?" the captain said in anger. "I'll be right there."

In less than a minute, Captain Garth was in the pilothouse. "What are you doing! Why are you on a course of 330? That will take us back to Miami. Where are we?"

"Uh, I don't know, Sir."

"Give me the helm! Go stand over there by the coffee table and call Yan to the bridge right away," he ordered.

Yan showed up in the pilothouse half-dressed and rubbing his eyes to get a clearer picture of what was going on. "Yes, Sir, Capt'n. What's up?" Yan asked.

"First, figure out where we are. Jones got us all screwed up. You see that piece of land just behind us. We are definitely not supposed to be here. Get us back on track, and then we'll talk about what happened," the captain ordered.

Yan took some bearings on the land mass, checked out the location indicated on the GPS navigation equipment and plotted the ship's position on the chart. Jones had steered the ship almost 20 miles off course in the vicinity of some islands and dangerous reefs. Quickly, Yan drew a safe course on the chart to return to their original track and advised the Captain to take up a new heading to get back into safe waters.

When things settled down a bit, Captain Garth turned to Jones and said, "Okay, tell us what happened on your watch. I want to know the details."

Jones shook with fear as he began his story. "I saw a light on the horizon. I watched it for a long time, and it never changed positions. It got closer, and it never moved from the same relative position. I was taught in marine school that if a ship doesn't change relative position and gets closer, you are on a collision course. I guess I panicked and changed our course to the right to avoid a collision. That seemed to help, and I maintained that new course for some time."

"For how long, Jones?" Yan chided.

"I don't know. Maybe an hour, maybe two. I lost track of time. I was more concerned about getting away from that ship."

"Well, ya got us away all right, but ya nearly ran us aground. That was stupid," Yan said in defiance.

"Who are you calling stupid?" Jones shouted back.

"Stop it, men! I'll take care of this," the captain asserted. "Yan, that will be all. Thank you for getting us back on track. You may return to the crew's quarters. You did a good job. Goodnight."

Captain Garth then turned to Jones. "Jones, stay here. I want to talk to you in private."

When Yan left the pilothouse, Captain Garth proceeded to give Jones a hard lecture on seamanship and responsibility for using good judgment.

"And finally, Jones, do you remember I ordered you to call me when things got out of hand and if any vessel got within two miles of us? You failed to do that, didn't you? Furthermore, good seamanship should have taught you that, in your situation, you should have turned to the left and let the other vessel pass to our starboard side. That would have kept us in safe waters and a mile or less off course in the end. Also, never change course for more than a few minutes without advising the navigator or me. That is a rule of the sea. Understand, Jones?" the captain concluded.

"Yes, Sir. I'm sorry, Sir. I'll do better next time," Jones mumbled. For a moment Jones considered telling the captain about the incident with Yan in the bow cargo hold ... to get even, but he paused and decided to keep his mouth shut. Squealing on Yan was not going to help his situation, he figured. He held tightly to the helm and stared ahead of the bow in silence. The captain retired to his cabin, and the ship became quiet once more.

CHAPTER 7

Jacksonville Bewilderment

"Cardinal 33223, turn left to a heading of 110 degrees, descend and maintain 3000. Do you have information Foxtrot at Jacksonville International?" Jacksonville Center asked.

"That's affirmative, left to 110, maintain 3000," Tom acknowledged.

"Roger, you can expect ILS approach to runway 13," the flight controller announced.

He explained to Chris and Renee over the intercom that the weather in Jacksonville was not good and that they'd have to make a landing under instrument conditions with a cloud cover at 700 feet and visibility 2 miles in rain and fog. He asked Chris to hand him the instrument approach charts for Jacksonville from his manual, and then he requested that Chris set up the instrument landing frequencies for the glide slope and outer marker. They descended into the thick clouds. Renee kept looking out the window, but there was nothing to see but the faint reflection in the mist of the red running light at the tip of the left wing. Everything outside of the cockpit windows was a whiteout. Descending through 4000 feet and 35 miles from the airport, they encountered moderate rain and turbulence.

"Hang on, guys. It's going to be bumpy a few more minutes until we're on the ground. Are you okay, Renee?" Tom asked.

"Yeah." Her voice came weakly over the intercom.

Tom had his hands full maneuvering the plane through the weather and getting set for the approach for the runway, so he couldn't look back to see what she was doing. One thought entered his mind about her at the moment—motion sickness. He hoped she remembered where the airsick bag was stored if she needed it, but he didn't want to bring up the subject for fear that the very power of suggestion would be a self-fulfilling prophecy. Rain now pelted the windshield hard as he reduced the plane's airspeed to 120 knots to ease up on the impact of the turbulence.

Chris looked out the window and saw nothing but solid white all around. Tom's eyes were glued to the flight instruments: the airspeed, the artificial horizon, the gyro compass, the automatic direction finder, the glide slope, the turn and bank and the vertical speed indicators and altimeter. Every few seconds he'd glance at the approach charts in anticipation of their next course change.

"Cardinal 33223, descend and maintain 2000, contact Jacksonville approach on 119.0."

Tom switched to approach control and confirmed that he was descending to 2000 feet. They were then instructed to descend to 1600 feet and turn to a heading of 160. When they reached 1600 feet, they were flying in and out of broken layers of clouds again, and the rain slackened to a drizzle. The tower cleared them for the final approach to runway 13 at the Jacksonville airport.

Chris looked out the window and saw nothing but clouds. Renee refused to look outside. She stared at her feet and chewed on her fingernails. Tom reduced the aircraft's airspeed to 80 knots and turned left to a heading of 130. According to the instruments, they were now lined up with the runway. At five miles from touchdown, he instructed Chris to lower the flaps ten degrees to slow down their descent.

At a point four miles from the end of the runway, they were socked in by the clouds again. Visibility was zero. He reported to approach control that they were at the four-mile marker, and they were instructed to change to the tower frequency for clearance to land. Chris lowered the landing gear, let down the flaps to 40 degrees and turned on the landing lights. They continued their descent using the glide slope indicator on the instrument panel to direct them to the end of the runway. When they reached 500 feet above the ground, they broke out of the clouds. The bright strobe lights at the end of the runway were clearly visible a mile ahead

"Can't do better than that,"Tom said to Chris.

A slight screech sounded as the main wheels touched gently on the wet runway, which prompted an audible sigh of relief from the back seat.

"Wow! I thought we were gonna crash!" Renee squealed.

Chris started retracting the flaps as Tom pulled the power all the way back and applied the brakes. At 60 knots and speed decreasing, the nose wheel touched down on the runway and held firm.

"Welcome to beautiful Jacksonville. Don't you love this weather?" Tom remarked sarcastically to the crew. "Renee? Renee, are you still with us?" He looked back to see if she was okay. She looked a little pale.

"What a wild ride!" she finally admitted.

"Thanks. That's a great vote of confidence," Tom said half-jokingly.

The tower instructed them to switch to ground control and gave them clearance to taxi to the general aviation ramp. A ramp attendant in yellow, foul weather gear stood at a tie down spot and directed them to swing around and park in front of where he was standing. Tom pushed on the brakes to bring the aircraft to a halt and shut the engine down. No one spoke in the cockpit for the next moment. Only the winding down of the gyros in the cockpit could be heard. Chris opened the door for Renee, and they made a dash through the rain for the general aviation terminal a few hundred feet away. Tom informed the attendant that they were going to be there for about thirty minutes and needed topping off with 100-octane fuel.

When Tom reached the terminal building, Chris and Renee were nowhere in sight. He headed over to the counter to fill out a fuel request for the plane, then got directions to the flight planning room down the hallway. But as he walked through the corridor, he heard Renee from a distance talking to someone. Even though he couldn't see her, she seemed to be around the corner in the next hallway. When he came to the intersection of the corridors, he spotted her apparently arguing with someone on a pay phone. Fortunately, she didn't see him, so he discretely went into the flight planning room next to the phone booth, where he could overhear part of the conversation.

"Will you shut up? I told you that I am going to take care of it!" There was a pause. Then, "Stop yelling! I can hear you just fine." Another pause, then, "I know what you said. Don't worry, I have a plan."

Just at that moment, Renee looked up, and out of the corner of his eye, Tom saw her glance in his direction. She immediately lowered her voice and turned her back to the planning room where he was, but he still heard her say, "Hey, I've got to go. No, I can't talk now. Trust me." She abruptly hung up the phone.

Tom pretended that he hadn't heard her. He sat down at a table just out of her sight for a few moments, then picked up the latest weather charts and thumbed through them. He had started to work on their flight plan to West Palm Beach when Chris walked into the room.

"How's the weather down the road?" he asked.

"Fine. Improving," Tom assured him. "Thank goodness the stationary front over Jacksonville is dissipating. The weather from Daytona Beach all the way to the out islands of the Bahamas is excellent—partly cloudy to clear for the rest of the route for the remainder of the day."

After filing a flight plan for the next leg of the trip, he pulled Chris aside and whispered, "Chris, have you noticed anything sorta funny about Renee since we landed? She seems to be bothered by something. Did she say anything to you while I was checking the weather?"

"Nope. I haven't even seen her since we left the plane. She took off for the restroom. Why?" he asked. "Maybe she has motion sickness," he added.

"I don't know. I heard her talking on the phone, and she seemed to be arguing with someone, upset about something. But who knows what it was? It's none of our business, I guess. Why don't you find her and see if she's ready to go," Tom said.

Chris spent a few fruitless minutes wandering around looking for Renee. When the rain stopped, he returned to the plane to supervise the refueling operations, while Tom went to the flight planning room to talk to the weather service people one more time to confirm the conditions en route. Renee still had not reappeared.

A few moments later, Chris returned to the pilot lounge and found Tom engaged in conversation with the weather specialist. Ground visibility and the cloud ceiling were improving faster than forecast, and instrument conditions at the airport had just been lifted. Tom made some minor amendments to their flight plan based on the revised forecast. They picked up some crackers from the snack machine and started their search in earnest for Renee. They searched the entire general aviation terminal without success.

"Maybe she's in the restroom again," Chris suggested.

"Maybe. I'll ask one of the ladies here to check. I hope she's not sick. She obviously was out of sorts about something," Tom said.

He approached the girl behind the front counter and asked if she could do them a small favor by checking for Renee in the ladies room. A few minutes later, she returned and confirmed Renee was not in the restroom.

As they passed a window overlooking the ramp, Chris abruptly grabbed the back of Tom's shirt and yanked him back to the window. Tom caught a glimpse of someone leaning over the nose wheel of their plane.

"Look out there! Is that Renee?" Chris asked.

"Could be. Let's go!" Tom said. Without further discussion, they ran down the hall and out the door to the ramp. As they approached the plane, they could see that the person hovering around the nose wheel was Renee.

"Hey! What are you doing?" Chris shouted.

Obviously startled, she jumped "Oh! Hi, guys! I ... I lost an earring. I heard it fall under the plane."

"Really? Funny? I hadn't noticed you wearing earrings," Chris said.

"No ... no. You're right. I had them right here in my hand, ready to put them on, and I dropped one of them."

"Oh. Well, hey, you look great without 'em," Chris said with some relief.

They helped her search for the earring but never found it. Then when they were both on the other side of the wing and Renee was behind their backs, she announced, "Oh, here it is." They turned around, and she was leaning over to pick up a small, bright-gold earring out of a puddle of water just beneath the wing.

"I'll be darned!" Chris exclaimed. "I could have sworn I already looked there. I didn't see a thing. You must have sharp eyes, Renee."

She smiled sweetly, then turned to Tom. "What's our next stop?"

"West Palm Beach," Tom said.

"How long will it take to get there?"

"About two hours."

"I guess I'd better make a bathroom stop before we go then. Excuse me, guys, while I go check out the ladies room for a few minutes." She walked quickly back to the terminal building and disappeared again.

"I thought she went to the restroom when we first arrived," Chris said.

"Who knows what's going on. I think she's still not feeling well. You know, it's that 'girl thing.' I'm not going to get into that type of conversation with her," Tom said.

About 10 minutes later, Renee returned to the plane.

"Well, are we ready to go?" Chris added. At their answering nods, the three of them piled into the plane and shut the doors. Tom tuned in to the automatic terminal information service to get the current field weather conditions and then obtained their clearance to the West Palm Beach Airport. After taxiing to the far end of the runway, they got clearance from the control tower to take off and head south. There were no delays, and when they reached 1000 feet, the tower instructed them to turn to a southeasterly heading and climb to 6000 feet. They flew through some scattered layers of clouds and were clear on top of the clouds at 5500 feet. The air was smooth at this altitude. Chris set the autopilot to level off at their final approved altitude of 9000 feet and tuned in their first radio beacon checkpoint in Daytona Beach.

Renee seemed withdrawn. Her face was blank and still.

"You okay, Renee? You seem so quiet," Tom attempted to draw her into a conversation. Chris peered over his shoulder to look at her.

"I'm all right," she replied. She said nothing more, yet the expression on her face and the look in her eyes gave her away. She was definitely concerned about something.

"We should be arriving in West Palm Beach in 2 hours and 10 minutes, which should be around 12:55 in the afternoon. West Palm Beach will be a good place to have lunch before we head across the pond to Nassau. The weather forecast is good the rest of the way with a few widely scattered showers en route, mostly inland due to the heating of the land. We can easily circumnavigate the isolated variety," Tom informed everyone.

They continued down the coastline of northern Florida, flying just above the innocent appearing, white clouds and admiring the fascinating view below. Tom kept thinking about Renee. Ever since they landed in Jacksonville, she had been acting strangely. He wanted to ask Chris privately what he thought about Renee's behavior, but there was no way he could disconnect her intercom headset without it being obvious. So he resolved to wait til they arrived in West Palm Beach.

Out the left window the sea looked like an endless lake with two coastal freighters and several sailboats scattered about on the surface, some moving northward, others moving toward the south. On the right side and just below them was the Florida coastline. Far to the west of their track, the hot haze above the Florida plains restricted their visibility to eight miles. Except for the strip immediately along the coastline, the land was mostly scrub wasteland with a few cattle farms carved out of the marshes. Tom noticed Chris' head was starting to get heavy, and before long he was leaning against the side window sleeping. Renee continued to meditate in silence in the back seat. He left everyone to their own thoughts for a while.

CHAPTER 8

Scarface's Thorn

It was mid-morning when the telephone rang in the sparsely furnished, second-floor warehouse office. A lone man leaned back precariously on two of the four wooden chair legs so he could prop his feet up on a box and look out the window. But the cracked windowpane was grimy and partially obscured the Atlanta skyline a mile away. He startled when the ringing phone broke the silence. He jerked so violently that he lost his balance and fell backwards slamming his head on the floor. Groaning and holding the back of his head with one hand, he managed to stumble to his feet and move quickly across the room to grab the phone off of a cigarette stained table.

"Yes?" he answered in a cautious voice.

"Scarface? Is that you, Scarface?" the distant voice at the other end inquired.

"Well, yes, who's this?" he asked.

"This is Boss, you zero brain ... from George Town."

"Oh, yeah. Sorry. I didn't recognize you at first, Boss. What's up, Sir?"

"I have got some questions for you. Did you take care of the situation I told you about?"

"Well ...."

"You know what I'm talking about, the little annoyance up the coast. Do you understand me, hollow brain?"

"Yes, Sir, Boss. I'm taking care of it," Scarface said in a nervous, unconvincing voice.

"When are you going to get the job done?"

"Soon. Real soon, Boss," Scarface assured him.

"So, why don't you tell me about what's happening?"

Boss probed further.

"Well, uh, I arranged to have two of our people fly there to fix it. I gave them detailed instructions on what to do. They understand the mission. Believe me," Scarface boasted.

"Oh, I do. I do. You know how much I trust you. That's why I'm calling you, you knucklehead," he said in a disbelieving tone. That's why I always have to ask you questions. Are you sure you don't have anything else to tell me, Scarface? Tell me exactly what you did. I want all the details."

A bead of sweat trickled down Scarface's left check, and he started pacing across the squeaky, wooden floor trying to find a way to calm Boss down. Scarface knew he wasn't convincing him. No one gets away with lying to Boss.

He hesitated for a few seconds to search for the right words and then continued, "Just like I said, Boss, I ordered comrade Rum Runner to fly her plane there a few days ago. An ex-aviation mechanic went with her. And don't worry about the mechanic. He's a fugitive and he's harmless. He needs us. He'll do anything we tell him to do, because his mechanic's license was revoked for making false log entries, claiming repairs and inspections which were never done. Now he's running from the law. I told him we'd protect him if he did some jobs for us … like take care of our plane for our island missions. It's just another job for him, no questions asked. Rum Runner knows she is the key to success between you and our contacts on the mainland. She won't do anything to mess up. And, Boss, just to make doubly sure there are no mistakes, I sent comrade Blondie there, too."

"I don't have to remind you, bonehead, that we've got a lot at stake here. No screw ups! Understand? NO SCREW UPS!" Boss growled.

"Yes, Sir. No screw ups," Scarface repeated. The line went dead.

Scarface hung up the receiver, reached in his hip pocket, pulled out a wrinkled, damp handkerchief and mopped his forehead. His telephone conversation with Blondie half an hour earlier haunted him, because he hadn't had the guts to tell Boss the mission with Rum Runner and her aviation mechanic had failed. Now Scarface was relying solely on Blondie to finish the job. Feeling desperate, he picked up the phone and dialed a number in Miami. An answering machine responded. At the beep, he shouted, "Sheila! This is Scarface. It's urgent. Call me."

He slammed the phone down and walked over to the oscillating fan on the table and stood in front of it for a few minutes to evaporate the sweat off of his face. Frustrated, Scarface strode to the cooler, retrieved a can of beer and placed it on the back of his head to ease the throbbing knot—his souvenir from the fall. Then he opened the can and guzzled down the beer.

Southeast of Andros Island, the ship's captain ordered the helmsman to turn right to a heading of 115 degrees now that they had safely passed the narrow cut in the reef at Ships Channel Light. The coastal freighter was already about thirty miles south of the light in the shallow waters of Exuma Sound. It was almost noon, June 15th. Yan walked through the port hatch of the pilothouse onto the bridge to talk to the captain.

"Capt'n, Sir, I confirmed our position on the chart. We're lookin' good, Sir. It's good water all the way to Devil's Point and the entrance to Cutlass Bay. There's no more reef problems until we reach the entrance to Cutlass Bay."

"Thank you, Yan. I can handle it now. Go get some chow and rest," the captain ordered. Yan had been up most of the night plotting continuous course changes through the dangerous shallow reefs north of the Exuma Cays.

"Aye, Capt'n."

Yan disappeared through the hatch into the pilothouse, climbed down the ladder onto the main deck and headed aft. The captain looked at his watch and did some quick calculations in his head. By now he felt confident of his estimated arrival time near sunset at Devil's Point. Taking three more puffs from his pipe, he removed his cap, walked into the pilothouse and headed aft to the radio room. The room wasn't much bigger than a closet but was full of radio equipment: two short-wave transmitters and receivers for long distance communications, two VHF transceivers for short range harbor communications, LORAN and Satellite navigation systems, a ship-to-shore telephone system and teletype. He closed the hatch door behind him, sat down by the table and started tuning the radio dial for a clear ship-to-shore telephone channel to make a call to George Town.

The phone rang several times before someone answered. "Conch Harbour, may I help you?" a voice said.

"Hello. I need to speak to Boss," the captain demanded.

"He's not here. Who's this?"

"Tell him the captain called. Have him call me when he returns. He knows how to reach me."

"Yes, Sir, Captain," the voice acknowledged.

He hung up the radiotelephone and left word for the helmsman to notify him when the call was returned. Forty minutes later, the helmsman heard the telephone operator radio the ship. He called the captain on the intercom in his stateroom.

"Captain? Jones here. There's a call for you."

"Thank you, Jones. I'll be there in just a second." Captain Garth hustled down the passageway to the radio room, slamming the metal door shut behind him.

"Hello, this is the captain."

"Where are you?" the voice in George Town asked.

"I'm thirty-two miles north of Cutlass. At my speed I should arrive at Devil's Point around four o'clock this evening. I'll drop anchor and wait for further instructions."

"Perfect," Boss replied. "Our supplies are low. Good work, Captain. I'll stay in touch." The conversation ended as quickly as it had begun. Security on the radio was not the best, and the less conversation, the better, over the airways.

Incident at Cat Island

In Miami, a summer thunderstorm had just passed over the old warehouse along the Miami River. It pushed swiftly inland toward the Everglades. Although the rain diminished to a drizzle, the relative humidity increased from 75 to 100 percent.

A black limousine drove up to the front entrance of the warehouse. A pair of slender, well-shaped legs were followed out of the back seat by a striking young girl wearing a miniskirt. She and two men in business suits exited and walked hurriedly along the open, wooden walkway to the riverfront side of the building. Ducking inside the large loading entrance and brushing the water droplets off their clothes, they weaved their way around pallets of large boxes and crates until they came to a rickety, wooden staircase which led up to a closed door on the mezzanine level. The warehouse was dark except for two lights hanging down from the ceiling at each end of the building. When they reached the top of the stairs, the girl knocked three times on the door, paused and knocked twice again.

An old man cautiously cracked open the door an inch and peered outside at the visitors standing on the stairs. When he recognized one of them, he opened the door wide and shouted, "Rum Runner! It's so good to see you. I hear you've been on a special mission up north. Come in, come in."

He jerked his head toward the two strangers, "Uh, who are these two guys?"

"I'm here to introduce you to two possible new partners. Gentlemen, I'd like for you to meet Rufus, our Miami dispatcher and supply scheduler," she replied.

The two gangsters shook Rufus' hand but didn't bother to introduce themselves.

"I can't tell you any more until I talk to Scarface," she continued.

The old man ran a hand over his stubbly chin.

"That reminds me, Scarface has been trying to find you. He sounded a little anxious when he called here looking for you," Rufus said.

"Yes, I know. I picked up his message on my answering machine a couple of hours ago. Let's call him now. I want him to talk to these two."

In Atlanta, Scarface already had downed five beers while sitting in his office and was two sheets to the wind when the phone rang. He picked up the receiver and just listened.

"Hello… HELLO. Is that you Scarface?... Scarface … answer me!" Rum Runner hollered into the receiver.

"Ooooh, now you lishen to me, you idiot. Don't you shout at me. You have the wrong number." He hung up the phone. A few seconds later the phone rang again. "Hey, I told you, cutie pie, you have the wrong ..."

"Wait, Scarface. This is Rum Runner, you know, Sheila. I'm in Miami. I've got a couple of men here I want you to talk to."

"Why didn't you say who you were? (hic). You make me look stupid sometimes."

"Shut up and listen to me," Sheila snapped. "They're interested in being our partners. They have big time connections in the financial world, with banks and loan companies. And they have connections to the syndicate. They're a perfect link for our operations. They're hot. It could mean millions for our operations on Cat. I wanted to run this by you before we face Boss."

Scarface was not focusing on the conversation. He belched loudly.

"Where in the devil (hic) you been, girlie? I've been trying to reesh you for days," he slurred.

"You know what I've been doing. Now listen to me. These guys here ..."

Scarface interrupted, "Why'd (hic) you mesh up your last mission? Huh? Made me look bad. Them yahoos up the coast are all over our operations. I promised Bossh this wouldn't happen. Bossh is extremely upset. (hic) What the heck are you doing now? Gotta get it all fixed up. Can't fail thish time."

Sheila turned her back on the two strangers and hissed into the phone. "Hey! Would you please pay attention to why I'm calling you?"

Scarface continued as if she hadn't spoken a word, "If Bossh calls again, and we don't have the answer he wants to hear this time, we're finished! Do you hear me?... Done for!" he whined.

Sheila tried to calm Scarface down. "No, no, no. Blondie's not stupid. She knows how important this is. Her life's at stake, too. She'll take care of it."

"You better be right, Rum Runner." Suddenly changing the subject, Scarface asked, "So, whatcha been doin?"

Sheila repeated the information about the two new prospects, and after a few minutes of conversation, arrangements were made for them to meet Scarface in the Atlanta office the next week.

"Listen, girlie. One more thing," Scarface mumbled.

"What?" Sheila asked.

"I've arranged for another shipment from Mexico to be delivered at two o'clock Thursday morning at Code Crocodile. Be there with the truck and take it to the warehouse for the next run to the islands. Unnershtand?" Scarface insisted. His voice trembled.

"Of course. No problem. We'll take care of everything. Don't you worry," Sheila said calmly, as though speaking to a small child.

The telephone line went dead.

CHAPTER 9

Foiled Plot

In south Florida, an air traffic controller gave new instructions to Tom, "Cardinal 33223, this is Miami Center. Descend and maintain 3000 feet. Contact Palm Beach Approach on 124.6. Good day."

"3000 and Approach 124.6," Tom acknowledged.

Chris had just finished listening to the Airport Terminal Information Service to get the latest weather and runway conditions at Palm Beach International Airport.

Tom contacted Palm Beach Approach Control and advised them they were in their airspace and were descending to 3000 feet as requested. He pulled back on the throttle and manifold pressure to reduce their air speed as they continued their approach to the airport.

He was momentarily distracted when Chris twisted around to look back at Renee who was staring out the window still in deep thought. She was chewing her fingernails again.

"We should be on the ground in about 12 minutes," Tom announced. "Make sure your seat belts are on." The weather was ideal with a few cumulus clouds scattered about and unlimited visibility.

"We can expect a little choppy air when we reach 3000 feet due to the heating effect from the ground, but it shouldn't be bad," he was quick to add.

Soon, Approach Control switched them to the tower radio frequency and gave them clearance to land on one of the parallel runways, and in a matter of minutes their wheels squeaked gently on the concrete.

"And here we are in sunny south Florida," Tom announced

happily. He requested the tower to give them clearance to one of the fixed based operators, and they were directed from the active runway onto a taxiway and to the ramp. A ramp attendant was standing in front of the parking spot with his arms straight up in the air to guide them to the tie down space. Tom swung the plane around to face the ramp attendant and slowly eased the plane up to within five feet of where he was standing. The attendant signaled for them to stop, and Tom shut down the engine.

Chris had already opened his door slightly to let some breeze blow through the cabin. When the propeller stopped spinning, he hopped out before Tom could take off his earphones, and Renee was close behind him. It was 1:55 in the afternoon.

"It's good to stretch out," Renee said as she reached for the sky with both arms. "Ow! The pain is killing me," she moaned, and she clutched her stomach. "I need to make a quick dash to the ladies room. I don't think I can hold it any longer!" She took off toward the terminal.

Chris and Tom exchanged silent glances. They remained at the plane to get out the life jackets and the charts for the water-crossing leg of their flight. Tom asked the ramp attendant to top off the fuel tanks with 100 octane and mentioned that they planned to be there only for about an hour, long enough to talk to Flight Service about the weather, file an international flight plan and grab a bite to eat.

Renee quickly disappeared inside the general aviation terminal and exited out the door on the other side of the building. She ran into the next building and found a pay phone in a hallway. Glancing back over her shoulder often, she dialed a number, waited a few seconds and then hissed into the phone, "Hey. Listen. I only have a minute. This is Blondie. I'm still working on my plan…. No. These guys are sharp. I need a little more time." There was a brief pause. And then she said, "Stop yelling! Will you listen to me? I'm not done. I did NOT fail. I still have time. Trust me! I'll take care of it before it's too late. NO! I'll call you later." She hung up and left the building.

Chris and Tom entered the general aviation lobby and felt

the atmospheric shock of cool, dry air on their skin after experiencing 90-degree heat and 80-percent humidity outside. Renee was nowhere to be seen, so they assumed she still was in the restroom. They sat down in the lobby to relax. After a few minutes and with still no sign of Renee, Tom suggested that Chris wait there while he went to check on the weather and file a flight plan. The weather briefing and filing of the flight plan took 15 minutes, so when he returned to the main lobby, he was surprised to see Renee hadn't made an appearance yet.

"Chris, any sign of Renee, yet?" he asked hopefully.

"Nothing," Chris said.

"Where does she go when we're on the ground?" he muttered. "We're running out of time. Let's go over to the snack shop and get a sandwich. Maybe by then she'll show up."

Conveniently, the snack shop was just down the hall, so they left a message with the counter attendant to send Renee their way when she returned. They ordered the soup and sandwich special for the day, figuring the order would be quick, and Tom briefed Chris on the weather for the Bahamas. There were no problems, just a few scattered cumulus clouds at 1500 feet over the islands and perhaps a widely scattered shower. They were expected to encounter a head wind of 25 knots at 9000 feet, but on the surface, the winds were out of the southeast at 10-15 knots. He told Chris their flying time to Nassau, their first stop to clear customs and immigration, should be about one hour and forty minutes.

Lunch was served within five minutes, and as they ate, their conversation kept drifting back to Renee. There still was no sign of her. They hurriedly swallowed their food, almost without chewing, and returned back to the general aviation lobby to continue their search for her. Chris headed in one direction. and Tom headed in another, and in about ten minutes, they met again without having found Renee.

"Let's check the plane. Maybe she has gone back there," Chris suggested.

"I doubt it," Tom said.

"Well, what else can we do? I'll check the plane myself

then," Chris said. He stomped off toward the plane while Tom searched the building and asked everyone he spotted if they had seen Renee.

A few minutes later, Chris came pounding up to Tom. He careened to a halt and leaned down on his knees to catch his breath. "Tom! Did you ... did you leave the doors open on the plane?" he gasped.

"No, I locked them. Why?"

"Both doors ... *both doors* were standing wide open," Chris exclaimed.

They rushed out of the building and headed toward the aircraft. When they arrived, Tom discovered the locking mechanism and door handle were bent on the pilot's side of the plane. When they searched inside to see what had been stolen, they saw that all of Renee's personal belongings were gone. At first glance everything else seemed to be there.

Tom shook his head, "Why would anyone just steal Renee's stuff?"

Chris smacked Tom's bicep with the back of his hand. "No one stole Renee's stuff! *She* took it. Anybody else would've taken the valuable stuff, not Renee's baggage. Renee jumped ship. She's gone! Something's been kinky about her from the start!" Chris ranted. Dang her and her big blue eyes!"

Tom ran a hand through his hair and paced back and forth on the tarmac. "I feel like an idiot. You're right, Chris We don't really know anything about her. This whole thing's been weird. I remember when we were in Jacksonville. She was arguing with someone on the phone. I overheard her say something like 'I'll take care of it' and 'I have a plan.' I let it slide because I figured it was none of my business—that maybe she was having a fight with her boyfriend, or with someone—but now? Who knows? What do you think?"

Chris blew out a breath. "I don't know what to think. You know me when I see a pretty face. She seemed nice enough, just a little different. But the episode with the lost earring under the plane ... I swear when I spotted her from the window of the terminal building, she was on her knees and had her hand inside the engine cowling next to the nose wheel."

Chris walked around to the front of the plane and pointed to the spot. "Remember, she claimed that she had dropped one of her earrings and heard it fall up here? Then when we showed up and started helping her look, she miraculously found the earring...." He turned and walked back to the wing and gestured underneath it. "... way back there."

Chris abruptly stopped talking and chewed his bottom lip for a moment, then blurted out, "And why would she desert us at this point in the trip? I can't figure her out. All I can say is 'good riddance.'"

Tom shook his head, just as confused as his friend. "She must have had a fight with her boyfriend or ... or maybe it was her boss. The only thing I can figure is she got so wound up with whatever was going on that she suddenly decided she had to leave ... in a hurry."

"But, she didn't even say goodbye or tell us she was leaving, or anything."

"I know. I can't figure it out either," Tom started pacing again. "Maybe we should report her as missing." Tom said.

Chris grabbed his friend by the arm and brought him to a stop. "Absolutely not! Forget it. She was the one who wanted to come along with us. She has been a pain in the neck from the very beginning, and no fun at all. She's supposed to be an adult, but she's acted like a child. Let her go. We're not responsible for her. Let's just go on to George Town, like we planned in the first place, and forget about Long Island."

Tom weighed his options, then a slow grin spread across his face. "Okay. I don't want to go to Long Island either. George Town it is."

Chris let out a whoop and the two exchanged a high five.

Chris hollered, "Roadtrip!"

Tom Laughed, "Um ... yeah. If you stretch the definition of a roadtrip to include flying, I guess you could call it that."

Chris grinned his lopsided grin.

Incident at Cat Island

Still laughing, Tom nodded his head toward the building. "I need to go back into the terminal and amend our flight plan and immigration papers. It will only take about 10 minutes. Meantime, find a mechanic and see if he can fix this door handle and lock. It looks like it's just bent and probably can be fixed without much fuss."

Chris got a mechanic from one of the hangers and had the door lock and handle fixed in about 20 minutes. Tom returned to the plane, checked the door locking mechanism himself, climbed in, shut the doors, listened to the automatic information service on the radio for the current runway in use and field conditions and turned the key to start the engine. Nothing happened, not even a single turn of the propeller.

Tom slapped his forehead in disbelief. "This plane must be jinxed!" he shouted to Chris. He tried again. The engine remained silent. There was no power to the starter. "All right, let's get out and see what's going on."

They exited the plane and looked under the cowling at the engine. Everything appeared normal. Then he thought, "No power, no battery power." Tom removed the panel behind the luggage compartment to check the connections to the battery.

Again, it was Chris' sharp eyes that spotted something odd just behind the battery box. Tucked underneath a wiring harness were a couple of red tubes wrapped with wires.

"Are those supposed to be there?" Chris asked, the look of sheer horror on his face making it very clear that he knew better.

Tom looked closely, reached inside and pulled the tubes out of the compartment. They were two sticks of dynamite wired to a small black box, then hand wrapped around the two battery cables.

"GOOD GRIEF!" Chris gasped. "Someone is trying to kill us! Renee is trying to kill us."

"No. It couldn't have been Renee," Tom explained, peering at the bomb. "She ... she was in the terminal. And besides, it would have taken a lot of time for someone to rig this up."

Chris snorted, "She could have brought it with her and then installed it while we were in the terminal. Remember, we haven't seen her since we landed."

"But I saw what she had in her suitcase, and it wasn't this," Tom said.

"You did? When?" Chris demanded.

"Uh, well, it was back in Wilmington. She was going through her stuff at the terminal before we left, " he lied, too embarrassed to tell Chris about his disastrous motel room encounter with Renee. "Look, what possible reason would she have to do something like this?" Tom asked.

Chris shrugged, then turned back to the bomb. Suddenly his face lit up like he had just won the lottery. "Hey, look here. This is interesting! Look at the battery cable. One of the terminals is connected to the battery, but the other one is loose." He pointed.

"And that's why the plane wouldn't start," Tom said. "Whoever did this must have been distracted, or they had to leave in a hurry without connecting that last cable."

"Yeah! Lucky for us. If it had been connected properly... well, we know the rest of the story," Chris said. "Let me see that black box."

They carefully opened the box and discovered a pressure switch inside it.

"Aha," Chris said. "I know how that works. When the plane reaches a certain altitude, the switch closes, and BAM!!"

He used his left forearm to wipe a trickle of sweat from his temple. "Tom, we need to call the police. This is like ... attempted murder or something." Scuffing the toe of his shoe across the tarmac, he suddenly looked up at Tom and added, "Hey, you don't ... you don't s'pose it was the fuel guy ...?"

"Why? Again, what's his motive? What possible reason would he have for doing this?"

Tom shook his head. "No. There may have been two people involved, though. We were in the terminal looking for Renee for quite a while. Someone was probably shadowing us while the accomplice was doing the dirty work out here."

Tom watched Chris drop his head and kick at a small tuft of grass growing up through the tarmac.

"And maybe that someone signaled the guy in the plane before he could finish making the last connection to the battery," Tom added.

"Man, we're so fortunate that the loose connection was loose," Chris exclaimed with a deadly pale face. "We gotta call the police," he repeated.

"This is definitely a criminal act. Tampering with the safety of an aircraft, especially involving an explosive device, is a federal offense. But we can't prove who did it."

Tom thrust his fingers through his hair again. "The real problem is that now we're talking about involvement with the FBI, the FAA, the local police, the base operations and who knows who else—maybe even the NTSB. The paperwork, the interviews, impounding our plane...." He slapped the flat of his hand against the plane's fuselage. "We could be stuck here in West Palm for the whole week. Maybe longer. Up to this point, no one has been harmed, right?"

He saw the suspicion on Chris' face even before his friend spoke.

"Noooo, but ... someone tried to kill us. This is serious."

"Right, but nobody actually got hurt," Tom stated firmly. "Look. I vote we continue our flight. We've found the problem. We can fix it. All we have to do is quietly dispose of the device, hook up the battery properly, do a thorough run up check of the engine on the ramp and take our vacation in the Bahamas like we had planned."

Chris' face was a study in emotions. "Are you serious? Just leave?"

Tom glanced over his shoulder to make sure no one was close enough to the plane to hear their conversation, then nodded. "I'm going to the islands. I need a vacation, not an investigation."

Chris didn't move for a moment, then shrugged, "Okay. Suit yourself. I'm with you, partner. But what do we do with the you-know-what? We can't just throw it away?"

After a brief discussion, Chris took a black trash bag from the plane and walked to the edge of the tarmac and scooped several handfuls of sand into it. As casually as possible, he walked back to the plane, placed it next to the battery, then carefully deposited the two sticks of dynamite and wires inside the bag and stowed the bag in the cockpit next to his seat. The black box with the pressure switch, he stuffed into a small paper bag and pushed it deep into a trash bin next to the terminal. When he was finished, Chris brushed off his hands and climbed into his seat in the plane.

Tom tightened up the loose battery cable, closed up the panel behind the luggage compartment, reloaded their gear, climbed on board and turned the ignition key one more time. After a couple of turns on the propeller, the engine fired up normally. He checked the engine gauges and flight instruments. Everything was working okay.

"We're good to go," he said to Chris. "One thing's in our favor with Renee gone. We're about 180 pounds lighter. That means we can fly a little faster and use less fuel."

"I don't suppose Renee paid in advance for her share of the trip?" Chris asked, grinning like the Cheshire Cat.

"Yeah, right! That would have made too much sense." Tom answered.

As they rolled down the taxiway, Tom's thoughts were a jumble of conflicting emotions about Renee and the bomb. He was so distracted that he missed the instructions from the ground controller to make a left turn at the next intersection and, instead, continued straight down the wrong taxiway.

Immediately, the ground controller's shrill, irritated voice squawked in his ear, "Cardinal 33223, WHERE are you going? You missed the turn onto taxiway Bravo. Do a 180-degree turn right there and proceed onto taxiway Bravo, as instructed."

"Yes, Sir. I'm very sorry. We're turning around now," Tom apologized. Soon the control tower cleared them for a straight-out departure toward the islands. Tom lifted the wheels off the runway when the airspeed passed 60 knots, and they were on their way.

As they proceeded east leaving the shoreline behind, the tower called them for the last time, "Cardinal 33223, you have traffic one and a half miles at your two o'clock position at 2500 feet heading in the same direction as yours. Do you have that plane in sight?"

"Yes, Sir, we have the traffic in sight. Looks like a DC-3."

"Roger, squawk 1200 on your transponder. Have a good flight to the islands."

"Thanks," Tom acknowledged.

CHAPTER 10

Whale Creek Anchorage

A few miles off the western tip of Cat Island, Captain Garth peered through his binoculars from the port bow and searched along the shoreline for Hawksnest Creek, a key landmark that identifies the island. When he spotted the peninsula, he took a compass bearing on the point and instructed his helmsman to alter his course slightly to the left. The helmsman guided the coastal freighter through the calm waters of Exuma Sound until the ship passed Hawksnest Creek entrance. The captain then ordered the helmsman to bring the freighter left to a course of 150 degrees. As the ship swung slowly to the east, Captain Garth looked through his binoculars again to find Devil's Point, the next turning point.

"Capt'n, remember, Sir, the barrier reef from Hawksnest Creek around Devil's Point to the eastern tip of the island extends out two miles offshore. According to our position on the chart, we're only half a mile from the reef. I kindly recommend you steady on course of 165 degrees, Sir, to stay clear of the reef," Yan pleaded.

"I know where the reef is. This is not the first time I've been here. We'll stay on a 150-degree heading. You can help keep watch for changes in the color of water ahead," Captain Garth grumbled.

"Aye, Sir, as you wish."

It was four o'clock in the afternoon with a steady southeast breeze of 20 knots. An hour later, as the freighter reached Devil's Point directly midship on the port side, the ship encountered a ten-foot, rolling surge from the open sea just ahead. The captain thought for a moment. Then he summoned Yan back to the bridge.

"Yan, I'm not concerned with the proximity of the reef, but I'm concerned with the ocean surge on the south end of the island near Cutlass Bay. We can't anchor and off-load under these sea and wind conditions. I want to turn around and head back to Hawksnest Creek and then swing to the northeast and proceed along the northern coast. We can anchor in the vicinity of Whale Creek on the north side and off-load our cargo there on the lee side of the island. I've been there in the past. Plot a course to clear the shallow sand bar west of Hawksnest Creek, please."

"Aye, Sir," Yan replied.

Captain Garth walked into the pilothouse and picked up the radio microphone. He tuned to a discrete frequency and made a call.

"Operation Asset, this is Code Dolphin, come in."

There was a minute pause with no answer. The captain repeated his radio call. The second time there was a response.

"This is Operation Asset. Go ahead."

"I'm just off Devil's Point heading northwest around Hawks then to Whale Creek. Estimated arrival at Whale Creek around 6:30 this evening. Over."

"Roger that. I'll have someone rendezvous with the barge offshore at Whale Creek around ten o'clock tomorrow morning. See you tomorrow, Captain," the voice on the radio assured.

Steady on a course of 300 degrees, the ship made its way toward the point at Hawksnest again. Since he knew it was going to be a long night, Garth decided to retire to his cabin for some chow and a couple of hours of sleep before anchoring in the harbor.

Soon the ship stopped rolling in the heavy swells when it reached the leeward side of the peninsula. The Cuban was at the helm. Yan decided to have a serious talk with him, since they were alone.

"You've been crewin' on this ship a long time, right?" Yan asked the Cuban.

"Yeah. So what?" he replied in a not-any-of-your-business tone.

"Well, Sir, I knows a lot 'bout navigatin' and stuff and been on other ships, sailed the seven seas, but I gots bad feelin's 'bout this trip. Capt'n don't tell me much 'bout whats we're doin'. Why are we goin' to Cat Island?" Yan asked.

"Oh, the captain didn't tell you, eh?" the Cuban said.

"Not 'xactly. He jest said I should stick to my navigatin' duties. But I knows what's in the cargo hold. It ain't jest lumber."

"Now, just how do you know that?" the Cuban asked.

"Well, I was … " He stopped in mid-sentence, as though realizing it would not be wise to tell him that he had been caught snooping around. "I was jest thinkin' that this is a lot of lumber for a little island. Maybe, someone's buildin' a resort or somethin'…. Ya reckon?" Yan asked.

"Maybe," the Cuban shrugged noncommittally.

"But there's more stuff on board than lumber," Yan repeated.

"Like I asked before, how do you know that?" The Cuban narrowed his eyes at the navigator.

"I jest knows. That's all," he said.

"That's between you and the Captain," the Cuban said. "It's his job whether to tell you about our cargo."

Yan kept quiet for a while until his curiosity overwhelmed him again.

"Okay, tell me why we're goin' to Cat Island? What's our job there?" Yan asked.

"Man, you are full of questions. Aren't you? Why don't you just do your job and let us take care of why we're going to Cat Island?" the Cuban said. He thought a few moments and then said, "Well, okay. I'll tell you this. Besides, you're going to find out anyway. We are bringing supplies to a business on the island."

"I thought so," Yan muttered.

"You what?" the Cuban asked.

"I mean, I thought we're jest bringin' lumber," Yan corrected himself. "But why are we bringin' so much high quality material for a little island shop?"

"So, Yan, you really do know more than you're tellin'," the Cuban said.

"All right. I did see the boxes and cartons in the cargo hold. But I wasn't goin' to touch nothin'. Jest curious, you see."

"We're going to make a bundle on this mission. This island

shop is a big international operation. That's all you need to know. The captain pays you well, right?" the Cuban inquired.

"Yeah, it's a good job. The capt'n didn't ask many questions when I was hired. Jest wanna know 'bout my navigatin' skills. I'm good at that, you see. So, he says, 'welcome aboard.' It was jest like that, an' I was a crewmember again. I'm happy here ... except for Jones. Don't like him much. He's no good."

"Why do you say that? Jones is a good seaman. He has been on this trip many times. He knows his job," the Cuban said in Jones' defense.

"Well, maybe him and me jest don't see eye to eye," Yan back-pedalled.

"Look, Yan, you'd better leave Jones alone. Stay outta his way. Stay outta his business. You get mixed up with him, and he'll throw you overboard. And everyone on board will cheer. The captain? He likes Jones. You mess up somethin' the captain likes, and you'll be spending the rest of your time with King Neptune at the bottom of the sea. Is that clear?"

"Yes, Sir," Yan replied. Yan had had enough of the Cuban's irritation and exited the pilothouse quickly. He headed down the ladder to the main deck and walked aft to the crew's quarters. Although he had been clearly warned by the Cuban, he felt a little better now that he had confirmed some of his suspicions about the mission to Cat Island. But he still had some unanswered questions. His burning curiosity was not yet extinguished.

CHAPTER 11

Nassau Quandary

Flying on a southeasterly heading with the Florida coast disappearing behind them, Tom mentioned to Chris, "I filed a visual flight plan instead of an instrument plan to Nassau and Cat Island. That means once we leave the control zone at West Palm Beach and the air defense identification zone along the coast, we can fly at any altitude we want. I know there won't be any weather problems across the water." They continued their climb to 9500 feet and aimed straight for Nassau 162 nautical miles ahead on a heading of 122 degrees.

The clouds along the Florida coast vanished behind them by the time they reached twenty miles offshore. Now that they were well over international waters, Tom slowed the plane to 60 knots—just above stall speed—and Chris pushed open the small vent window on his side of the plane with one hand and reached down beside his seat with the other. He picked up the weighted black trash bag that contained the dynamite and pushed it through the gap. It caught in the propeller slipstream and was shoved behind the plane so quickly that it was almost as though it had never existed at all.

Soon, they could see a cluster of clouds on the horizon to the left of their course, which they knew was over Bimini, since cumulus clouds tend to hover over islands. The air was smooth as the propeller slowly, yet steadily, pulled them toward Nassau. Forty minutes into the flight, there was no land in sight. They suddenly felt isolated from the world—just the two of them over a vast sea. Endless, monotonous waves below were very conducive to daydreaming about the excitement of snorkeling and sailing in the clear, warm waters of the tropics. Thoughts of Renee were gone, and Chris and Tom had little to say to each other on this leg of the journey as they closed in on the islands.

An hour and twenty minutes went by in silence except for the steady drone of the engine before Tom started their descent into the Nassau controlled airspace. They had already passed the northern tip of Andros Island, so they knew Nassau wasn't far away. They could see large clusters of clouds ahead, which they assumed were over the island of New Providence.

Chris tuned in a radio frequency to get the airport information and local weather. Field conditions were good. "2500-foot broken cloud cover, visibility 8 miles in haze, wind out of the southeast at 12 knots, gusting to 18. Runway 14 in use," he heard.

Chris handed Tom the microphone to report in with Nassau Approach Control.

"Nassau Approach, this is Cardinal 33223 twenty-two miles northwest, descending to 2500 feet, landing at Nassau." He paused for a few seconds, but there was no response to his call. He could hear approach control talking to other aircraft, so he repeated his call. Still, there was no response. He asked Chris to switch to transmitter number two, and again, he called Nassau Approach... and again, no response. He tried another frequency listed on his charts, but to no avail.

By now they were entering the traffic control zone for the airport. Tom called the control tower directly. Still there was no response. He listened to the tower give instructions for landing to the commercial airlines and to smaller aircraft in the area, but no one responded to Tom's calls.

"Chris, I don't know what's going on, but we have to land in Nassau. We have no choice. In my early days of flight instructions, my instructors drilled into my head how to handle emergencies like this, particularly communication failures. The procedure is to fly at 3000-feet elevation over the field in a triangular pattern. The air traffic controllers are supposed to recognize that flight pattern as a radio failure, and they should give us landing instructions by signal lights from the tower. Let's give it a try. We'll at least be above the landing and take-off traffic pattern; so we'll be out of the other pilots' paths."

They flew over the field at precisely 3000 feet above the airport elevation, flew a left-hand triangular pattern around the airport and watched for traffic and light signals from the control tower. They continued this flight pattern for fifteen minutes, but no light was seen from the tower. Boeing 747's, 727's and other commercial aircraft were landing and departing just below them, but they made sure they remained clear of all traffic.

In desperation, Tom told Chris that they were just going to have to find a slot in line of the landing traffic and land without a clearance. Tom was tense, not so much that they might cause an accident, but more so that they were on an international flight and were breaking regulations. They had to make sure they were well clear of the traffic, particularly the fast jets. Tom could see the line of planes, stretched out for several miles at sea, which the control tower had sequenced for landing. They headed away from the airport on a course parallel to the incoming line of traffic until Tom discovered a large gap in the line. He made a 90-degree left turn and headed toward that gap. He tried one more time to contact the tower by radio. It was no use. Yet, he could hear the tower giving landing clearances to other aircraft. So far, the tower controller had not spotted them.

Finally, they were in line with the runway five miles away. A plane had just landed in front of them, and Tom maintained the Cessna's airspeed at 120 knots to keep anyone behind them from catching up. Suddenly, the tower spotted them on final approach and realized that he hadn't given them clearance to land. But the tower operator didn't attempt to contact them by radio or light at this point. Tom continued his rapid approach and touched down his wheels on the runway at 100 knots, 40 knots above the normal landing speed. He jammed on the brakes while Chris retracted the flaps to give them better braking power. As quickly as he could, Tom exited the active runway onto the first turnoff and slowed down on a parallel taxiway. They kept a close eye on the control tower for any light signals for clearance to taxi. Still, they heard and saw nothing from the tower.

Incident at Cat Island

Tom told Chris that he shouldn't go any further, because he was specifically instructed in Palm Beach that he must go directly to the Bahamas Customs ramp for entry into the Bahamas. If he made the wrong turn or went elsewhere on the airport, he could be heavily fined and possibly detained. He brought the plane to a complete stop on the taxiway and watched for light signal instructions from the tower. Still no response.

Chris noticed a trash truck approaching nearby on another taxiway and suggested they flag the driver down for help. Tom knew the truck driver had to be in contact with the control tower in the middle of the field, so he gave it a try. He shut off the engine, climbed out of the plane and waived to the driver to help them. The driver of the truck noticed and drove up to their plane. Tom explained that they couldn't contact the tower, so the driver agreed to call ground control on his radio and request clearance for them to taxi to the ramp. Soon they spotted a flashing, yellow light from the tower. That was their signal to taxi to the ramp. But which ramp? They wanted to go to the customs ramp. They decided to taxi directly to the base of the tower instead.

Tom taxied the plane to the tower and watched an air controller come out on the top catwalk and motion for them to continue on to the next ramp where all of the other general aviation planes were parked. He started up the Cardinal again and moved over to the next ramp, found a parking spot, shut down the engine, sat and waited.

"Chris, I know we've broken some rules, but at least everyone is safe. Let's sit here and wait for customs or the police or someone to come to our rescue. I'm afraid if we get out of the plane and wander around the airport without going through customs and proper immigration procedures, our problems will be compounded immensely."

Chris agreed. They waited for about twenty minutes, but no one came out to investigate.

"Oh, the heck with it," Chris said in disgust. "Let's get down from this cockpit and go find customs ourselves. Apparently no one cares what we've done!"

"You might be right. Okay, let's go," Tom said.

Chris and Tom walked in the first door they saw at a building at the end of the ramp. Tom asked for directions to the customs and immigration office for general aviation planes and was told they were located in the building next door. As they approached the other building, they finally saw the sign, *Bahamas Customs*. The official gave them some forms to fill out, asked them if they had anything to declare and if there was anything still in the plane.

"Yes, Sir. We have our luggage and some food for our vacation stay in George Town."

"Go out to the ramp and bring everything in here from your plane. I mean bring everything, please," the official demanded.

When they returned to the aircraft, there was another customs official waiting for them beside the plane. He showed them his badge.

"Good afternoon, Captain. Mind if I search your plane while you unload it?" he asked.

"Of course not. Help yourself," Tom politely obliged.

The inspector not only checked the storage compartments, but also looked under the seats, in the seat pockets, and opened the fuel tanks to be sure only fuel was being stowed there. Tom assumed he was looking for drugs or any other things illegally smuggled into the country. Apparently satisfied that they had nothing illegal, he returned to his office.

Chris and Tom loaded up a cart with all of the grocery bags, and their suitcases, cameras, snorkeling gear, flight charts and life jackets and hauled it across the ramp to the customs office.

The inspector searched each bag for illegal or taxable items. Satisfied with what he saw, he commented, "You sure have a lot of groceries here. How much did you pay for them?"

His question immediately reminded Tom of the hefty import tax the Bahamian government had on food. He thought for a few seconds and responded, "It cost us $65, Sir."

"It did not! Tom and I paid an arm and a leg for all those groceries—$185 to be exact … and most of it came out of my pocket." Chris cheerfully volunteered.

Incident at Cat Island

Tom cringed. Thanks to Chris, the official had caught Tom in a bare-faced lie.

The inspector stared at Tom with a grim, poker-faced expression, then broke into boisterous laughter.

"That's okay, Mon. Go on to George Town and ya have good time," he said smiling. He stamped all their papers *cleared* and handed them back to Tom, who politely thanked the inspector for his services and started loading their stuff back on the cart. The official also gave them a cruise permit which allowed them to fly throughout the islands for the duration of their visit, and the immigration officer stamped their papers to allow them entry as visitors. They were free to head south.

But there was another matter to take care of ... the radio problem in the plane. They obviously had to get it fixed before they could go any further.

Tom asked the customs official, "Is there an avionics repair shop on the field?"

"Yes, Sir. There's a radio shop next door," he replied.

"Thanks, Gentlemen. We'll see ya in a week," Tom said.

After reloading the plane and topping off the tanks with fuel one more time, Chris and Tom walked across the ramp to the radio shop and met the avionics technician.

"Hello, my name is Tom Hannaford, and this is my friend, Chris. We seem to have a problem with our radios in our Cessna Cardinal. Any chance you can help us right away?" Tom asked hopefully.

"Sure, if it's nothing too major. Let's go see what you got," the technician replied. He picked up a tool kit and walked with them to the plane. In less than two minutes he found the cause of the communication failure. It was a bad microphone. Tom had a speaker and earphones, two transmitters, two receivers, but only one microphone. Of course, the weakest link, the single microphone, had to be the cause of the communications failure with the control tower. He sold Tom a new microphone, and soon they were ready to continue their flight south.

But Tom had one more matter to settle. He had a sinking

feeling the air traffic controllers in the tower had written a citation to them for violating their air space. Tom wanted to find out. After locating a telephone in the avionics shop, he dialed the control tower directly.

"Hello, Sir, I'm the pilot of Cardinal 33223, the plane that landed without a clearance about half an hour ago. I'm very sorry, but we had a radio failure, and I ..."

The controller interrupted, "Oh yes, I remember. Don't worry about it, Mon. Just get your radio fixed before leaving the field."

"Thank you, Sir, for understanding. Do I have to come up to the tower and fill out any paperwork? I'm really sorry this happened, Sir," he said, apologizing again.

"No, forget it. You're okay. Like I said, get your radios fixed before you leave."

"As a matter of fact, we've already found the problem. It was a bad microphone, and it's been replaced," Tom reassured him.

"Okay. You're all set then."

George Town was one hundred thirty miles to the southeast and one hour's flying time. Chris and Tom filed a visual flight plan with flight services, completed their preflight check on the ground and climbed in the cockpit for the last leg of their journey. When the ground controller cleared them to taxi to the active runway 14, Tom looked at his watch. It was 5:15 in the afternoon.

They took off from Nassau and headed southeast toward Exuma Islands at 3500 feet with excellent visibility. They stared out the windows and exulted over the endless coral reefs. The water was so clear they could see sand patches in the shallows just off the coastline of New Providence Island. Since radar coverage in the Bahamas was limited only to the Nassau area, they chose to continue their flight under visual flight rules. That meant that they were on their own again until they closed their flight plan by telephone when they arrived in George Town.

The air continued to be smooth, and when they approached the western coast of the Exumas, the water was clear enough for them to spot several dolphins swimming southward. As they gazed

Incident at Cat Island

out the window, the transition from flying across the US mainland to flying over the tranquil, transparent waters of the central Bahamas sparked excitement between the two friends. The ocean looked almost as intoxicating as a tropical rum punch, and earlier events of the day faded rapidly from their memories.

CHAPTER 12

Miss Pendella

Flying low along the western shores of the Exumas Islands, Tom spotted the village of George Town just ten miles ahead. A few minutes later the airport came into view. He asked Chris to radio the airport base operator to get the weather conditions at the field.

"George Town Radio, this is Cardinal 33223. What are your weather conditions and active runway today?" he broadcasted. There was no answer. He tried again with no response. Then he tried the Stella Maris airport on Long Island a few miles away.

"Aircraft calling Stella Maris, read you loud and clear, go ahead," the voice responded with a German accent.

"Stella Maris, this is Cardinal 33223. Thanks anyway. Just wanted a radio check," he said.

"Chris, watch for any other air traffic in the area. We're going to fly directly over the George Town airport and look at the direction the windsock is pointing to determine the runway in use. Apparently no one is attending the radio on the ramp," Tom said.

When they descended to 2000 feet and flew over the field, Chris noticed the windsock was pointing toward the northwest favoring runway 15. They circled around and entered the down-wind leg for the runway, then flew outbound for a mile, made two left turns and lined up for their final approach to runway 15. There was no air traffic in the vicinity. The moment the wheels touched the pavement, Chris opened his window letting hot, humid, tropical air flood the cabin. He was already unbuttoning his shirt and pants to get ready to put his bathing suit on.

"Chris, what the heck are you doing?" Tom shouted. "We'll be on the beach shortly. There are a few hours of daylight left. Don't even think about changing in the plane. If someone saw you naked out here…? Ugh! Haven't we already had enough setbacks? Do you know how slowly things move in the islands? We'd be sent to jail and questioned a month later. We're not going that route."

Chris mumbled something unintelligible in response.

As they taxied onto the ramp, they saw a young boy with his hands straight up the air standing in front of one of the parking spots. He started waving his arms for them to approach him as they drew closer. Tom eased the plane slowly up to him until the boy crossed his arms overhead signaling him to stop.

"We've arrived! Hooray!" shouted Chris.

"Yeah."

Tom shut down the engine, turned off the lights and radios, unbuckled his seat belt and followed Chris, who was already out the door with feet firmly planted on Bahamian soil. The boy approached Tom.

"Afternoon, Mister. Need service?" he asked.

"Yes, please. Can you top off the tanks with 100-octane fuel?" Tom responded.

"Roger that, Mon. Stayin' long?" he asked.

"Yeah, we'll be here for a week."

"Okay," he said.

While Tom and Chris began to unload the plane, the boy ran over to the office and returned a minute later with a couple of wooden blocks.

"Want a chock to put under the wheel?" he asked Tom.

"Yes, that's a good idea."

"Right. That'll be one dollar," the boy said.

Without hesitation, Tom reached in his pocket and gave the kid a dollar.

"Do you want another chock for the other wheel? It's better to have two. The wind blows hard many times," he suggested.

"Sure."

"Okay. That'll be another dollar," he said.

Again, Tom dug into his pocket and gave the boy a dollar. Tom and Chris continued unloading for a few more minutes while the boy placed the two wooden chocks under the wheels. Then he stood by and watched.

"Need someone to watch your plane while you are on the island? Jest five dollars," the boy chimed in again.

"What! Are you kidding me?" Tom snapped.

"Wait. Let's talk about this," Chris grabbed Tom's arm and pulled him just out of earshot of the boy.

"Look. He is just a young kid trying to make a little spending money. Give him a break. He doesn't mean any harm. Let's give him the five dollars. Besides, what do think might happen if you turn him down? What's a few dollars? You were a teenager once, remember?" Chris said.

"Fine," Tom growled. "But you can pay him."

This time, it was Chris who reached into his own pocket and gave the boy a crumpled bill.

"What's your name?" Chris asked the boy.

"Jeremy."

"Let's see, Jeremy. I would guess you are thirteen years old. Am I right?" Chris asked, trying to strike up a friendly relationship with the boy.

"Nope," Jeremy said.

"Well then, how about fifteen?" Chris asked.

"Nope," Jeremy said again.

"All right, how old are you?" Chris asked in frustration.

"Almost fourteen," he said proudly.

"Ah. I was close then," Chris said.

"Nope," Jeremy replied.

"Okay, you win, almost fourteen it is," Chris said, anxious to end this conversation.

"I'll be fourteen tomorrow," Jeremy said.

"Oh! Happy birthday … a day in advance," Chris said.

While this discussion was going on, Tom was unloading the plane. He was getting ready to pull out the last of the gear when an agitated man in the office caught his attention. He was standing in the doorway of the office talking on a telephone. He seemed to be very animated, gesturing wildly with one hand, but was too far away for Tom to hear what he was saying. Tom turned back to the plane. Shouldering the snorkeling gear and picking up a bag, he started toward the airport office.

"Here, let me help carry your luggage," Jeremy volunteered.

"How much will that cost me?" Tom asked.

"Oh, nothing, Sir. That's my job," Jeremy said.

"Yeah? Then feel free to help," Tom said.

The three of them proceeded to carry everything into the airport office, and then Jeremy disappeared to take care of refueling the plane. The man standing in the doorway had disappeared into a back room. The airport lounge was furnished only with the bare essentials: a table in the center of the room tucked in by two straight-back, wooden chairs, a counter, a water fountain along one side wall and a couple of stuffed chairs next to one of the windows. All of the windows were wide open with no panes or screens, and there was a large ceiling fan running at medium speed. On the counter top was a white cat, curled comfortably and sound asleep in a straw basket. A small, handwritten sign was taped to the front of the basket—*Not for sale.*

They sat down in one of the lounge chairs by the window and waited for someone to come out of the back room and assist them with their arrival. Tom leaned back, rested his head against the top of the chair. He took a deep breath and blew it out in a deep sigh. "Well, we're here at last."

Chris sat forward on the edge of his chair, swinging his head from side to side, looking from the window to the door and back again. "Yeah, but where is the operations staff? I want to hit the beach before dark."

"There's someone here. I saw a man standing in the doorway when we arrived on the ramp."

Tom spotted a telephone behind the counter, so he called Flight Service to close their flight plan from Nassau. As soon as he had given the information to the agent on the telephone, the man appeared in the doorway, hesitated for a moment, then approached the counter.

"Hi. We've arrived in the Cardinal out there, and we plan to stay here a week. Can we leave our plane here where it's parked?"

Tom asked.

"Yes. Let's see, you came here from North Carolina. Right?" he said.

"Why, yes. How did you know that?"

"Oh, well, we knows lots of things in da fambly islands of da Bahamas," he said without actually answering Tom's question and burst into laughter.

"Wait, I'm serious. How did you know where I came from?" Tom frowned.

"Like I say, Mon, these islands are small. We keep track of what's happenin' here. We knows what people do, we knows where people go, we knows where people came from.... You knows how it is. It's a small island. Welcome to George Town," he said casually. "Please fill out the arrival registration form." He handed Tom an official looking document. "Where are you guys staying? At da Conch Harbour Inn, perhaps?"

"We don't have a place to stay yet. We thought perhaps you could help find a place for us." Tom said.

"Okay. The Conch Harbour is a good place. Ya want me to call Conch Harbour for reservations?" he quickly volunteered.

"Uh, no, we'd like to rent a small cottage, a two bedroom place with a kitchen and bath, preferably near the beach. We have our own food," he said.

Tom filled out the registration card and handed it to him.

"Gentlemen, jus' wait here. I hafta go an' make some calls to find you a place in our settlement. Please have a seat," he said. He disappeared again to the back of the building. Chris was itching to get to the beach and started pacing back and forth around the room. Fifteen minutes passed before the man returned.

"Oh, Mr. Hannaford. I have a message for you … from Mr. Roberto, I believe." He held a note in his hand, and Tom quickly snatched it from him and read it.

"Chris!" he shouted with excitement. "Roberto says he did get my letter, and he can meet us here at the end of the week. He'll be at the airport on Thursday around noon. Hot diggity dog! I've been wanting to meet him for years."

Incident at Cat Island

"Okay, Mr. Hannaford, I found something for you. It's a two-bedroom cottage just a block from da beach. The rent is $500 a week, payable on da first day. Do ya want to see it?" he asked.

Tom looked at Chris for his thoughts.

"Yeah. Sounds good to me. Let's take it. I don't need to see it first. I'm sure it'll be okay. Besides, I want to hit the beach. I don't want to spend the last hour of daylight house-hunting," Chris said.

They agreed to take it sight unseen.

"Fine, Mon. Go to da Pink Shell Bar on Coconut Street, four blocks from here. Ask for Miss Pendella. She has da key. You can pay her," he said.

Not knowing exactly where the cottage was, they decided to leave their things at the airport until they had arranged to rent the cottage. They headed down the road to the Pink Shell Bar and found the bar's door standing wide open. It was dark inside. Entering the door they noticed a large ceiling fan swirling in the tropical breeze and a large counter with several barstools placed at random out in front. Two men, drinking mugs of beer, were sitting at the counter. A middle-aged, but very striking, dark-skinned lady with long, black hair was working behind the bar.

"Hey, boys," she greeted as they walked up to the bar. "What kind of beer you like?"

"No beer, thanks. We're looking for Miss Pendella," Tom said.

"What business you have with her?" she asked cautiously.

"We want to rent her cottage near the beach. We were told that she has a place for rent," Tom said.

"I'm Miss Pendella," she said. "You're Mr. Handfield, the flyboy from the airport?" she inquired.

"Hannaford," Tom said.

"Okay. Do you want to see the house first?" she asked.

"No thanks."

"Well then, I charge $500 a week," she said. "And that's payable in full in advance, Mr. Hannifore," she explained.

"Will you take a personal check?" he asked.

"Yes, but I hafta charge another $10 to cash check at bank," she added.

Tom gave her the check including the extra amount. She handed him the key and gave them directions to the beach house. "Oh, by the way," he said. "We have some luggage and groceries at the airport. May I call a taxi from here to take us to the airport and get our stuff?"

"I'll go get your luggage myself if you tell me where it is. You go to beach house. I'll be there in about an hour with your belongings."

Tom told her the luggage and groceries were in the airport lounge, and they walked down the road to find the beach house. It turned out to be a nice place … small, but just right for them.

Thirty-five minutes later a car pulled up in front of the cottage. Miss Pendella got out and began carrying their bags to the front door until Chris and Tom spotted her and helped her with the remaining bags. Tom thanked her and gave her a tip for her help. As soon as she left, Chris immediately threw open his suitcase, got out his bathing suit, yanked off his clothes and slipped on his suit. He was out the door in two minutes flat and racing to the beach.

It was 7:30 in the evening when they returned from their swim. They prepared a simple meal at the cottage, and as they sat at the table digesting their dinner, Tom reflected, "Can you believe just thirteen hours ago we were in Wilmington, North Carolina? And here we are, in a tropical paradise. I'm so glad we chose to press on. This is absolutely heaven."

"Yeah, man. This is cool. But I still can't figure out where Renee went … and why she left us. She's missing out on a fabulous vacation. She sure was weird," Chris added.

"I'm not going to worry about her," Tom said. "She obviously had her own problems. We really didn't need to get involved with whatever was going on in her private life. I say, 'good riddance.' We won't call her and she won't call us. And I'm especially glad we didn't end up on Long Island. I had my heart set on George Town from the beginning, and I am happy we're where we wanted to be in the first place."

"So, why did she disappear?" Chris asked. "You don't think

she disappeared because she was tired of flying with us, do you?"

"I have no idea what she was up to," Tom said. "But I can tell you this, I'm not going to let her spoil our vacation. Let's change the subject." They finished their dinner in relative silence, and by nine o'clock Tom was so tired he went to bed. Chris stayed up a while and read.

CHAPTER 13

Code Crocodile

In Florida, at midnight, Sheila and Rufus headed out of the dimly-lit warehouse along the Miami River in an unmarked truck and drove through the back streets of the city's south side toward the Everglades. They drove through the suburbs for thirty minutes until they reached a two-lane highway that led them to the marshes. They turned off onto a primitive, sandy, one-lane road and approached a chain that was stretched across the road about 300 feet from the entrance into a pine forest. Rufus got out and searched in his pocket for the keys to the padlocks that secured the heavy chain to the metal post. Using the headlights of the truck, he unlocked the two padlocks and hopped back into the driver's seat. Rufus pulled forward past the gate and stopped while Sheila got out and relocked the chain across the road. Mosquitoes attacked them like they hadn't eaten in a week. Sheila rushed back into the truck, swatting her face, neck and arms. Rufus handed her a can of bug spray, and she opened fire, spraying inside the entire cab of the truck.

They proceeded down the narrow, sandy road for another four miles, then turned right onto another road overgrown with two-foot tall weeds. They continued down the road for another six miles until they came to a cleared area in the middle of the pine forest. In the center of the open area were two parallel ruts in the grass that stretched almost a mile in length. It was a rugged, grass runway carved out of the tall pine forest, deep in the heart of the south Florida marshlands. Rufus pulled the truck along the edge of the tree line and looked at his watch. It was 1:45 in the morning.

They sat patiently inside the truck until 1:55 when they heard a plane approaching at treetop level from the southwest over the Everglades. The dark, shadowy, unlighted plane flew directly over the field and continued outbound for a couple of miles. Rufus and Sheila could barely make out the plane's silhouette against the new moon as it passed overhead. Rufus drove to the end of the grass strip, swung the truck around in the direction of the runway and turned on his headlights to light up the landing path. The plane circled behind them and made a straight-in approach to the runway. With full flaps extended on the wings and a steep descent, the captain settled the DC-3 hard on the grass and slammed on the brakes to bring the plane to a halt just 200 feet from the pine trees at the opposite end of the field. The plane turned around and taxied to the spot where Rufus and Sheila were waiting. The pilot eased the plane next to the pickup truck, shut down the sputtering engines, got out of his seat, walked down the aisle and opened the door of the aircraft just behind the wing.

When the pilot appeared in the doorway, Sheila shouted, "Another amazing landing, Captain Jenkins. Welcome to Code Crocodile International Airport."

"A pilot yourself, you know how it is. Any landing you can walk away from is a good landing. Right?" Captain Jenkins shouted.

Within seconds the mosquitoes began their vicious attack on Captain Jenkins. Slapping his face and arms in a useless attempt to ward them off, he motioned for Sheila to bring him the bug spray.

"Here, use this. These darn mosquitoes are so hungry that within a matter of minutes you could be be so anemic, you'd need a blood transfusion," she exaggerated. Jenkins opened the cargo door and hauled the wooden crates to the doorstep. Rufus and Sheila began carrying the wooden crates from the plane to the truck. In less than thirty minutes the transfer was complete.

"I'm curious, whatcha doing with all of these crates of paper and chemicals?" Jenkins asked.

"Oh, we sell these stolen goods out of our warehouse in Miami" Sheila said.

"I see, but who buys this stuff? Looks to me like this is high quality merchandise. I bet it's expensive," Jenkins continued.

Sheila remarked, "Yep, but there's a good black market for

it. As you can see from the stenciling on some of the crates, these have already been sold in another country. Other crates are destined for shops in Miami where they'll save money buying it directly from us rather than going through a distributor. I can't go into the details. You know… company's confidential trade secrets, and all that kind of stuff."

Sheila glanced at the luminous dial of her watch. "Sorry to cut this short. I've got a deadline to meet in Miami."

They shook hands. Jenkins climbed aboard, shut the door of the aircraft and crawled into the cockpit. A few minutes later, the right propeller began to rotate slowly until the engine let out a loud bang and a burst of smoke from its exhaust. The engine backfired a couple more puffs of smoke before it started running smoothly. Captain Jenkins revved up the engine to boost the electric power needed to start the number two engine. In less than a minute, he had both engines running, and Rufus turned on the truck lights again to light the path on the ground. The DC-3 taxied to the edge of the tree line, turned 180 degrees and stopped. With the brakes held down firmly, Jenkins ran up the engines to full throttle, breaking off small tree limbs and blowing a cloud of dust, sand and underbrush through the woods behind him. At just the right moment with his engines roaring at full rpms, he released the brakes and the plane shot out of Code Crocodile like a rocket, just clearing the tops of the pines at the other end by about 10 feet. With running lights extinguished, the DC-3 disappeared over the treetops and headed southwest across the great swamp toward the Gulf of Mexico.

Rufus and Sheila drove the loaded truck slowly down the sandy road, carefully dodging the deep pot holes to avoid shifting of the load. By four o'clock they had unloaded the cargo at the riverfront warehouse and gone their separate ways in the dark of the night. Sheila desperately needed some sleep before her flight to the Exumas in a few hours. She had made the run between Tamiami and George Town many times ferrying the finished payloads back to her partners on the mainland, but the flight still demanded a long 2 hours and 15 minutes of constant vigilance and avoiding detection from ground radar. This morning's trip to the Islands wasn't routine, however. She had an appointment with Boss in George Town. He wouldn't disclose the details of the meeting, just that it was urgent.

At 6:30 in the morning, Sheila woke up and looked at her watch. She was late as she rushed out of her apartment and headed to the Tamiami airport. Racing into the parking lot on the general aviation side of the airport, she leaped out of her car with her flight bag in hand, locked the doors and ran to the ramp where her Cessna Centurion was tied down. Foregoing the preflight inspection, she hurriedly untied the plane, jumped in the cockpit, slammed the door and started the engine.

"Tamiami Ground Control, this is Cessna 77052 at the ramp. Taxi instructions for a local visual flight, please," she radioed.

The tower controller instructed Sheila to taxi to runway 9 left and hold for further clearance. She raced down the ramp to the taxiway at almost take-off speed and headed to the runway while doing her engine and cockpit checks. By the time she had reached runway 9 left, she told the controller she was ready to go.

"Cessna 77052, what will be your initial direction of flight and altitude?"

"It will be southbound along the coast at 2500 feet for a local flight," she lied.

"Okay, you're cleared for take-off," the operator said.

Sheila shoved in the power controls to the maximum and the plane leapt into the air in less than 1000 feet of runway. It was 7:20 in the morning. By the time she reached 500 feet, she turned right and continued her climb to 2500 feet and headed down the coast toward the Florida Keys. As soon as she was clear of the airport control zone, she turned off her radar transponder and descended to 500 feet above the shoreline.

She flew south for another 30 miles along the Florida Keys, descended further to 300 feet in order not to be detected by radar and turned left to head out to sea for the central Bahamas. The skies were clear and the flight smooth as she flew southeast over Andros Island and then well south of Nassau.

CHAPTER 14

The Discovery

The following morning in George Town, Chris and Tom woke up at sunrise to the songs of the tropical birds, the rhythm of the surf and the palms rustling in the breeze. Tom had dreamed he was staying here for the rest of his life ... a very pleasant thought.

After breakfast he suggested to Chris that before they searched for a sailboat to rent, they fly around the nearby islands and check out the interesting places to sail and snorkel.

"It would be a lot better to see the layout of the channels and coves from the air than from the deck of a boat," he said. "We could look for a sailboat rental later this afternoon."

Chris agreed, so they decided to pack a lunch and some drinks in case they wanted to land somewhere to explore the area.

They hiked to the airport and checked in at the office to inform them they were planning a local flight around the area and would be back in the early afternoon, or sooner perhaps. The plane had already been refueled and was ready to go.

"Chris, this may sound crazy, but just to be sure, I want to check the battery compartment one more time."

"Good idea," Chris agreed.

Tom opened the luggage compartment again and removed the back panel. After searching very carefully for any evidence of tampering, he was convinced that everything looked normal. Chris secured the panel back in place and set their backpacks with their lunches in the back seat. Tom climbed into the pilot's seat, organized his charts for the central Bahamas, followed the preflight checklist and started up the engine. All the instruments indicated that the systems were operating properly, and they began their taxi to runway 15.

Incident at Cat Island

At the same time, six miles to the west of George Town, Sheila spotted the airport and started her preparations for landing. She flew over the airport to check which direction the windsock was pointing, and then flew outbound for a mile to begin her approach to runway 15. She noticed a plane taxing from the ramp to runway 15, a Cessna Cardinal.

Chris scanned the horizon for other aircraft in the vicinity of the airport and reported to Tom that he spotted another Cessna that just flew over the field and headed outbound preparing to line up with the runway.

"Okay, keep an eye on it. I think we'll be airborne before the plane lands," Tom replied.

Engine run up check completed successfully, Tom turned onto the runway and applied full power for take-off. They lifted off the pavement and continued their climb toward the southeast. Sheila landed behind them a minute later. At an altitude of 2500 feet, Tom and Chris turned left and followed the shoreline of the Exuma Islands. The weather was typically tropical … few scattered clouds hovering over the landmasses at 1000 feet with clear skies over the water. They flew around to the east side of the island then turned to an easterly heading toward Long Island and Stella Maris, approximately 23 miles from George Town. From 2500 feet, the shallow water between George Town and Long Island was transparent all the way to the sandy bottom. They approached the north end of the long, but narrow, island and made a few circles along the shoreline while Chris made mental notes of the coves and beaches as potential places to drop anchor and visit in their sailboat if they went there. Then they turned to the north and headed toward Cat Island 28 miles away.

At the George Town airport, Sheila swerved her plane off the runway and raced to the ramp. Before bringing the aircraft to a full stop, she shut down the engine and had the door open when the wheels finally rolled to a halt. Not bothering to tie the plane down, she leaped out of her seat, ran into the building and immediately called for the airport manager.

"Well, about time you reached here. Boss has been steamin' waitin' for you. He's extremely unhappy," he informed her.

"Yes, I'm not surprised. Where is he now?" Sheila asked.

"At da Conch Harbour Inn."

"Can you take me there right now?"

"Yeah, let's go," he said.

They hurried to the parking lot, jumped in his car and drove down the road about a mile to the Inn. Sheila hopped out and ran inside. Boss sat in an empty lounge drinking a tropical rum punch. Her quick glance told her that he hadn't changed any since the last time she'd seen him. As ever, he was impeccably groomed, from his Panama hat to his white linen suit. Boss thought himself the reincarnation of a turn-of-the-century, island plantation owner, and he always dressed the part, right down to the cigar clamped between his teeth. But this time his close-set eyes were narrowed with anger.

Sheila forced herself to smile, and she took another step forward. "Sorry I'm late. It took a little longer to unload the plane last night. I've only had a couple of hours of sleep, but I know how important this meeting is ..."

Boss snaked out one arm and clamped a fist around her bicep. He yanked her toward the French doors at the end of the room. "Shut up," he growled, shoving her out onto the deserted patio.

He jerked Sheila back toward him and hissed, "I don't care why you're late. The fact that you are says quite enough. I gave you a job to do. And then I let your dimwit friend back you up. Neither one of you took care of it. What happened? Huh? Get scared? Break a nail? Couldn't handle it? Go girlie on me?"

With each insult, the large man thrust his finger hard into Sheila's breastbone forcing her backward. Even when she abruptly came up against the rough, stone exterior wall of the building, that didn't stop the man. He still kept coming. He cupped her face in one hand—the same one that held his cigar squeezed between two fingers, its wet end now pressed into her cheek.

"You have twenty-four hours to finish the job. Do you understand? Twenty-four hours. You get it done, and we'll talk again. If you don't ..."

Boss took his hand and pressed the palm flat against her nose and mouth. She couldn't breath. She struggled to push his arm away, but he leaned his weight against her, and she heard him laugh softly. Then as suddenly as he'd placed his hand over her mouth, he let go and turned away.

"Twenty-four hours," he said.

Sheila left the Inn and walked back to the airport. She needed some time to think of a plan.

Approaching Cat Island from the south, Tom and Chris descended to 2000 feet so they could get a closer view. Tom turned the plane north and flew to the north side of the small island where they spotted a small coastal freighter at anchor near Whale Creek. Continuing toward the east, they saw a sailboat anchored 100 feet from the beach in a well-protected, isolated cove about one mile from Whale Creek. From the air, the entrance to the cove looked like it was completely blocked by coral reefs, but obviously the boat captain had found a passage to the anchorage. The water in the cove was so clear that it looked as if the sailboat were suspended in air. They searched the beach for any signs of life, but no one appeared to be in the area. Perhaps there were people on board, but out of sight. They flew across the center of the island to the southern coastline until they reached Cutlass Bay—a beautiful harbor lined with pure white, sandy beaches, coconut palms and a magnificent barrier reef surrounding the harbor.

"Now, this is truly Paradise," Tom said.

He slowed the plane down to 80 knots and circled the Bay several times to take in the view as long as possible.

"Would you look at that!" Chris exclaimed. "If there's a perfect place to sail, THIS is it! We have to put this down as number one on our list of possibilities. And the best thing of all, it's not that far from George Town ... maybe just a half day's sail."

"Yes, it's gorgeous," Tom agreed.

They flew inland half a mile and discovered an abandoned airport near the shore of Cutlass Bay. It was indeed grown up with weeds, except for a narrow dirt path down the center that looked like it had been used recently. There was a smaller path that led from the landing strip into the adjacent jungle hillside beneath the tropical canopy.

"Tom, isn't this the place that you kept bugging me about when we were at home ... something to do with that piece of wood you found on the beach? What was it, Barrington something?" Chris asked.

Tom snorted, "You didn't ever believe my story anyway. So what difference does it make?"

"Just curious," Chris shrugged.

After a pause, Tom said, "Yes, this is supposed to be where the old Barrington Plantation was located 200 years ago, but I'm through talking about it. Besides, I don't see anything down there that even gives us a hint that a plantation existed."

They circled Cutlass Bay again while Chris continued surveying possibilities for sailing there from George Town. As they flew over the abandoned airstrip one more time, Tom couldn't resist temptation and said, "I'll tell you what, I want to get a closer look at that dirt strip. It'd be fun to land and explore the area for a couple of hours. We brought our lunch. We could even have a picnic at the top of the hill overlooking Cutlass Bay ... if the airport is suitable for landing."

Tom descended to 1000 feet and then made a low pass over the strip while Chris carefully scanned the pathway for possible obstructions—holes, ditches, rocks, tree limbs.

"I just don't know, Tom. The strip looks pretty rough to me.

What if there are some big rocks or holes hidden beneath the tall grass? We don't want to get stranded here," Chris said.

They continued their descent to 500 feet and flew the length of the landing strip again. The urge to land there just for a quick exploration visit was overwhelming Tom.

"Well, I didn't see any obstructions on the strip, did you?" he asked Chris.

"No, it seemed okay from here," Chris agreed.

They made a 180 degree turn past the runway and flew back to the field. Tom slowed their airspeed to 75 knots, lowered the flaps to 30 degrees, extended the landing gear, reduced the power and propeller settings and set up the glide to the end of the pathway.

"Here goes, Chris. I'd really like to give this a try. Here goes nothing!"

"Okay, hold on, baby!" Chris said nervously, as he held tightly on the arm rest.

At 70 knots airspeed and 200 feet from the end of the runway, Tom slowly raised the nose of the plane to allow the main wheels to touch the dirt first. He gently let the plane settle to the ground. The dirt strip was bumpy but manageable. He brought the plane to a halt halfway down the strip where tall weeds on both sides of the plane stood up almost to the base of the wing tips. He turned the plane completely around and taxied to an open area along the edge of the strip that led to the woods. The grass had been smashed down by another plane sometime recently, so they followed the trail to the edge of the woods.

"Most likely someone like us has landed here to explore the area," Tom rationalized.

As they approached the edge of the forest, they noticed a cleared area that looked like it used to be a parking ramp. It was now covered with grass and tall weeds. They taxied to the spot and shut down the engine.

"Well, we're here," Tom said as he exhaled a deep breath of relief.

"Yeah, Now, I hope we can get out of here in one piece," Chris said.

"Look, it's tougher to land than to take off under these conditions. If we got here, we can get out of here. It's that simple," Tom said, trying to make him feel better. "Let's grab our lunch packs and go for a hike."

They climbed out of the plane and plowed through the tall grass until they discovered a well-worn trail that led into the woods and up the hillside.

"This path looks like it's been freshly used," Tom remarked. "It looks like it heads to the top of the hill. Let's try it."

"Might as well. That's why we're here," Chris agreed.

Chris led the way as they hiked along the twisting path beneath the jungle canopy. Halfway up the hill, Tom paused and looked back to see the plane and the landing strip, but the dense foliage limited his view to about 50 feet. Continuing on to the top, they reached a partial clearing where they noticed rows of bushes that looked like they had been planted by someone long ago. Chris walked up to one of the trees for closer examination and hollered, "Hey! These are pineapple bushes. Notice how they were planted in rows. I bet someone lived near here many years ago and this was their pineapple farm."

"Sure. If we keep looking around, we might find an old foundation of some sort, the remains of where they lived," Tom said. "One thing's for sure, the view from here of Cutlass Bay and this lush surrounding hillside is incredible. This would be a perfect place for a house."

They searched the area for another thirty minutes but didn't find further evidence of people living there in the past. They continued around to the north side of the hill and stumbled on another clearing of trees. Although the area was grown up with tall weeds, they could see, in the center of the clearing, an old, crumbling stone-wall foundation, with some of its surviving structure only rising about three feet above the ground. The structure appeared to be a mixture of oyster shells, limestone and sand.

Out of curiosity, Tom said, "I wonder if this was a part of the old Barrington Plantation that was located somewhere near Cutlass Bay?"

"Probably not," Chris said. "You told me that Barrington was a cotton plantation. There are no cotton fields around here ... not even a single cotton plant. I know a cotton plant when I see one, and they ain't here."

"Well, maybe not on the top of this hill, but I bet the fields are here somewhere on this island. Maybe they were in the flat areas along the coast line," Tom said, trying to support his theory about the existence of Barrington Plantation in the area.

Chris pointed toward the ruins, "Look ... there, along the base of the foundation, there are a couple of windows just below ground level. There's some kind of cellar underneath those crumbling ruins."

They walked over to one of the windows and found a ditch dug down to the base of the window to allow light into the cellar. The ditch was about three feet in length, and just wide enough for someone to crawl down and take a peak inside. Tom lowered himself into the hole and squinted through the dirty, imperfect glass pane.

"WOW! Chris! Look at this," he whispered.

Chris crawled in the hole next to him and peeked inside. In the dim light, they saw tables with rolls of paper, cutting boards and two printing presses on them. On the floor they spotted drums of ink. And most shocking, on the far side of the room, they discovered several tables with stacks of freshly printed money.

"Good grief! I can't believe what we've found!—a sure 'nuf counterfeiting operation! And look over there! Shhhhhhh! A man is standing next to the table counting money. Let's get out of here before he sees us!" Tom whispered in a panic.

They turned around and scrambled out of the dirt hole as quickly as they could, but as Chris reached the top of the ditch, his shoe dislodged a small rock, which rolled down the slope and tapped the window. The man inside heard the noise, looked up at the window and must have caught a glimpse of Chris' leg, just as he reached the top edge of the ledge. The agitated, apron-clad man ran out the door on the other side of the cellar and stomped up and down for a few seconds, shaking his fist and cursing loudly while they vanished into the underbrush nearby.

"Hey. Stop! Whatcha doin' here? Come back here ya dirty sneaks!" he yelled. He continued shouting at them as they ran down the path toward Cutlass Bay. Now that they had been discovered, they knew that they had only a few minutes to make their escape in the plane. Halfway down the hill in the thick of the jungle, they heard an explosion. It came from the direction of Cutlass Bay, and Tom's heartbeat quickened. They ran even faster through the jungle to reach the area where their plane was parked.

Tom began to panic. What would they do if they couldn't climb in their plane, start up the engine, taxi to the end of the strip and take off before they were caught? He knew for certain that they'd be shot if they were captured. They reached the edge of the clearing at the airstrip only to see the most horrifying scene they could imagine. Their plane was on fire. Huge flames shot at least twenty feet in the air from all parts of the fuselage.

"ARGH!" Tom shrieked. He started toward the plane.

Chris grabbed his arm and pulled him back into the shadows of the trees and held him there. "How could this happen?" he asked over and over again.

As the shock receded, they spotted a larger, single engine plane parked in the grass about 500 feet away from the blaze, and standing between the two planes was a woman who watched their plane being consumed in the fire.

"Tom, look closely at that woman there. The long black hair, that long nose … doesn't she look familiar? Do we know her?" Chris asked.

Tom squinted his eyes and tried to focus through the sweat streaming down his face. "We saw her in Wilmington. That's the girl in the pilot lounge," he answered angrily, feeling as though he'd fallen down the rabbit hole with Alice. Nothing made sense any more.

"Yeah. That's right. Sherry or Shelly … No, Sheila," Chris replied. "Remember, she told us the story about some conversation she overheard in George Town regarding Cutlass Bay and the old plantation. She asked you about your plane … and where it was parked. I remember that part really well. And now she seems to be helping to destroy it ...!'"

Tom interrupted, "We don't have time for this right now. We have to get out of here. They'll be searching all over this island for us. Our most urgent thing is to get away from the airstrip and hide somewhere on the other side of the island ... and think, and then maybe we can figure out a strategy of how to get out of here."

They ran into the jungle-like hillside and headed east, away from the path that led to the hilltop counterfeit operations. They glanced back at Cutlass Bay for a second to make sure they weren't being followed and noticed a speedboat racing out of the bay toward the entrance of the harbor. After they covered about two miles under cover of the tropical underbrush along the coast, they turned north and climbed up a hill. At the top they saw a coastal freighter at anchor in a partially sheltered bay on the north side of the island. Something else caught their attention, however. There was a small boat dock just inside the entrance to a creek near the freighter's anchorage.

"If I remember the charts and what I saw when we flew over this side of the island, that dock is in Whale Creek. Maybe there's a boat there or someone there who could help us escape," Chris said.

Tom shook his head. "Don't count on it. I don't trust anyone on this island. I bet everyone here is involved in this operation. I mean, look how easy it was for us to find out what was going on. Anyone living here would also have discovered it long ago. We're just lucky we didn't get caught when we landed ... or maybe we weren't so lucky." He blew out a breath.

"Chris, we're in a bad situation. The odds are really stacked against us. Let's sneak over to Whale Creek to see what we can find."

They crept their way down the north slope of the hill as if they were playing a game spy versus spy, only this time the stakes were higher—it was a much deadlier game. When they reached the beach and inched their way toward Whale Creek, they anticipated they might find someone near the creek, friendly or unfriendly.

Twenty minutes elapsed before they stumbled upon a dock. Here, lying on the beach, they found piles of scrap lumber, pieces of wooden crates and boxes destined for the printing operation at the top of the hill. They searched for anyone in the area but found the place to be deserted. Then something on the beach caught Tom's eye. Wooden boards partially buried in the sand were stenciled with *INK-BARRINGTON PLANTATION*. He paused for a moment, forgetting about their present danger and pursuit. His mind linked the discovery of the flotsam found in the surf at Wrightsville Beach with the boards found here in the sand.

"Chris, look at this," he quietly called.

"We don't have time to stop and explore, my moron friend" Chris said. "They're on our trail. We've got to keep moving and find some safe place to hide for the night. And it can't be here near the dock. This place could be crawling with the wrong people any time now. Come on, let's get out of here!"

The enormity of their situation washed over Tom. Reality set in hard with a vision that they were *not* going to escape. There was no one there to help them. There were no boats to take them off the island. The nearest land, George Town, was forty miles away— much too far to swim. Despair chilled him to the bone.

Chris recognized the abrupt change on Tom's face, the blank stare in his eyes. He walked over and threw an arm around Tom. He felt the slight trembling that rippled through his usually strong friend. For an instant, *he also* wondered whether they would ever get off this island alive.

CHAPTER 15

The Sailboat

Chris kept his arm around Tom's shoulder for several minutes. Then he said, "Hey, listen. As long as we can keep our wits, we'll be okay. We still have some of our food left, so we're ahead of the game. Remember the sailboat we saw on the north side of the island when we flew over the area?"

Tom nodded slowly, "Yes."

"Well, it's a bit of a hike from here, but it may be our best chance to escape. We didn't see anyone around the area when we were in the airplane. The boat is still there. It was only a few hours ago when we spotted it in the tiny cove just east of here."

"What if the boat owner is part of this operation?" Tom asked.

"Well, I think we'll cross that bridge when we come to it. If there's no one on the boat, that won't be an issue. Now will it?" Chris pleaded.

"No, I guess not," Tom said. "Okay, let's go."

They continued their trek through the jungle, and from atop a small hill, they paused to reaffirm they were going in the right direction to the cove. Suddenly, Tom spotted three people at the bottom of the hill running toward them on the same path. One of them was Sheila, and another was the man they had seen operating the printing presses. They didn't recognize the third guy. The gangsters were running along the pathway, searching every likely hiding place along the way. It was painfully obvious to Tom and Chris that these criminals were out for the kill, and that unless they took evasive action quickly, they wouldn't likely have a second chance.

There was no point turning back to the airstrip. Yet, for the moment, they could find no suitable place to hide. They were left with only one choice—to climb a tree and hide in its branches until their pursuers passed by. Chris chose one tree and Tom chose another one next to him. Soon, they could hear the gang coming up the path, cursing and threatening to kill them. As they passed beneath the tree where Chris was hiding, the limb under his foot cracked from his weight. The pressman stopped instantly with his back to Tom, looked up and spotted Chris. Immediately, Tom jumped out of his tree, hurling himself toward the operator's back.

The other man shouted, "Rafael, look out behind you!"

But it was too late. In one second, Tom's feet slammed into the top of Rafael's head, and they fell into a heap on the ground. Tom scrambled to his feet while Rafael lay flat on the ground with his face down in the dirt. The other man charged toward Tom in retaliation. Chris leaped out of the tree, ran up behind the man and grabbed his arms just as the gangster reached out to swing at Tom. While Chris held the man's arms behind his back, Tom slugged him with his fist, hard across his chin. His hand throbbed in pain, but the blow was just powerful enough to flatten him to the ground. Chris came over and hit him once again across the back of his head. That finished him off. Both crooks lay unconscious on the ground.

During this melee, however, Sheila retreated down the path into the dense jungle underbrush. They didn't see which way she had run but suspected she ran back to the airport. They were too exhausted to chase after her and didn't know what other dangers were lurking in that direction.

"Wow! That was too close. Let's beat it down the hill before they come to," Chris said.

They raced along the path on the north side toward the cove where they were hoping the sailboat was still at anchor.

"Soon everyone on the island will be searching for us," Chris exclaimed. "We gotta get off this island pronto!" They remained under the cover of the dense jungle canopy as much as possible to avoid further detection.

By sunset, it seemed apparent they weren't going to locate the cove before darkness set in, so they began their search for a safe place to sleep. They assumed the ruthless gangsters would continue their hunt well into the night since they knew the island well. Tom and Chris found, about five hundred feet off the path, a thicket of low-lying brush that looked suitable for hiding. They threaded their way into the center of the thicket but made certain they left no trace of their path behind them. They cleared a tiny area on the ground under the brush and piled up some leaves to make a bed.

During the frantic hours of trying to escape, they had not touched the food in their backpacks, but now that they finally could let their guard down, they realized how hungry they were. Chris opened his pack, found a sandwich and almost swallowed it whole. He then guzzled down a pint of water. Tom did the same. They saved their apples, crackers and candy bars for the next day.

Tom looked at Chris straight in the eye and said, "Thanks, pal. You boosted my spirits today. I was just about ready to give up."

Chris blushed immediately, and he kicked at a leaf on a nearby bush.

"Yeah, I know. But we're going to get out of here. We gotta stay alert and be smart. We'll get out. I know we will," Chris said firmly.

"You're right. I'm … I'm okay now," Tom replied.

Exhausted, they laid their heads on piles of leaves and quickly fell asleep.

The next morning when the first hint of dawn appeared, Tom turned over stiffly and caught a glimpse of daylight out of his blurry eyes. He rolled over and attempted to sit up, but every muscle screamed and every joint in his body ached. After sleeping on the hard ground overnight, it was nearly impossible for him to stand on his feet the first few minutes. He slowly stretched, then poked Chris with his toe and said, "Hey, wake up; we have to get going. If we start now, we may be able to get a jump on those headhunters before they come after us."

Chris and Tom cautiously made their way around to the north side of the island toward the point where they thought the sailboat was located. Silently maneuvering under the cover of the jungle canopy, they reached the north shore, but the sailboat wasn't in sight.

"All right, Tom. Which way do we go now, left or right?"

"I have a hunch we need to turn right and walk along the shore just inside the tree line," Tom said.

Several hours passed while they tromped through the jungle without sighting the boat. By mid-morning, they rounded a point, and the cove and sailboat stood before their eyes.

"Hot dog! What luck!" Chris cried and leaped forward as though he was going to jump into the water and swim to the boat.

Tom grabbed the back of his shirt and held him back. "Chris, listen to me! The owner of the boat may be on board and is probably part of this counterfeiting operation. There's got to be a network of mobsters working here. We've stumbled into a very sophisticated and deadly hornet's nest." Tom swung his arm in a wide sweeping arc. "And everyone on this island is a suspect. Let's see if anyone is on board or if anybody returns. Of course, the crew of this boat could be just innocent visitors to the island."

"I don't think the crew are just visitors," Chris replied. "We saw this boat anchored here yesterday. And we didn't see anyone on the boat or on the beach. And we still don't see any activity around the boat. I say the sailboat owner is someone working at the abandoned plantation."

"Right. That's my point. It would be suicide to walk on board and say to the bad guys, 'We need help. Save us!'"

They remained out of sight all day behind the underbrush and watched for activity on the boat or anyone going to and fro. By late afternoon nothing had happened. They concluded the boat must belong to someone involved with the printing operation on the hill. Otherwise, any visitors would have returned to the boat by now.

"Chris, I've got an idea. This boat has been at anchor here for at least two days. No one seems to be on board, and I think this boat probably belongs to the man we saw in the cellar running the printing press yesterday. If no one shows up by midnight, let's steal this baby and head for George Town."

"What! Wait a minute. That's a lot easier said than done," Chris exclaimed. "Yeah, I know how to sail, but what if we get caught in the act? Sailboats are painfully slow. Why we would be sitting ducks! A man can swim faster than a sailboat can sail in a light breeze. 'Sides, what if the keys to the engine are still in the owner's pocket? We couldn't start the engine without the keys."

"We don't need keys. We'll just raise the sails and scoot out of the cove," Tom suggested.

"At night? Are you nuts!" Chris responded. "There are reefs all across the entrance of this cove, Tom, and they're scattered everywhere between here and George Town. I saw them from the plane. We'd have to turn on the electric power to enable the electronic depth sounder and the lights to read the depth gauge and to steer by the compass. The running lights would be on, too. And if we did all of that, someone from shore would see us. Do you see where I'm going with this? It would be like turning on a lighted sign that says 'Here we are, come get us!'"

"Listen to me!" Tom snapped. "It's our only chance. You saw the reefs from the plane. Think! Visualize where you saw those coral heads, 'cause hitting a coral reef would spell disaster. But we can't turn on any lights. We have to do this in the dark. You're supposed to be an expert sailor. Now's your chance to prove yourself."

"I'm thinking, I'm thinking," Chris said, waving him away. "Let me figure out a way to avoid crashing into the reefs in the dark with no depth sounder."

They searched the area for a dinghy, because Chris thought surely the crew had a small boat hidden along the beach somewhere. By sunset, however, they hadn't located one. They had no choice but to swim.

The sun finally sank below the horizon leaving only a vague silhouette of the boat in the harbor, barely visible in the light of the new moon in a clear sky. The boat sat silently in the harbor less than 300 feet from the beach. They waited until midnight. After scanning the area very carefully one more time for any living being and finding none, they quietly slipped into the water, fully clothed, and began treading their way to the boat. They were careful not to break the water's surface with their feet or hands for fear that someone on shore might hear them.

When they reached the stern of the boat, Chris grabbed the swim ladder, slowly raised himself out of the water and climbed over the railing. He quickly looked around the cockpit and decks to make certain no one was on board. Then he silently crept to the hatch door that led to the cabin below. Carefully, he opened the hatch wide and signaled to Tom to climb up the ladder and come on board.

"So far, so good. Looks like we might make it after all," Tom whispered.

"Yes. But we still have the reefs to negotiate, and we still have to get all the way to George Town without being caught," Chris hissed back. "But there's one other problem we didn't figure on." He held up a hand. "There's no wind here in the cove. It's going to be a turtle crawl out of here. We may have to paddle."

"Maybe we'll be lucky and find the keys. Then we can start the engine, with the lights off, and zoom out of the harbor, wind or no wind. Surely, we'll pick up at least some trade winds outside of this protective cove," Tom said hopefully.

"Don't hold your breath. Don't count on finding the keys."

While Chris worked getting the sails ready, Tom searched the cabin for keys. In the darkness, his fingers probed through drawers, cabinets and shelves, but he couldn't find any keys. He returned to the cockpit and gave Chris the bad news.

"I'm not surprised," Chris said. "I'm still working on the sails. Fortunately, the sails are already rigged. All I have to do is loosen the tie downs and make ready to unfurl the jib. I think I'm about ready now."

Tom said to Chris, "I found a paddle in the cabin. It's probably a spare for the dinghy, wherever that is, but maybe I could help move us out of this harbor by paddling. Thank goodness what little breeze we have is blowing out toward the cove entrance. Will you be able to see the coral heads in the dark without the depth sounder—if they're just below the surface of the water?"

"You're joking, right?" Chris replied. "No way, man. At night, water is as black as tar. The moon is no help either. The soft reflected light doesn't penetrate much below the surface. I'll stand on the bow and look ahead into the water. I might be able to see some suggestion that a reef is there or hear the water breaking across the surface of the coral. I'll just have to try to remember where I saw them from the plane. It's going to be mostly luck. I can just barely see the opening to the channel. At least we won't slam into the rocky shore or hit a tree. I'll be your lookout while you steer."

Tom stood behind the helm while Chris went forward to the bow and quietly hauled in the anchor. Fortunately, it was easy to dislodge it from the sandy bottom. He then scurried back to the cockpit and unfurled the jib. With the port jib sheet pulled in just enough to allow the sail to form a cup to capture the tiniest wisp of air, the boat began to inch its way toward the opening of the cove at glacial speed. Tom imagined he could paddle faster than the sail was pushing them. Chris hauled up the main sail and let the boom all the way out to starboard to capture whatever breeze there was. Their speed through the water doubled, from 1/2 knot to 1 knot.

Behind them, the beach was quiet. Chris returned to the bow to search as diligently as possible for any visible coral heads or audible signs of water splashing over rocks ahead of their path, while Tom steered the craft toward the cove's almost invisible opening.

"Be prepared to make a sharp turn if I see or hear anything," Chris advised, knowing it would probably be too late anyway.

While Chris leaned over the bow intently listening and keeping a keen watch, Tom kept the boat steady on course. Every minute or so he looked back, expecting to see someone running along the beach screaming at them. But then, he thought, *It's after midnight. No one will be stirring about at this hour.*

"Let out the main a little more," Chris requested. "We need to slow down a bit. I think I remember some coral heads just inside the entrance to the channel on the left. If we hit them, maybe it will just be a gentle bump and not a jab through the hull."

Tom released the main sheet until the mainsail started to sag in the light breeze. He was aware this meant the sail was no longer pushing the boat ahead; only the jib was working. The boat slowed down. CRUNCH! The boat came to an abrupt halt.

"Well, we hit it, Chris. Good job!" Tom said sarcastically. "It's probably the only coral head in the cove."

"Want to come up here and do this job yourself?" Chris replied, raising his fist at him.

"Okay, I'm sorry. I know it's tough up there. I just want us to get out of here," Tom sighed.

"Yeah, like I want to stay here forever," Chris retorted. "Turn the wheel hard to the right; swing the boom all the way over to port as far as it will go. Maybe we can twist the bow off the reef to the right. We certainly can't go backwards."

Tom cranked the wheel hard to starboard at the same time he pulled the main sail and boom across amidship to the port side. The boat heeled to port slightly as the breeze filled the main sail again. Then the boat turned to the right and ground its way over the reef until it freed itself.

"I don't think we poked a hole in the hull. We were going slow enough that I hope all we did was scrape a little paint off the bottom. At least we're free for the moment," Chris said. Everything was silent again.

They passed through the channel entrance without hitting another reef and continued outbound on a northerly heading. The southeast breeze increased once they left the shelter of the land and sailed into the open area of the bay.

"Turn left about 20 degrees, let out the main and jib sheets until the sails start to flutter, then haul them in a little and cleat the lines," Chris ordered.

As soon as Tom had completed these tasks, their speed increased significantly. He estimated they were doing around five knots by now based on the sound of the water rushing past the bow. Off to the left, less than a mile away, was a dim, white anchor light shining from atop a ship's mast. They could barely make out the dark silhouette of a coastal freighter perhaps a quarter of a mile off the shore from Whale Creek.

"Chris, turn on the instrument lights so I can see the compass headings and the depth sounder," Tom requested.

"Heck no. Absolutely not!" Chris stated firmly. "The instrument lights and running lights are on the same circuit. I've got a hunch the freighter over there has something to do with this counterfeit operation, too, and I don't want them to spot us. We'll steer on a northerly course for a while to circle well around him before we head southwest to George Town."

The trade winds continued from the east at a steady pace for the next several hours as they made good speed through the night. When they were well out of sight of the freighter and Cat Island, Chris agreed to turn on the running and instrument lights. He went below to search for any charts that would help them decide where to make landfall near George Town. They had agreed, however, that sailing into George Town would not be wise. In a drawer Chris found a chart of the central Bahamas, and he sat down at the galley table and plotted a course of 209 degrees to Conch Cay, just four miles north of George Town. On the east side of the Cay was a navigable entrance to Elizabeth Harbour. He estimated the distance from their current position to the harbour entrance to be forty miles or about an eight-hour sail. That would have them arriving near the coastline just after sunrise. It was perfect timing.

"With a little luck, we should beach the boat early, before people are up and about doing their daily chores," Chris said.

"Let's hope so," Tom said.

They steadied on a course headed directly toward Elizabeth Harbour, adjusted their sails to optimize their speed, secured the jib and main sheets and relaxed for the first time in more than twenty-four hours. They knew it would only be a matter of time before someone discovered the sailboat missing. Then the search would be expanded beyond Cat Island. But for now, they felt encouraged they might make it back to George Town.

"Tom, I've been thinking," Chris said. He sat with both arms folded behind his head. "I think that both Renee and Sheila are conspirators, responsible for all the misery that we've been going through since we left Wilmington. Remember when Sheila was there? She didn't get in a hurry until after she found out where your plane was parked. She wanted you to identify the Cardinal to her. She had something to do with the cut magneto wires. Either she did it herself, or she had someone else do it, like an aviation mechanic. After all, it's obvious now that she's a pilot herself.

"And remember when Renee said that she heard about us through a friend in Wilmington? Well, that friend must have been Sheila! Who knows if Sheila is really from Miami, or Wilmington? For that matter, how do we know Renee is from Atlanta? I think Sheila was trying to prevent us from flying to Cat Island."

Chris sat forward and leaned on his elbows.

"Renee must have stepped in as a backup so she could sabotage our plane en route when Sheila's efforts failed. That could possibly explain why she was arguing on the telephone in Jacksonville. She was probably catching flack from her boss for taking so long to stop us. Then she must have arranged to have the dynamite placed in our plane in West Palm Beach as a last ditch effort to derail us. And that's why she disappeared. She figured we'd be blown up as soon as we reached 5000 feet. This whole thing was to keep us from finding and reporting their counterfeiting scheme on Cat Island."

"Maybe. It would make sense ... except for one thing. Who tipped off Sheila that we were going to fly to the Bahamas and Cat Island in the first place?" Tom asked. "How in the heck did this whole thing get started?"

"Oh, yeah. That's a very good question. I don't know," Chris shrugged. "But one thing's for sure. In a few hours they're gonna realize that we escaped in their sailboat, and it'll be a no brainer to figure out we're on our way to George Town. All of our stuff is in George Town."

Chris yawned and rubbed a hand across his stubbled chin before he continued. "Right now I'm more worried about being overtaken and captured at sea by a swift boat."

Incident at Cat Island

"I know. That scares me, too," Tom said quietly.

The first hint of sunrise appeared across the eastern sea as a faint, orange glow flooded the water all around them. They kept scanning the horizon for signs of boats, but they saw nothing. Tom looked ahead to try to get a glimpse of the eastern coast line of Exuma Island, and for a moment, he thought he saw a light on shore, but then it disappeared in the haze. They continued on the 209-degree heading, and in another thirty minutes the sun lifted out of the sea and created a floodlit path straight ahead of them. Approaching eight o'clock, Chris spotted land ahead. Because of the morning haze, he estimated the coast to be only five miles away.

"Tom, let's beach this boat in a remote area as soon as we can, swim to shore and make a run for it. We'll be caught for certain if we sail south into Elizabeth Harbour or on into George Town. Someone will recognize this boat...."

"Yep, you're probably right about that," Tom said.

They were a mile off the coast of Conch Cay when Chris looked at the charts again and decided to proceed to Simons Point just inside the entrance to Elizabeth Harbour. Like all of the islands in the Bahamas, the entrance channel was full of dangerous coral heads, which demanded that they keep a keen eye on the water ahead. Chris volunteered to station himself on the bow again to serve as a lookout. They zigzagged their way through the reef cut successfully until they located Simons Point Beach. Inching their way into shallow water across a sandbar, Chris saw an area of dark water ahead just on the north side of the point.

"Head for that dark area," Chris pointed out to Tom. "It could be deeper water, or it could be a reef. In either event, it's close enough to shore we could swim from there."

With only the mainsail raised, they eased the boat into the dark water. It was a deep hole. Then they proceeded to the sandy beach straight ahead for another two hundred feet, until they came to a gentle stop as the keel dug into the sandy bottom and beached itself.

"We did it!" Tom wanted to shout for joy. "We made it! I feel better already!"

"Don't let your guard down. Let's get our bods out of here," Chris grinned. "Leave everything as is. The boat will be discovered soon enough."

They climbed down the stern of the boat and slid into the water. Chris swam ahead of Tom, and when Chris reached the shore, he scurried toward the bushes and sat down on a rock to catch his breath and wait for Tom, immediately behind him.

"Okay, I got us this far. Now what?" Chris asked.

"We have to find our way back to George Town. I figure the village is about four miles from here. Want me to call a taxi?" Tom said jokingly.

"Ha, ha, ha! You're so funny!" Chris said.

Based on the position of the sun, they knew they had to turn left and head south to get to town. Already the day was hot. The scrub trees along the dirt road offered little or no shade and blocked what precious breeze there was moving across the island. If not for the humidity, they could have been in a desert in August. They chose not to run, to conserve their energy and not become dehydrated. They set out at a moderate but steady pace. In about twenty minutes, they saw a cloud of dust on the road, perhaps a mile north, moving toward them.

"Hey, do we dare hitch a ride with someone?" Chris asked.

"Why not? It's probably okay. I doubt anyone here knows yet about our escape from Cat Island. Let's go for it," he said.

As the dust cloud came closer, they could see that it was headed by an old pickup truck. Chris stood on the side of the road and held out his thumb. The truck slowed down and stopped about twenty feet beyond where they stood. The thick dust cloud caught up with them and prevented them from seeing the truck driver inside. Coughing and wiping their faces, they struggled to walk forward to meet the driver.

"Hi. Any chance we could get a lift with you to George Town?" Chris asked.

"I reckin. Where 'bouts youse guys goin' in George Town?" he asked.

"Well, uh, I'll have to show you when we get there. It's hard to explain from out here. We're staying with a friend," Chris said, stretching the truth.

"Okay, git in. But one of youse'll hafta ride in the back. Alright?" he said.

Tom hopped in the back, Chris climbed in the front seat, and they headed down the potholed, dirt road to town. The driver kept staring at Chris until he finally struck up a conversation.

"How come yur clothes are wringin' wet? Git caught in the rain, did ya? Ain't seen rain here in many days," he probed.

"Well, uh, I fell in the water while standing on a rock at the water's edge back there at Simon's Point," Chris lied.

"Oh, I see." There was a long pause. The driver narrowed his eyes and fixed Chris with a look. "Then how come yur friend's all wet, too?"

"Well, see, he was standing next to me, and when I slipped, I reached out and grabbed the nearest thing around to get my balance," Chris laughed. "Just so happened that was my friend's arm. I pulled him right in with me. And let me tell ya, he was none too happy about it."

The driver stopped firing questions at him for a few minutes. Then he asked, "What were youse doin' at Simons Point?"

"Just exploring the area ... looking for a good place to do some snorkeling along the reef." Chris raised his left arm and rested it casually across the back of the bench seat.

Apparently not yet satisfied, the driver kept on shooting questions. "How'd ya get there? Where's yur car?"

"Oh, our friend dropped us off," Chris answered.

"So, where's that friend now, boy?" the driver continued.

Chris was getting extremely uncomfortable with all this third degree questioning. If this dragged on much further, he might inadvertently reveal what was really happening. He squirmed in his seat so much so that the driver started noticing that, too.

"Yur sure wiggling around. Got sand crabs in yur pants?"

"Right. The salt water is really itching my skin. It's horribly irritating," Chris pretended.

"As I say before, where's ya friend? Ya say a friend brung

ya here," the driver persisted.

"He had other things to do today. We told him we'd hike back. It's not that far. But that was before we fell in the water."

Chris chuckled, then leaned toward the driver. "Look, it's really not a big mystery. My friend and I are working on a special project that involves us studying marine life around a coral reef in the tropics," he said, hoping that would stop the interrogation.

It worked. They continued driving down the road in silence until they reached the outskirts of George Town.

"Okay, we reached the settlement. Where'd ya say youse were goin'?" the driver asked again.

"Turn left at the next intersection. We're staying at a house just a couple of blocks on the next street," Chris said, making it up as they drove along. He didn't want to reveal the place where they were actually staying, so when the driver turned left and went two blocks, Chris said, "Stop. This is it. We can walk from here. Thanks so much for the ride."

The driver stopped, Chris and Tom got out and stood in front of a house for a few moments pretending to carry on a conversation before they went inside. The driver proceeded to the next corner, turned right and disappeared. Chris and Tom immediately walked the other direction toward the house they had rented. After several blocks, they found their cottage and went inside. The first item on the agenda was to strip off their wet, salty clothes, take showers and put on clean ones. Then they fixed themselves something to eat and drink.

As they sat at the table finishing the last few bites of ham sandwiches, a thought suddenly flashed through Tom's mind. He said to Chris, "I've got it. I think I know how these crooks knew we were flying to Cat Island. I made a phone call to the George Town airport and to the Conch Harbour Inn a month before we left Wilmington to ask about Barrington Plantation!"

"You did? I guess I did hear a little about that," Chris said

Tom held up his hand. "Listen, the guy at the airport and the inn manager both repeatedly told me that the old Barrington Plantation site was abandoned, and they insisted that it was not worth going there. In fact, they even said it was dangerous. They kept saying the area was unoccupied. Then the manager asked me to repeat where I was calling from … to verify where I lived."

Chris' eyes widened, "Are you serious?"

Tom nodded, "Wait; there's more. That night, I had a hang-up call. I could hear a faint hissing, like the call was long distance. Someone asked whether I was Tom Hannaford. I said, 'Yes.' Then the line went dead. Now that I think about it, I bet the call was from the Conch Harbour Inn manager. He was probably calling me back to verify where I lived through my phone number listing. When he became convinced that we were going to fly to George Town and possibly on to Cutlass Bay, he got worried. That must be when they sent Sheila and Renee to try to stop us."

At Chris' frown, Tom waved a hand. "I know this is all just speculation, but it's the only way that everything fits together."

Chris responded, "If you're right, we have to get out of here. Somehow we have to get the authorities involved to find out who's who. But first we have to get out of here," he repeated.

"I think right now we have to get out of this house ..." Tom said, "and find a more secure place to hide until we can figure out how to escape. Half of George Town could be in on this counterfeiting job or is being paid hush money to stay quiet about it. I'm sure the airport staff is involved, because the printed money is being smuggled out of the Bahamas somehow. The Conch Harbor Inn is involved, too… maybe even Ms. Pendella who owns this house. I don't think we can trust anyone. By the end of the day, the word will be out about us, and we'll be hunted down like hounds chase a coon."

"Yep. Sounds about right," Chris agreed as he looked grimly at Tom.

"Okay. Then let's pack up and hit the road. We'll be safer finding a house in the country where the owner would rent us a room for a few days," Tom suggested.

They stuffed their clothes and some food into their suitcases and left the house. They knew they had to do some fast hiking over a long distance to find a suitable hiding place. They stayed on the less populated streets and headed out of town toward the northwest. After having trudged for about two hours, they felt confident that they had gone far enough away from George Town into the rural areas of the island. They started looking for a possible place to stay.

Just ahead on the right of the road they spotted a small shack with a man and a woman sitting in rocking chairs on the porch. In the front yard, some chickens pecked and a couple of pigs rooted along the ground looking for bites of food. Clothes hung on a line along the side of the house. At the driveway entrance, an abandoned car rusted in the ditch, and right next to the car was a mailbox with the name, *SIMMS*, hand painted in white letters on the side. A bent television antenna was strapped to a weather-beaten roof. The windows had no screens or panes, and the front door stood wide open. Chris and Tom looked at each other and shrugged their shoulders.

"Why not?" Tom said. "This could be a perfect hideout. Who would think to look for tourists here?"

"Okay, but what are we going to tell them?" Chris asked.

Tom thought a few seconds. "How about we tell them we're post-graduate students doing a research project on rural life in the central Bahamas, and one of our requirements is to live in a home with a local family for a few days and learn how they live. We could agree to pay them for our stay. How much money do you have with you?"

Chris looked in his wallet. "I've got $200. How about you?" he asked.

Tom examined his cash situation and found $350. "We could start by offering them a little money for a brief interview. If everything goes well, we could ask them to let us stay for a day or two, say for $200 more. If they want more, we can go higher. We might even find help while we're here."

Chris agreed and they headed to the driveway entrance and toward the house. The dogs immediately woke up and bounded down the steps onto the dirt driveway to greet them. They weren't sure for a moment whether they were going to be attacked, but the dogs' tails were wagging at the same time they were barking. They came up to Chris first and licked his hand.

"I guess we're accepted … by the dogs anyway," Tom said.

They waved at the couple still sitting in their chairs. The couple didn't wave back, apparently not as trusting as their dogs. Tom and Chris continued until they reached the bottom of the porch steps.

"Good afternoon, Ma'am, Sir," Tom smiled politely.

"Hey," the man responded.

"Uh, Sir, my name is Tom and this is Chris. Could we come up and talk to you for a minute?" he asked.

"Maybe. What do you want?" he asked with skepticism.

"Well, we're post-graduate students doing some research in this area, and we have some questions we'd like to ask you. Do you have a few minutes? We can pay you for your time," Tom offered.

"How much you pay?" the man asked.

"It depends on how much time you have. Let's say for half a day of your time, we can give you $25," Tom offered.

"You pay $30," he said.

Tom looked at Chris and he nodded his approval. They walked up the steps carrying their suitcases and used them for chairs as they sat in front of the couple. Tom handed the man the money.

"You must be Mr. Simms," Tom said, remembering the name on the mailbox.

"You got that right," he answered. "Joshua Simms. And dis is ma wife, Cora."

"Pleased to meet you. Is it okay if we call you Josh and Cora?" Tom asked.

"Well, I reckin you can. Whatever you want," he said.

Tom and Chris had to do some very creative story telling, so they started asking them questions about daily life in the rural areas of the Bahamas. They asked them about their ancestors, how long they had settled this area and what they did for a livelihood.

After a hour of questions and answers, Tom said, "You both are absolutely fascinating. We sure would like to learn more."

Tom looked at Chris and cleared his throat, "Um, well, our doctoral thesis…." He waved his hand between himself and Chris. "*Anthropology, A Study of Indigenous Peoples in Their Native Environment,* would be so enriched if we could actually spend a few days living here with you to experience first hand what it's like on a daily basis, what kind of food you eat, how you go about your daily chores. We could even help you with some of them."

Tom paused. He'd caught a glimpse of his Chris' telltale twitching nostrils as he'd spun the fictional name of their fictional doctoral thesis, and he knew Chris was on the verge of laughing out loud and blowing the whole thing.

"Tell you what," Tom rushed on. "Suppose we offer you $200 to stay with you for a few days? We promise to help some so we won't be a burden. And we don't need a bedroom to ourselves. We can sleep on the couch or even the floor if that's all right with you. How about it?"

Josh motioned to Cora to get up, and then he said to them, "If you excuse us for a moment, we need to talk. Stay here. We'll be right back."

They left the porch and went inside the house. A few minutes later they returned, and he said they had agreed, if Tom and Chris gave them the money up front. Then he added, "You can stay three days. For longer, you pay more, in advance, okay?"

"Yes, that's perfect. Where can we put our suitcases?" Tom asked.

"Come with me. You can put your belongins in da front room. We've got two sofas in this room. You can sleep on dis one, and your friend can sleep on dat one over thar. We don't have no fancy food, so if yur expectin' some big city restaurant food, it ain't here," his eyes shinning proudly. "And da toilet is in da backyard ... in dat shed by da fence," he added, pointing to it through the open window. "And der ain't no bath here neither. Jest a shower on the da porch. We'll give you a towel."

"That's fine with us." Chris said solemnly. "We can manage it. Like Tom said, we want to experience your lifestyle ourselves for our dissertation."

CHAPTER 16

The Search

Sheila climbed up out of the old cellar on Cat Island. She and Rafael were both nervous that Federal Agents would come swarming onto the island at any time if Tom and Chris weren't caught soon. Destroying their plane at the Cutlass Bay airstrip was a significant step in assuring their capture and being out of Boss' reach at the moment. Sheila now felt confident that it would be only a matter of hours before Tom and Chris would be flushed out of the jungle and finished off. Even Rafael agreed that there was no way they could get off the small strip of land in the middle of the Atlantic. Their avenue of escape was blocked off.

At ten o'clock in the morning these murderous crooks from the Barrington Plantation operation had planned to meet the boat from the freighter carrying crates of printing paper and ink at the Whale Creek dock. Half an hour before the scheduled rendezvous, Sheila and Rafael left the old ruins and headed down the well-hidden, dirt pathway along the north side of the hill to the creek. In twenty minutes they reached the dock, just in time for the arrival of the supply boat.

"How was your voyage here from Miami?" Sheila asked the Cuban.

"Boring as usual."

"Listen," Sheila said. "I need to talk to Captain Garth. Is he still on board?"

"Yes."

"Good, I need to catch a ride to the ship as soon as we've delivered these goods to the top of the hill, okay?" Sheila said.

"Sure. Fine with me. Is he expecting you?"

"No, but something urgent has come up, and I don't want to

talk to him about it on the radio," Sheila continued. "Here, let me help you break down these pallets. Then we'll take the paper and ink to the site."

The Cuban, Jones, Rafael and Sheila pulled out their long knives and began cutting the straps loose that held the containers to the pallets. Using a crowbar, they broke free the wooden slats from the sides of the ink cartons and tossed them on the beach. Two of them walked up a narrow, overgrown path leading away from the creek for about one hundred feet until they reached a patch of thick brush. The Cuban thrust his arm deep in the underbrush, grabbed the handle of a wooden cart and pulled it out to the cleared area. Then he reached in the brush again and pulled out a second cart. The Cuban and Jones towed the carts back to the dock, and the four of them filled them with the paper rolls and ink containers. When the carts were full, one person pushed and another pulled the loads up the hill. Because the hill was steep and the loads heavy, it took them nearly thirty minutes to reach the top and another fifteen minutes to off-load the supplies into the printing cellar.

Finally finished, they rested under the canopy of trees. Sheila waited a few minutes, then spoke to the small group of men gathered there.

"Two days ago, we had unexpected visitors—a couple of real cowboys from the States. They flew their private plane into the abandoned dirt strip at Cutlass Bay and hiked up to this spot. I don't know if they expected to find something here or accidentally stumbled on our operation, but we've been discovered. Rafael caught 'em near the window."

At the collective rumble from the men, Sheila waved them all down, and continued, "We don't know what they saw, but we have to assume that they saw everything. Unfortunately, they got away and have hidden somewhere on the island. Now, I took care of their plane, so they can't fly out. And we're too far from the nearest land for them to swim. So we know they're still here. We should be able to catch them today. They can't hide forever."

Sheila looked from face to face at the group of men. These were tough, beefy men, who were used to a life that sometimes included bloodshed. Nothing she said was going to shock them.

"They have no food, and the local people are on our side. So, we're going to get them—Boss's orders! No matter what! They can't get off this island. We have to end this fiasco today. I need your help and the help of your crew."

Sheila turned to Jones and the Cuban, "That's why I have to talk to Captain Garth. We have to track them down today. Are you with me, guys?"

There was a unanimous, "Aye."

Rafael and Jones agreed to stay at the Barrington ruins while Sheila and the Cuban headed back down the hill to the dock. Upon reaching Whale Creek, the Cuban loosened the rope that had secured the boat to the piling on the dock while Sheila climbed on board. With a couple of pulls on the starter cord the outboard engine roared into action. He steered the boat out the channel entrance into the bay and headed straight for the freighter at anchor a short distance away.

"Are you scared? I mean, do you think those boys could escape and turn us in?" the Cuban asked."

"Nah. They'll be caught today. Trust me." Her brilliant blue eyes glittered as she swung a cold gaze back toward the island. "I just hope I'm the one who has the privilege of taking them out."

They approached the starboard side of the vessel and spotted Yan leaning over the railing from the second level of the deck.

"Yan, give us hand. Get the crew together for an urgent meeting," the Cuban shouted.

Yan lowered the ladder and climbed down to help them secure the boat to the lower platform. Then the three scurried up to the main deck and requested to see Captain Garth.

In a few minutes the captain appeared on deck and agreed to convene all hands in his cabin. Meanwhile, Yan went aft to gather up the remaining crew. Sheila, the Cuban and Captain Garth entered the captain's cabin. They pulled up some chairs around his table in the center, and Sheila began her tale. Within minutes, the remaining crew arrived. The captain interrupted Sheila to bring the others up to speed about the events happening on shore. Then

Sheila continued with her story.

"So, we have to find them. It's not a matter of *should*. It's a matter of *must*. They are endangering our operations, and we can't let them escape. I need everyone's help. Are you all with me?" Sheila concluded.

"Aye," the crew responded.

When Sheila finished, the Captain agreed the matter was of the utmost urgency. He ordered the entire crew to go ashore and conduct a search for Tom and Chris. The crew and Sheila lowered themselves into the boat at the bottom of the ladder, and the Cuban restarted the motor. Quickly, the Cuban steered the small boat back to Whale Creek dock. It was nearly noon when they climbed the hill to the plantation to meet Rafael and Jones. They split up into three search parties of two people each.

Rafael's coworker volunteered to stay and guard the print shop. Jones had the foresight to bring whistles with him to aid in the search and suggested that whenever Tom and Chris were spotted, the crew should blow their whistles as loudly as possible to alert the rest of the search parties that the fugitives have been located.

By one o'clock the hunters had dispersed down the hillside to the north, south and west. They had arranged to return to the Barrington operation by 5:00, with or without their quarry. Sheila and Captain Garth paired up and headed down to Cutlass Bay and to the airstrip, with the idea of heading east along the coast line from there. Rafael and Jones headed over to the north side of the island in the direction of Whale Creek and then east, while the Cuban and Yan headed to the beach on the west side of the island.

As Sheila and the captain trotted down the winding path, she said, "Capt'n, I'm sorry I had to involve you and your men in this, but I really appreciate your help. Quite frankly, Boss is on a tear, and he's holding me responsible for this situation. I don't even know if I'd still be alive if I hadn't blown up their plane yesterday, so the intruders can't get away. When I told Boss I'd destroyed their plane, I assured him they'd be caught. He told me, 'Good, I don't ever want to hear about them again. Finish them off!'"

"Can't blame him, can you?" the captain said. "Look at it this way, if those two get to the authorities, we're done for. It's all over for all of us, period."

"Right," Sheila shivered. "We'll catch 'em."

She shivered again when the captain fixed her with a hard stare.

"You better hope so."

They reached the airport, checked the Cessna Centurion to be sure it was safe and started to walk away. Captain Garth stopped suddenly. "Wait a minute. This Tom guy is a pilot, right?"

"That's right," Sheila said.

"You burned their plane up, but yours is sitting here, purdy as you please. What's to stop 'em taking off in it?"

Sheila gritted her teeth.

"I say again. Their plane is over there looking like a piece of burnt toast, and your plane is waiting for them to steal it "

"Hey, I'm not stupid. I knew that was a possibility when I set their plane on fire. I disconnected one of the wires to the starter of the Centurion in such a way that they'll never find it. I'm guessing neither one of 'em's an aviation mechanic, so he won't know where to look for something like that."

Sheila reached into the pocket of her cotton shorts and pulled out a key ring and twirled it around and around her finger. "And I have the keys. My plan is obviously working. There she sits!" Sheila sputtered.

"Not so fast, fancy pants. In retaliation they could easily have sabotaged your plane as revenge for what you did to theirs, perhaps wired it to catch fire on ignition," the captain countered.

The color drained from Sheila's face. "I … I don't think they're that smart," she stammered. "Besides, I think their first priority is going to be to escape from the island, not to sabotage my plane. Don't you think that would be a waste of their time and energy?"

"I don't know. Might be," the captain shrugged, then jerked a thumb toward the beachhead. "They're obviously not here."

Silently, they trekked to the east along the sandy beach.

Rafael and Jones approached Whale Creek and then headed east along the shoreline toward the small cove on the north side of the island. In about thirty minutes they rounded the point and faced the protected cove.

"Oh, no! I don't believe this! Where is my sailboat?" Rafael wailed. "It was here two days ago. I checked on it. It was here."

"Are you sure? Could it have sunk?" the Cuban asked.

"Are ya kidding me? Of course not! It's too shallow. We'd be able to see the mast sticking up if it had sunk. They *stole* it! Those idiots stole it!" Rafael shouted. He ran over to a clump of brush along the beach and pulled back the branches of a scrub tree. "The dinghy is still here. At least they didn't find that."

"Then maybe they didn't steal the sailboat. How could they have gotten out there?" the Cuban asked.

"They swam, ya dimwit! Anyone can swim out to the boat. Ya don't have to have a dinghy," he said. "Boss is gonna kill somebody! This is not good. This is not good at all!"

Rafael clapped one hand over his mouth and paced the path for a second, then almost skidded to a halt as a chill crept up his neck. "Blow the whistles!" he shouted, reaching for his own. He turned and raced back up the steep path toward the old plantation. "Blow the whistles!"

By 4:45 the last of the search party had followed the sound of Rafael's and the Cuban's whistles up from the woods to the crumbling foundation. They met inside. The Cuban spoke first. "I have some bad news. Rafael discovered his sailboat missing this afternoon. We don't know how long it's been gone, but he says it

was there two days ago. Since none of you came back with those scums in hand, we have to assume they escaped in the boat. We got no reason to think anyone else would take it. Right?"

"Captain Garth, did any of your crew spot a boat leaving the cove in the last couple of days?" Sheila asked.

The crew looked at each other for a second, and then, "Not me" Yan said. The rest all shook their heads.

"How could anyone slip a sailboat undetected by a freighter at anchor just a mile from the cove? That's unbelievable!" Sheila snapped.

"Hey! We weren't assigned, or expected, to have someone on watch twenty-four hours a day, lady," Yan retorted.

Sheila exploded toward the navigator with both her fists clinched. The Cuban leaped behind her and grabbed her hair. He yanked her backward and pinned one arm back, then forced her into a chair. He leaned over her and said, "Sit there and shut up."

"All right, that's enough!" Captain Garth's voice cracked through the room like a rifle shot. "Let's look at our best plan of action. Now, I figure they headed back to George Town, the closest island, for help."

"That would be dumb. Why would they go to George Town? If I was them, I would sail far, far away from here," Jones said.

"You ain't got your head on straight, Jones," the Cuban snarled. "It's like this. The longer they are out at sea, the more likely they'll be caught. You forget, sailboats are snailboats."

"Shut up, you two," Sheila said. "I agree with Captain Garth. All of their personal belongings are there in a cottage they had rented in town. I'm sure they headed in that direction."

"But how long ago could that have been? Maybe they're still at sea and haven't made it yet to George Town," the Cuban suggested.

"I destroyed their plane two days ago. They've been on the run ever since. We lost track of them after our fight on the hill right after Rafael caught them at the window. If they were smart, they stole the boat at night. It could have been the first night, or with a little luck maybe as recently as last night. It would have been too risky to try to sail out of here during the broad daylight," Sheila reasoned.

"Okay. If they sailed outta here the first night or last night, they would be in George Town by now," Yan concluded. "We gotta contact Boss and have him organize a search party in the village."

"Do you think for one second they would be stupid enough to sit around at their rental cottage and wait for us to catch them?" Captain Garth said. "They knew we'd discover the sailboat missing, and we'd start looking for them in George Town. It's the old cat and mouse game, isn't it? They're smart. So, now we have to move our manhunt to George Town. Any volunteers to call Boss and tell him the bad news?" A deathly silence fell over the room. All eyes slid toward Sheila.

"NO, no, no, no, NO! Not me. Don't look at me like that. I'm already in enough trouble with Boss. Please! Someone else has to do the dirty work this time," Sheila pleaded. The gang continued looking around the room for a volunteer. The silence was deafening.

Finally, Captain Garth said, "All right, I'll do it. I'll call him as soon as I return to the ship. We'll catch those boys in George Town. Boss will make certain of that."

He shifted his gaze back and forth between Rafael and Sheila, then said, "Since we've already off-loaded your supplies, I'm going to weigh anchor early in the morning and sail back to Miami. When are you flying back to George Town?"

Sheila replied, "I guess I'll go in the morning. Hopefully, Boss and his people in George Town will have finished the job by then. I'll stay here with Rafael tonight. I have to fly a load of money to Atlanta tomorrow anyway." She looked at Rafael and then said, "You can come along with me to George Town and maybe we can find your boat."

The captain intervened, " I wouldn't be too optimistic about finding your boat, not in one piece anyway. I wouldn't consider sailing into George Town Harbour with a stolen boat, would you?"

Rafael's face fell. "Yeah, you're probably right about that, but maybe I can borrow a boat from friends to run back and forth between here and there for hauling whatever supplies we need until this gets sorted out," Rafael said.

"Suit yourself," the captain said.

The Captain and his crewmen left the cellar and headed down the path again toward Whale Creek. The Cuban untied the small boat, everyone climbed in and motored out to the anchored freighter. The crew climbed on board, hauled in the ship's ladder. Captain Garth retreated to his cabin to call Boss. The phone rang at the Conch Harbour Inn several times until the booking clerk answered with her usual spiel about reservations.

"Stop," he interrupted. "This is Captain Garth. Let me speak to Boss."

"Oh, sorry. Boss isn't here. Is there a message?" she asked.

"Where is he? This is very important. I need to talk to him right away."

"He's at the airport, but ..."

Captain Garth hung up the phone without saying goodbye. He called the airport.

"Hello. This is the captain. Is Boss there?"

"Yes, as a matter of fact he is, Captain. Hold on," a polite voice on the other end answered.

A couple of minutes went by. Then, "Capt'n, how are you? How did the off-loading of supplies go? Let's see, was that today or yesterday?"

"Everything went as planned. You're well stocked for now, and the presses are running on schedule." There was a long pause. Then the captain said, "Uh, Boss, there's something I need to tell you. It's about those creeps from North Carolina...."

Boss interrupted, "Yeah, what about 'em? My boys should have 'em taken care of by now? I've been waiting for news all day. I'm mad as a hornet. What are those dimwits doing over there?"

"Well, as you know, the good news is that Sheila destroyed their plane," Garth continued. "Sheila assured you that they were trapped on the island. And we expected to flush them out of the jungle quickly.... Uh...."

"Get to the point, Captain. What are you trying to tell me?"

"Today, we discovered Rafael's sailboat missing, and we

now think they stole his boat and headed back to George Town."

"WHAT!" Boss shouted.

"Now, before you blow your top, let me assure you, they can't escape from George Town, because your buddy, the airport manager, is there guarding the airport. Secondly, they can't escape by boat because you control the marina, too. Thirdly, they can't hide in Rafael's sailboat because everyone on the island knows it. And they certainly can't make a swim for it. So, see? You've got 'em right where you want 'em. It'll be a piece of cake for your guys to catch them now. Isn't that great, Boss? See, they gotta be running around like rats in a cage, in your own backyard, and I plan...."

There was a loud click and then a dial tone.

"Boss?... Boss!... BOSS!" Captain repeated. The captain rested the phone down on his chart table and called the crew to his cabin. A few minutes later, when they'd once again gathered around the table, Captain Garth relayed the gist of the phone conversation.

"So, obviously Boss is on a rampage," he concluded. "He's unpredictable and dangerous. I don't have a clue what's going to happen in George Town. One thing is certain, however. We are going to set sail for Miami immediately."

Yan went on the bridge and plotted the course from the anchorage in the bay at Cat Island to the entrance to the Miami River, while the Captain checked on the weather conditions from reports on the ship's radio. The ship's ladder was pulled on board, and the shore boat was secured on deck. The captain ordered all hands to make ready to get underway. Although the sun was lying low on the western horizon, the captain had made this run many times and didn't need the aid of daylight to navigate through the reef fields.

The Cuban walked up to the bow, released the locks on the anchor chain and waited for the signal from the bridge to weigh the anchor. A few minutes later the captain yelled through his bullhorn to pull up the anchor. The Cuban leaned over to the anchor windless, put it in gear and pulled back on the large lever, and slowly the windless began to turn. The noise of the large chain grinding past the wheel, sliding across the metal deck and falling through the hole into the chain locker below was almost deafening. In about three minutes, the Cuban signaled to the bridge that the anchor was free of the bottom. A black belch of smoke spewed out the top of the stack as the ship's propeller began to move the freighter slowly forward. Meanwhile, the windless continued to pull up the heavy chain until the anchor was out of the water and nestled inside the bow chamber. The Cuban secured the chain on deck and shut down the anchor windless.

As the freighter turned slowly to the northwest, Captain Garth told the helmsman to steady on a course of 290 degrees. He called down to the engine room and ordered full speed ahead, and in thirty minutes the ship disappeared over the horizon and headed for their home port on the Miami River. The crew manned their workstations with extreme anxiety, concerned about how things would work out over the next several days. The tension on the ship was almost palpable.

CHAPTER 17

The Phone Call

In George Town, as evening approached, Tom began to have second thoughts about the fabricated stories they had told the Simms. For reasons he could not explain, he trusted them—trusted them to the point that he believed they'd stand a better chance of survival if he and Chris confessed the reasons why they were really there. They had to have help to get them out of this horrible mess, and Cora and Josh didn't strike Tom as the kind of people who would be involved with counterfeiting.

"Chris, listen; come with me. Let's go for a walk. I've got a plan," Tom said.

They headed off the porch, down the driveway and up the road for a short distance. When they were out of earshot of the Simms, Tom picked up a small stone and threw it out across the field.

"I know we're planning to ask Josh to take us into town tonight to make a telephone call to the States for help, but I've got another thought."

"Wait, you *are* going to call the police tonight, aren't you?" Chris asked. "Cause if you don't, then I will. I want to get out of here … now!"

Tom held up his hand, "I know. Just let me finish. We're going to call the authorities tonight as promised. But I have another plan. I don't think these good people have any idea what's happening on Cat Island. They just don't seem to be the type. Not only that, they wouldn't likely be so willing to take strangers like us into their household if they were in with counterfeiters. It would be too risky. So, I think they could help us escape if we tell them the real reason we're here."

175

Chris looked thoughtful. "All right, I can buy that. So what's this big plan? After we announce that we lied to them, of course?"

"Well, it's simple," Tom began. "By now half of George Town and certainly everyone on Cat Island is hunting for us. It could be just a matter of hours before we're discovered. If we don't get help fast, we can kiss our lives goodbye. This mob's gonna be out for blood, now that we found their operation. They have nothing to lose by killing us, and everything to lose if we escape."

"I know that. So, does telling Josh and Cora help?" Chris asked.

"If we tell them the whole story, they could play a role in getting us out of here and halting the counterfeit operation. They might be in line for a big reward," Tom said. "In the meantime, we get a little more time hiding here on their farm."

Tom watched while Chris digested this information.

"Okay, I agree," Chris said finally. "Hiding in George Town, getting a commercial flight to the States or jumping a boat in the marina to a port in the States would be impossible right now."

They turned around in the road and headed back to the Simms farm. Their walk up the drive was slowed while they waited for a mother hen and six down chicks to scurry across in front of them. Tom thought for a second about how simple life was for those chickens. If only their lives could be that simple. They stepped up on the front porch where Josh was sitting in his rocker. Cora wasn't anywhere in sight.

"Josh, may we talk to you for a few minutes?" Tom asked.

"I reckon you can. What's up, Tom?" he responded. "Got more questions 'bout what we do 'round here?"

"No, not exactly," he said. "We're in major trouble and need your help."

"Oh? What you guys been doin' dat make you in trouble?" Josh's eyebrows shot up.

"Okay if I sit down? It's a long story."

Josh got up and moved the empty wooden rocker closer to his chair. Then he went inside and retrieved another chair for Chris, and they sat down in a semicircle. Tom began his story. As soon as he mentioned their discovery of the counterfeiting operation on Cat Island, Josh's facial expression immediately transformed to one of intense interest.

Josh interrupted, "Wait! Let me git ma wife. She gotta hear what you say." He quickly got up out of his chair and ran into the house. Tom and Chris could barely hear them talking in the kitchen, but they were too far away to tell exactly what they were saying. Five minutes elapsed before they returned to the porch. Cora was carrying a chair, and she sat besides Josh.

"Okay, move on wid ya story," Josh insisted.

For the next twenty minutes, Tom told them why they were there and the events that led up to the counterfeiting discovery. Then he explained how they ended up at their farm.

"We desperately need your help. We trust you and Cora and think you are our only hope to survive and put an end to this criminal operation. It could even mean a reward for you. So, will you help us?" Tom pleaded.

Josh and Cora looked at each other in silence. They seemed to be in deep thought, and a decision was not forthcoming. Josh put his head down and stared at the floor for a minute. Finally, he said to Cora, "We hafta talk. Let's go inside, jest me and you, and talk 'bout it." He turned to Tom and said, "You boys sit here. We come back afta we talk. Sorry for our manners."

Chris and Tom nodded agreement.

But Chris squirmed in his chair. "I'm more scared now than I was on Cat Island," he admitted.

"At least they didn't say *no*," Tom said.

"They didn't say *yes*, either," Chris retorted. "I vote we make a run for it right now. I don't have a good feeling about this."

"No, we're not running. I'm telling you I don't believe that they're involved," Tom said.

"But what if they decide to help us, and then we get caught by the gang? They'll be in the same boat we're in. We're asking them to risk their lives for us."

"We'll have to make sure they understand the risk they'll be taking," Tom said, rubbing a hand across his chin. "Hopefully, they'll be on our side, the right side, and this will all be resolved before anyone gets hurt."

Tom and Chris could hear them mumbling in the back room. Time seemed to stand still as they sat in intense anticipation of the next words that they might hear.

Finally, Josh emerged from the back room without Cora.

"Okay, we's willin' to hep you boys git off our cay. But, we don't want no part of what dem hoodlums are doin'. Understand?" he stated.

"Yes, Sir! Absolutely. We don't want you to have any dealings with them either," Tom was quick to reassure him.

"Ya hafta see our life on our farm has always been peaceful, simple, and we don't want no trouble here," Josh said.

Tom shook Josh's hand while Chris blew out a sigh of relief.

"So, boys, more 'n all, how ya gonna bust free?" Josh asked.

"I think the most urgent thing now is to drive into George Town tonight, after dark, and try to telephone Federal officials in the States. Surely, the police, Secret Service or some international law official will come to George Town and Cat Island and address this problem," Tom said hopefully. "Meanwhile, we need to stay in hiding until they get here."

"Well, okay, but if any of dem counterfeit guys come runnin' around here and starts askin' questions and snoopin' 'round, we agree we will say nothin' 'bout nothin'. Okay? And you lay low."

"That's a promise," Chris said. "You don't have to worry about that!"

Cora shouted from the kitchen that supper was ready, "I've got some fixins on da stove. Come to da table. I'm servin' up."

"Sounds good to me," Chris said, realizing that he had not eaten in almost ten hours. Chris, Josh and Tom got up from their chairs on the porch and followed Josh into the dining room. Josh sat down at the head of the table while Cora suggested Chris and Tom sit on opposite sides next to Josh. The room was furnished simply with a worn, wooden table in the center and a chest against the wall opposite the window. A family picture hung on the wall above the chest. Cora opened the chest to get out some china serving dishes and took them to the kitchen. The window was bare of any shades or curtains and offered a clear view of the farmyard outside.

"I have steamin' rice, okry and pinto beans. I'll set them in the middle. Dig in, boys," Cora said. She returned to the kitchen and brought back another dish of food for the table. "Here's some more to fill those bellies—a plate of baked fish and hot biscuits. What wud you boys like to drink?" she asked.

"Do you have iced tea?" Chris asked.

"Yes, I can fix ya some," she volunteered.

"I'll have the same," Tom said.

In a couple of minutes, Cora brought from the kitchen a pitcher of iced tea. "You'll hafta put sugar in it if you want it," she said.

Cora sat down and joined the rest of them. Tom and Chris were so hungry they could have eaten anything. But the simple fare was absolutely delicious. It was difficult to remember their manners once they started eating. They hadn't had a real meal in days. The beans and biscuits were so good, Tom could have eaten three servings. But he held himself down to two.

When they finished their meal, Chris offered to wash the dishes, but Cora laughed and refused his offer on the pretext that only she knew where her dishes were kept. Tom suspected the real reason was that Cora was afraid Chris might break too many dishes in the process of washing them.

The sun finally set and darkness began creeping across the island. They started thinking about their mission in town. They had agreed to leave the house around 10:00. Out of curiosity, Tom asked Josh if he knew anyone at the airport or the Conch Harbour Inn, but he denied having any friends there, although he knew the names of people who worked at each. Tom told him he had a hunch that the management at the airport and the Inn had something to do with the operations at Cat Island, so he was glad to know that Josh had no close friends at either place. In his wallet Tom found the only United States Government telephone number he had ... the Federal Aviation Administration Flight Service Station in Raleigh, North Carolina. This was the same agency he had called to obtain weather briefings and file flight plans.

Josh informed Tom that Cora had to go to her weekly sewing social at her friend's house down the road around eight o'clock that night and wouldn't be joining them on their journey into town. When the 10:00 o'clock hour arrived, Josh, Chris and Tom left the house and headed down the dusty road in Josh's truck to George Town. Tom and Chris were anxious to make that rescue call but at the same time frightened that help would not arrive in time to find them before the gang caught them. Josh knew of a pay phone outside a general store just on the edge of town and assured them the store would be closed, since it was late and in a quiet neighborhood. After twenty minutes of driving, they had reached the outskirts of the town. The streets were deserted as they had hoped. The dirt road soon gave way to a broken asphalt pavement full of potholes.

They came to a deserted intersection with a street light on the corner. Josh turned left at the corner and headed away from the population center of George Town. At that moment, a car pulled out of a driveway and started following them. They continued east until they reached sparsely settled neighborhoods. The car began closing its distance behind them until it was almost touching their rear bumper. Chris and Tom noticed the car but paid little attention to it until it suddenly pulled alongside on their left and remained there for several seconds driving at the same speed as Josh. Tom could barely make out two dark-skinned men sitting in the front seat.

Then the car lurched forward, swerved in front of them and slammed on its brakes forcing Josh to bring his truck to a skidding stop. The two men leaped out and ran over to Josh's truck. Quickly, one of them grabbed the door handle on Tom's side of the truck, threw open the door, reached for his arm, and dragged him out of his seat and onto the ground. The other man abruptly grabbed Chris and manhandled him to the ground. Surprisingly, Josh stepped back in silence and just watched. Before they could stand up and defend themselves, the men managed to tie their victims' arms together behind their backs and drag them into their car. Tom and Chris were so stunned over the sudden turn of events that they had hardly

Tom Hudgin

mustered any resistance before it was all over. Their worst fear had become a reality—they'd been caught by the mob, and they hadn't had a chance to make their call. Just as the gang began to drive away, one of the men opened his window and looked back at Josh standing in the road.

"Thanks, Josh," he yelled back. "You'll get a reward for this." He waved at Josh as they sped away in the darkness. Josh limply waved back. Tom and Chris found no comfort in the fact that it was obvious, from the look on Josh's face, there was no joy in what he had done.

The driver jammed the accelerator to the floorboard and drove the car to George Town so fast that it was nearly out of control. Still stunned, Tom leaned over to Chris in the back seat of the car and whispered, "I think I can open the door by pushing up on the door handle with my knee, kick the door open, roll out of the car while we're moving and then run behind the houses. Do you think you can do the same thing when I give you the signal?"

Chris looked carefully at the door handle and nodded. A couple of blocks later, the driver slowed down to turn the corner. Tom signaled Chris by nudging him with his knee. It was time to make their move. They cautiously leaned forward, then violently knocked the handles upward with their knees. Both doors flew open, and Chris rolled out the left side of the car while Tom fell out on the right. Before the driver could stop, they rolled to their feet and ran toward the backyards of the houses.

"Hey, you!" One of the gangsters swore viciously, "You guys won't get away with this!"

By the time the two men screeched the car to a halt and ran back to where Tom and Chris had rolled out, they had vanished behind a nearby house. They kept running across the next road and into the backyard of an abandoned shack. There they found a tool shed, with the door cracked open, at the far end of the yard. They ducked inside and closed the door. Soon it was quiet. Tom cracked the door open to let in a little light from a street lamp that was several yards away, and Chris found a sickle standing in the corner of the shed. He held the sickle steady behind his back while Tom slid over to him and used the blade to cut the rope from his own wrists. When Tom's hands were free, he was able to cut the ropes from Chris' wrists with ease. They stayed in the tool shed for another fifteen minutes until they were certain it was safe to move about outside.

Cautiously, they opened the door, made certain that no one was in the vicinity, and moving from shadow to shadow, they crept closer to town where they were more likely to find a telephone. Periodically, they spotted the two men driving their car frantically up and down the town roads searching for them. After an hour had passed, they began to feel more confident they had successfully engineered their escape. But the fact they hadn't been able to find a telephone began worrying them. They had to find a phone somewhere soon.

By midnight they stumbled onto a small, dirt parking lot with a general store at one end. There were two gas pumps in front of the store. Between the pumps, a dimly-lit post light beamed across the lot. A little bit of the light flooded the store's porch. Barely visible was a pay phone mounted on the wall adjacent to the front door. The store was dark inside except for a small security light near the meat counter. They remained motionless in the shadows of the coconut palm adjacent to the lot for a few minutes to make sure no one was milling around the area. Tom's heartbeat raced in anticipation of their chance finally to call for help. "I must not fail," he sighed. After Chris signaled all clear, Tom made a dash to the telephone.

He pulled from his wallet the piece of paper with the Flight Service number on it and squinted to read the numbers in the poor light. He picked up the telephone receiver and dialed the operator in Nassau. Chris stood guard nearby watching for anyone who might be approaching the store.

"Hello, how may I help you?" the soft voice said.

"Hi, I need to make an emergency call to the United States … to Raleigh, North Carolina, and I'd like to charge this call to my home number in Wrightsville Beach, North Carolina … and please hurry. This is an emergency," he said.

She asked for, and Tom gave her, his name, address and telephone number. Then she asked him to wait for a few seconds while she verified his home telephone number.

"Okay, Mr. Hannaford, what number do you want to call?" she asked.

He gave her the Raleigh number and waited for someone to answer.

"Raleigh Flight Service, may I have your aircraft number, please?" the agent said in a routine voice.

Suddenly tears filled his eyes. The agent triggered a vivid picture of his Cardinal burning at the Cutlass Bay airstrip.

"I'm sorry, Sir, but I have an emergency, and I need your help. Yes, I'm a pilot. My plane number is… er… was Cardinal N33223. But that's not why I'm calling. My life is in danger, and I must contact the FBI, CIA or some official immediately. I'm in George Town, Great Exuma, in the Bahamas, and I don't have any telephone numbers with me. Can you get me in touch with someone to help us? I'll tell you what happened to my plane later."

"Yes, I can. What's the nature of your emergency so I know which authority can help you best?" he asked.

"I accidentally discovered a money counterfeiting operation at an abandoned plantation. Some of the gang members burned our plane to prevent us from escaping. Now we're trapped and being hunted down at George Town on Great Exuma Island. Please give us a number to call for help immediately. We don't have much time left. We're at a pay phone and are being hunted down right now by a mob."

"Yes, Sir, a quick question. What is your name?"

"Tom Hannaford," he said.

"Mr. Hannaford, I'm going to switch you over to the Secret Service Department. They're the agency that handles money crimes. Standby. I'll come back to you," the FAA agent said.

A minute later a Secret Service Agent answered the telephone, and Tom explained their crisis as quickly as possible.

"Mr. Hannaford, where can we find you if we decide to send a team in after the gang?" the agent asked.

Incident at Cat Island

For the moment, Tom couldn't come up with an answer. He wanted to say Josh and Cora Simms, but he now had seen that Josh was a conspirator in this operation, too. He couldn't suggest the Conch Harbour Inn, the airport or even the cottage owned by Miss Pendella. Everyone seemed to be involved.

"By the end of the day, I hope to find a hideout where we can be reached, but at the moment we are on the run," Tom explained.

"Okay. I'll discuss this with my team. Can you call me back by nine o'clock in the morning so that we can coordinate a plan of action?" he asked.

"I'll try, but I can't guarantee the time," Tom responded.

"Good. Now, one more thing. What is the location of the plantation where the money is being printed?" he asked.

The phone line went dead before Tom could answer. He hung up the telephone and slipped back into the shadows of the woods to rejoined Chris. Tom feared the worse.

"I got through to the Secret Service, and he wants me to call him back at 9:00 A.M. to follow up. I told him where we were, but the phone connection was cut off when he asked me where the printing operation was," he explained to Chris.

"Good grief! What rotten luck!" Chris said in dismay.

"Hey, that's no problem. We'll tell them all about it when we meet them here in George Town," he said."

It was already after midnight, and Chris and Tom were so exhausted that they could barely muster up enough strength to find a place to hide and get some sleep. They quickly located a thick cluster of scrub oak trees in a rustic country area, which hopefully would provide the perfect cover until daybreak. They crawled into the thicket on their hands and knees to the center of the underbrush, cleared a small opening to make a nest, lay down and tried to get some sleep.

CHAPTER 18

Rendezvous In Atlanta

Shortly after midnight, a plane flew over George Town at 1000 feet. It circled the airport, banked around the northeast side of town and lined up with the active runway for landing. Chris and Tom heard the plane and looked up to see what kind it was, but all they could see were green, red and white running lights emanating from a black object against a black sky. As quickly as it appeared above them, it disappeared beyond the trees.

A minute later, the plane landed at the George Town airport and taxied to the parking ramp. Sheila shut down the engine of the Cessna Centurion, stepped out of the cockpit and walked quickly across the ramp to the airport office. The fuel attendant was the only person on duty, and he greeted her as she rushed in the door.

"Where's Boss?" she asked, glancing around.

"He's in town hunting down those two brats from up north," the attendant said. "We had them earlier this evening, but the stupid thugs we sent out to catch them let them escape. They won't get far. They're somewhere in town. We'll get them today for sure."

"We have to catch them and finish them off. Our whole operation is in danger. They must be done away with quickly," Sheila insisted in a state of panic.

"Of course," the attendant agreed. "We're lucky that Josh and Cora were afraid of us. They knew they had better tip us off that the boys were coming to town last night. They've seen first hand, from sad experience, how Boss handles his enemies."

"In the meantime, I've got a million dollars in $100 bills in the plane, ready to be flown to our center in Atlanta ... tonight," Sheila said. "Boss wants to go with me. He's got an appointment with a new client from Chicago at our Atlanta warehouse tomorrow.

So, what the heck does he want me to do now? Just wait for him? I need to get going and get this trip over with so I can get some sleep before the day begins in a few hours."

"Just cool it. He'll be here. Sit down and have a cup of coffee. I made a fresh pot a few minutes ago," he said. "I'll top off your plane for you while you're waiting."

Sheila nervously paced the small office and drank cups of strong coffee while she waited. A few minutes after one o'clock in the morning, Boss suddenly roared into the parking lot, locked his brakes, leaving a ten-foot skid mark on the pavement, and jumped out of his car. He stomped into the airport office and glared at Sheila.

"I'm in a rotten mood. Don't talk to me. Don't ask me any questions or say a word. I'm ready to get out of here. Is the plane ready?"

Sheila wasn't sure whether he was serious about her not saying a word, or whether he expected an answer. She swallowed hard, "Yes, Sir. The plane is loaded and fueled, and the weather is cooperating."

They stormed out the door and headed across the ramp to the plane. Boss abruptly stopped in his tracks, turned around and shouted to the attendant, "Listen, spread the word. When they catch those yahoos—and they will catch them today—take them to Cat Island and hold them there at the cellar shop until I get back. I want to deal with them myself when I return. If I didn't have an urgent matter to take care of in Atlanta, I'd stay here for the hunt. But I'll be back later. Understand? Let the boys know. They are mine!"

"Yes, Sir, Boss," the attendant said dutifully.

They climbed into the plane. Sheila started the engine and taxied out to the active runway. In less than a minute she turned the plane onto the runway and pushed the throttle and power controls all the way forward to maximum. Halfway down the runway the plane lifted off the pavement, and when the plane was 100 feet in the air, Sheila banked the Centurion to a heading that would take them to the mainland of Florida.

Thirty miles off the Florida coastline, an hour and a half

into the flight, Sheila nosed the Cessna Centurion downward and reduced the power settings to begin her descent. When the altimeter read 500 feet above the water's surface, she eased back on the control wheel to level off and pushed the power settings forward again to a cruise speed of 180 knots. There was a new moon that evening so it was impossible to see the surface of the water from the cockpit. Sheila had to rely totally on the instruments in the plane to stay above the dark water. Finally leveling off at 200 feet above the surface and out of range of the ground radar stations, she headed for the central area of the Florida Keys.

"What time will we arrive at the airport?" Boss asked.

"I estimate our arrival around 4:30," she said.

They spotted the lights from the Florida coast line just ahead. Boss breathed a sigh of relief. He was not fond of flying, especially over water at night, and the sight of land ahead made him only a little less nervous. Sheila tuned the radio to listen to the current weather and forecast weather throughout central Florida and Georgia. The remainder of the route was reported clear except for some developing, patchy ground fog around the Atlanta area at daybreak.

"Well, Boss, looks like the weather is in our favor. We should be landing at the strip just west of Atlanta before fog sets in," Sheila said.

When they crossed the coastline of the Keys, she turned the plane to a northwest heading and flew toward the Everglades avoiding the densely populated Miami, Fort Lauderdale and West Palm Beach areas. They continued northward through central Florida maneuvering around the restricted airspaces and the controlled airports on into southern Georgia. Flying at 2500 feet, they soon saw the distant lights of the Atlanta metropolitan area. Sheila altered the course of the plane slightly to the northwest toward the grass strip located about sixty-five miles west of the city. The field was marked on the aeronautical chart as *abandoned*, but Sheila had paid off a local farmer to use the strip under the guise of calling it a secret government project.

The Centurion circled over the field to get a sense of wind

direction, and she then lined the plane up for landing to the west on the runway. Sheila touched the wheels onto the grass so softly that Boss hardly knew they were firmly on the ground until she pulled the power back to idle position. She brought the plane to a halt in less than half the length of the strip, then taxied back to a small dirt road that led off the runway toward the tree line. She shut down the plane, and the two of them got out to stretch their legs. Boss headed to the woods while Sheila called her contact to meet them at the airstrip. Then it was a waiting game to off-load the money and then head to the Atlanta warehouse for the meeting.

Soon, they heard the distant whine of a car that turned off the county road onto the dirt road that led through the woods to the airstrip. It was only a moment or two before Scarface and Renee drove the car up to the plane where it was parked next to a grove of pine trees. They got out and walked up to Boss.

"Hi, Boss. Nice trip?" Scarface asked.

"Too long, Scarface," Boss snarled. "But I'm here all in one piece. That's the important thing. Is this morning's meeting all set with Mussini?"

"Yes, Sir. Eleven o'clock," Scarface said.

"Good. Let's get going. I want to get a couple of hours of sleep before we meet," Boss demanded.

They opened the back doors of the plane. Renee helped Sheila unload the counterfeit money from the plane and stash it in the car. Soon, the four of them sped off into the early morning darkness toward the south side of Atlanta.

"Boss, I heard a rumor that you'd caught Tom and Chris," Renee said.

"More or less. No thanks to you. You were supposed to keep them from ever going to Cat Island in the first place," he growled.

"So, what are you going to do with them?" she asked.

"What do you think I'm gonna do? I'm going to finish them off when I get back to the islands."

Boss leaned his head back against the seat and closed his eyes. "And the pleasure will be all mine," he added.

CHAPTER 19

Return To Cat Island

The sun peeked over the ocean horizon beginning another day in George Town. Chris woke up first and rolled over to poke Tom like a physical alarm clock.

"Hey, we need to get moving. We gotta find a safer place to hide out for a day or two." He sat up and stretched. "And man! I'm starving! What I wouldn't give for some fresh scrambled eggs, toast and jelly, orange juice, bacon and a large cup of coffee," Chris said wistfully.

"Stop torturing yourself. And while you're at it, please stop torturing me," Tom mumbled. He pushed himself up to a sitting position and blinked his eyes in the early morning light. "Let's head back to that general store. We should be able to find something there that will get us by for a few hours," Tom said.

They crawled out of the thicket and walked to the little country store a few blocks away. No one was roaming around the streets at that hour in the morning, so they had a clear run at the isolated shop. When they reached the dirt parking lot, they saw someone move past the window on the inside. They walked up to the porch and pulled on the latch of the door. It opened and they stepped inside. A voice from the back of the store responded to the tinkle of the bell over the door.

"Good mornin'. Need some help?" the store clerk asked.

"Good morning. No thanks. We're just looking to buy some breakfast," Tom said.

"Well, the cereals are on the first aisle half way down on the left, and if you want fresh baked cinnamon rolls, they're over with the bread on the next aisle. Jenny just made 'em this morning. Try some. They're good," he said.

Incident at Cat Island

Tom's mouth began watering at the description of the rolls. He decided they were his best bet. "Do you have any fresh coffee?" he asked.

"Yes, Sir, there's a table next to the meat counter with coffee, sugar, and cream. It's fifty cents a cup with free refills. Say, aren't you new around here? You visiting from the States?" he asked.

"Yes, we're here on vacation. Nice place ... George Town," Tom said.

Chris and Tom helped themselves to coffee and the cinnamon rolls.

"So, where are you from?" the clerk asked again.

Chris started, "We're from ..."

"Florida," Tom finished.

"Have you tried your cinnamon bun yet, John?" He said to Chris and nudged him toward the other side of the store.

As soon as Chris' back was turned to the store clerk he broke out in a huge grin, and answered. "Um ... no ... Monty, I haven't. Are they good?"

"Monty" glared at "John" and whispered. "Don't volunteer any information about who we are, or why we're here, you idiot. We're in hiding, remember?"

"Sorry, I was just trying to be friendly with the guy," Chris looked genuinely wounded. He turned back toward the clerk. "How 'bout you?" he called. "Are you from here? You don't sound like you grew up here," Chris asked the clerk.

"No, actually I was born in Key West. But I married a native Bahamian lady; we moved to George Town years ago. She inherited the shop from her family," the clerk answered.

"That worked out well. You've got a nice little place here," Chris said.

"It keeps body and soul alive," the man said.

Tom looked at his watch. It was only 6:30, still too early to call the Secret Service. He made a pretense of studying a tin of imported English biscuits.

"Chris, we have to concentrate on finding a place to stay until the Federal Agents come to rescue us," he said under his breath, while pretending to point out something fascinating on the label of the tin.

Chris bent his head over the tin. "What about this guy? He seems to be nice enough," he whispered.

Tom set the tin back on the shelf and turned toward the next aisle. "No, he's too risky. I'd rather go back out to the country in a different direction and take our chances with some other rural family. There's got to be someone here who's not involved with the criminal operations at Cat Island."

"I wouldn't bet on it. These islands are small. It seems like everybody knows everybody," Chris said.

In spite of the early morning heat, cold chills ran down Tom's spine. "Yeah, that's what I'm afraid of. And it's too dangerous to hang around here to make my nine o'clock call to the Secret Service. We'll have to find a phone in the country ... on another farm perhaps."

"Yeah, I agree," Chris said.

They finished their coffee and rolls, paid the store clerk and headed back to the parking lot. It was still quiet outside as they started walking east to the less developed part of the island. They had been on the road for about thirty minutes when they noticed a car heading toward them. They dashed off the road and ran for the woods nearby, but not quickly enough. The car screeched to a stop, and four men piled out and followed them. Tom and Chris ran as fast as they could.

They were almost to the cover of the trees when Chris stepped in a hole and went down hard. He cried out and grabbed his ankle between both hands. Tom turned back and raced to Chris' side. He wrapped one arm around Chris and practically hauled him to his feet, but that was all the delay their pursuers needed. They were tackled from behind and slammed to the ground.

With four-to-two odds, the fight was over before it began. Within seconds, both Tom's and Chris' hands were bound tightly behind their backs.

They were escorted, none-too-gently, by their captors back to the road and thrown into the back seat of the car—but this time, the bad guys seemed to have learned from their mistake of the previous night. One of their men sat in between them as a guard. In absolute silence, they were driven to the marina, blindfolded and led down a dock to a waiting boat.

Tom could hear several people talking, but none of the voices sounded familiar. Snatches of several different conversations were audible, most liberally salted with swear words and raucous laughter. He tried unsuccessfully to untangle the thread of the various conversations and figure out what was going to happen to them. But there was too much going on, between the talking, the tread of heavy feet as men walked up and down the wooden dock, boats moving in and out of the marina in the distance and the constant lapping of the water against the sea wall.

They were shoved onto the deck of a boat and forced through a hatch into the cabin. Tom suspected they were being pushed under the bow of the boat. Soon he felt the engine start and the boat pull away from the dock. They could hear the rumble of voices on deck, but due to their distance and the roar of the engine, they couldn't hear what the men were saying. The boat moved slowly at first, presumably maneuvering out of the harbor. Then it picked up speed. Soon, the boat was racing at full speed across the water. It seemed like they were trapped there under the bow for an eternity. Tom remembered the last time he'd looked at his watch. It had been 7:15. Trying to guess how much time had elapsed since then, he figured around a half an hour. A short time later, the boat finally began to slow down, and he estimated that they had traveled perhaps some forty miles based on a typical small boat's speed of eighteen to twenty miles per hour. *That's about the distance to Cat Island*, he thought. He swallowed hard and prayed they were not really being taken back to where it had all gone so horribly wrong.

The boat crawled forward and then suddenly bumped into a dock or piling of some sort. The engine was shut down. All was deathly silent for a few moments. Then Tom heard voices again and someone opened the hatch and walked up to them. He grabbed them by the arms.

"You're coming with me," a strange voice said.

Tom Hudgin

Tom and Chris were dragged blindfolded out from under the bow and off the boat onto a dock. They were handed over to pairs of two-man escorts who led them up a long, steep, dirt path. Tom became more and more convinced as they stumbled along blindly that they were back on Cat Island. In the central Bahamas, only Cat Island had steep hills like this. He guessed the men were taking them back to the counterfeit operation. *But why?*

Chris constantly complained that his ankle was hurting him severely, and he pleaded with his captors that they at least remove his blindfold so he could see to walk. They ignored him. Tom and Chris were pushed and prodded up the path until they reached the top and were led down a short stone stairway through a door into a large room. They could smell fresh ink and paper. They knew where they were. They had indeed been taken to the printing room in the cellar of the old Barrington ruins.

In the tight confines of the room, they were pushed to a back corner, and they each had one ankle chained to a ring in the wall. When their blindfolds were removed, Tom's worst suspicions were confirmed.

"Why did you bring us here?" he asked.

"Ya don't really expect us to answer that. It oughta be obvious. Yur days are over, my friend," Rafael sneered

"Gosh! There's been some kind of mistake," Chris quipped. "We can't help you. Don't know a *thing* about printing."

"Yur some real joker, ain't ya?" Rafael moved over fast. He pressed the blade of a knife against Chris' throat.

"Back off, Rafael!" One of the hoodlums stepped between the angry man and Chris. "C'mon man. Boss wants to take care of this personally when he gets back from Atlanta. We're just s'posed to keep 'em here."

Tom watched with his heart in his mouth. His pulse went even higher when Chris continued to goad the men.

"Oh yeah? Well, when's that gonna be? 'Cause I've already got plans for this afternoon."

"Listen, punk, it's none of your business 'bout Boss," Rafael growled, starting toward Chris again. "Just keep your mouth shut."

"Why should I? Your days are numbered, too," Chris said.

"Chris! That's enough," Tom snapped.

"Yeah, Chris! Even yur buddy thinks yur a babbling idiot," Rafael laughed.

Tom let his shoulders droop. "So, tell me, is Atlanta where y'all take all of this hot money?" he asked.

Rafael snorted. "Ha, ya really do think I'm a fool? What we do with the money is for us to know and you to find out. But since ya only have a few hours to live, ya won't have a chance to find out, will you?" Rafael shook his head and poked out his lip. "When Boss gets here, it's all over for the flyboys from the Carolinas."

"So, if we're gonna die, what difference does it make if you tell us about the money?" Tom sighed and leaned his head back against the wall, apparently defeated. "I mean, what difference does it make now?"

Another of the gangsters joined the conversation, "Aw, he's right, Rafe. It don't matter what we tell these guys. They're dead anyway." He turned toward Tom and Chris. "Yeah, we fly our money to Atlanta, where we work closely with what you'd probably call the underworld bosses. From there, our associate sends it out for distribution worldwide."

"And your boss man is in Atlanta making more deals to buy his fake money right now. Right?" Tom asked.

"Maybe," Rafael said.

Chris chimed in with a question of his own "And just where do you get the ink and paper?"

"From various places, brought in by freighter from Miami. Now does that make ya happy? I guess it would be a nice thing if ya died happy, wouldn't it?" Rafael said, the sarcasm dripping form his tone.

"Ya ask too many questions," one of the older gang members threatened. "If ya don't shut up, I'm gonna stuff a rag down yur throat. Your choice."

Chris' mouth clamped shut. They gave up their conversation and sat there silently for the next several hours.

CHAPTER 20

The Mussini Deal

In a seedy warehouse section of south Atlanta, Boss, Sheila, Renee and Scarface waited for their meeting with Mussini. He was already twenty minutes late, and Boss was highly agitated. No one made Boss wait. At 11:30 A.M. a black car pulled into the warehouse and drove to the bottom of the old wooden staircase in the back that led to the second floor offices. Two men wearing dark sunglasses and black hats got out and climbed the stairs. They knocked on the door using the code from Boss' instructions ... two taps, a pause, four taps, a pause, and then three taps. Scarface opened the door and let the two men into the office.

After a brief introduction, they took seats around a table to begin their discussions. Mussini had a network of gangs in Chicago, Denver and Los Angeles that wanted the money. He was second in command of a large crime syndicate, which gave him the authority to negotiate the purchase of the counterfeit cash. Sheila opened the boxes and allowed Mussini to examine it closely with a magnifying glass and feel the money between his fingers. He was satisfied that it looked and felt legitimate enough to be passed as real currency. They agreed on a price and Mussini handed Boss a large bundle of cash to consummate the deal. In a few minutes, they shook hands, and the group carried the bags of counterfeit bills down the stairs to their car. Mussini assured Boss that he was delighted with the transaction and felt his bosses back in Chicago, Denver and Los Angles would be pleased as well. They drove out of the warehouse and disappeared into the back streets of Atlanta.

"All right. Let's get back to the airport. I've got unfinished business to take care of back at Cat Island," Boss said to Sheila. Scarface and Renee accompanied them down the stairs to their car, hidden in a dark corner of the warehouse. They climbed in and headed out the door for the primitive airstrip on the west side. An hour later Scarface turned down the dirt road that led to the plane and parked his car next to the Centurion. Sheila and Boss got out, said goodbye to Scarface and Renee and boarded the plane. In a matter of only a few minutes the plane took off from the dirt strip and headed east.

"We have to stop at Charlie Brown Airport near Atlanta to get more fuel. We only have about thirty minutes of fuel left," Sheila explained.

"Whatever you have to do. Does that mean we don't have to stop after that until we get to George Town?" he asked.

"That's right," she said.

Soon, they landed at the airport and taxied to the ramp of the fixed base operator. Shutting down the engine, she climbed out and requested the services of a fuel truck. When the lineman pulled up to the plane with the fuel truck, she insisted that she handle the refueling herself. She didn't want the ramp employee peeking into the back of the plane and becoming suspicious of her cargo.

"I'm sorry, but company policy doesn't allow pilots to refuel their own planes. It's a safety issue, you see. We're trained to ground the plane properly, to prevent fuel spills, and ... well you know what I mean," he said to Sheila.

"No. I don't care about company policy. I want to refuel my plane myself. I want to make sure the tanks are full and the fuel cap is on tight. You know what I mean, too," she insisted.

"You'll have to talk to the manager of this operation, then," he said.

"All right. Where is he?"

"I'll call him on the radio and let him know you're coming. He's in the first office on the left after you enter the building," the attendant said.

Sheila left Boss in charge of the plane and hurried into the office to talk to the manager. When she returned a few minutes later, she was smiling.

"Your boss said it's okay to let me refuel my plane," she said.

"Yes, I know. He called me on the radio. So here is how you do it," he said and proceeded to give her instructions.

Sheila finally waved him off. "I know how to do it. Done it a hundred times. Just relax. Go get some coffee. I'll go back in the office and pay you when I'm done."

The ramp employee left the truck and headed back to his office. Meanwhile, Sheila grounded the plane to the truck and filled both tanks with 100-octane, low-lead fuel. The plane was equipped with long range tanks, so it took about ten minutes to fill them up. Sheila paid cash for the fuel, climbed back in the cockpit and started the engine again.

"Boss, I'm sorry about the delay, but I didn't want to take a chance of anyone snooping around and getting suspicious about what we're doing. I feel safer this way," she apologized to Boss. "Okay, now I'm ready to go."

She told the ground controller she planned a visual flight southbound at an altitude of 3500 feet even though no flight plan was on file. Ground control then cleared the Centurion to the active runway. As they taxied, Sheila saved time by doing the run up checks and instrument checks "on the roll." When she reached the runway, she switched radio frequency to the control tower and requested clearance for take-off. Moments later she applied full power and was airborne in less than 1000 feet. She turned the plane southbound and bade farewell to the tower controller.

At 3500 feet Shelia and Boss wove their way southward over Georgia and Florida. Two hours later they had reached the Everglades and had the Florida Bay in sight ahead of them. Sheila slowly descended the plane to her usual 500-foot altitude and flew south along the west coast of the Florida Keys until they reached midway between Miami and Key West. She banked the Centurion southeast, and when they flew over the beach on the east side of the Keys, she lowered the plane's altitude to 200 feet and headed out to sea. It was not until they reached fifty miles off shore before she felt she could safely climb up to 5500 feet, out of range of U. S. radar. Thirty miles southeast of Bimini Island, the Centurion flew over a rusty coastal freighter heading westward toward Miami. Captain

Garth spotted the plane, but neither Sheila nor Garth recognized the other, as the two vessels passed in the midday sun, going in opposite directions.

As the plane approached the south side of Andros Island, Boss was becoming agitated. He began muttering about the intrusion of the boys from North Carolina and berating Sheila about needing to get back to George Town to take care of those brats personally once and for all. He wondered if somehow they could still be running loose in George Town....

Boss got so upset at one point, he pounded his fist on the armrest several times in a fit of rage … hard enough to shake the plane.

"Boss, you're going to destroy the plane. We'll be at George Town in less than an hour. Please calm down," Sheila pleaded.

"Don't tell me what to do, you, YOU BLOOMING IDIOT!" Boss bellowed.

Sheila cringed and clamped her mouth shut. She stayed absolutely silent for the next few minutes until Boss spoke again.

"I can't believe I have so many incompetent dimwits in my operation. How could anyone with half a brain let those two escape from Cat Island, and then to add insult to injury, let them escape again right there in George Town? They are nothing more than bumbling twits!" Boss shouted again. It was obvious he was getting angrier the more he thought about the situation. Sheila was now getting so frightened by Boss' rage that she was beginning to fear for her own safe arrival at the George Town airport. Boss was so violently unpredictable. Anything could happen.

Boss continued his rant, "And you … you are just as stupid as the others. You promised those flyboys would never reach George Town, much less Cat Island. I blame you for most of this. And you will pay dearly. You better pray that they've been caught by the time we land in George Town… or you, my dear, will suffer the same fate as they do. You understand me?" He was shouting so loud Sheila could hear him over the drone of the engine even with earphones on her head.

"Yes … yes, Sir," she stammered.

Fifty miles east of the Exuma Islands, Sheila told him, "Boss, we should be at the airport in about 20 minutes."

"Good! But just remember, YOU had better not disappear tomorrow. I've got some unfinished business with you … whether I've found the boys or not," the red-faced man wheezed.

"I understand, Boss." Sheila felt cold sweat trickle down her back.

Sheila flew the remainder of the flight to George Town in silence. She was so distraught over the threat on her own life that she had difficulty concentrating on the flying skills needed to finish their flight. Twice, she let the plane drift off course towards the Abaco Islands, losing more than 1000 feet of altitude before she realized what was happening and corrected the situation.

CHAPTER 21

Tom's Offer

At the old Barrington Plantation, Rafael was alone with Chris and Tom. He started up the noisy presses for another million-dollar run. Chris and Tom, still confined to a corner of the large cellar, watched intently as the printer clacked out pages of green bills.

"So, you were gonna tell us who buys your funny money in Atlanta." Chris said.

"No I wasn't. Do ya think I'm a numskull?" Rafael said.

"Of course not. As a matter of fact, it's obvious that you're a skilled professional. You're good at this. But, I just wanted to mention that I, myself, have underworld contacts, looking for this kind of money. I can set you up with some very lucrative deals. Probably better than you have now," Chris boasted.

Tom almost choked when he heard the lies coming out of Chris' mouth.

"Yur nothing but a fool," Rafael said. "Shut up. Ya don't know anything about our business."

Chris shrugged. "Hey man, I know more than you think. I'm telling you I have contacts with the mob in Boston. That's the hot spot right now. But you have to tell me who your current contacts are, 'cause I don't want any problems between your guys and mine," Chris said. "We don't want any violence between families, you know."

Tom leaned his head forward on his knees. He couldn't risk cracking a smile at this point. Chris was going to make him laugh out loud if he didn't tone down. As serious as their situation was, Tom knew Chris was playing a head game with the gangster, and Tom was willing to play along.

"Okay. I'll bite. Who are yur contacts in Boston?" Rafael

questioned.

"No way! I asked you first. You get my information after I get yours."

Rafael laughed. "Bluff ... all bluff."

Chris laughed, too, which seemed to confuse the printer. "C'mere," Chris said. "I like you, man. Let me tell you something. Not only do I have contacts, but they know exactly where we are. And if I don't call them tonight, they're gonna be swarming all over this island tomorrow."

Tom peeked out at the gangster, and this time he did laugh. The look on the man's face was priceless. He was buying all that Chris was selling!

"Seriously, man," Tom added. "That's why we're laughing. They sent us down here to scope out your operations. You don't think it was a big secret, do you?"

Rafael's eyes shifted from Tom to Chris and back to Tom. "You an' yur buddy there are great storytellers."

"Oh, he's telling the truth, all right," Tom said. "That's the only reason why we're here. Boston sent us here to check you out." Tom leaned forward and looked around as if he were about to impart a secret to Rafael, then whispered, "You see, you have a couple of rats in your organization who squealed on you. Why do you suppose we suddenly showed up at Cat Island? Did you really think it was mere chance?"

Rafael's face drained of color.

"Starting to get the big picture now? We exposed your game plan when we first arrived in George Town. We contacted our gang in Boston two nights ago and confirmed what's going on here. The truth is, we have people poised in Miami waiting for the word to zip on over to George Town to settle matters here ... if you don't cooperate...." Tom let that sentence hang in the air.

Chris picked up where Tom had left off, "Or, one simple phone call will let them know we've all become dear friends and formed a partnership."

"I ... I don't believe ya!" Rafael said, but it was obvious that he was beginning to waver.

"Suit yourself," Chris leaned back against the wall, and this time it was his turn to shut his eyes. "We could all be big winners, but instead it sounds as though this time tomorrow all of us will be dead."

Tom could tell Rafael was thinking.

Rafael whispered, "Okay. But what's in it for me? And what do ya want from me?" he asked.

Tom whispered back, "It's simple. I've been authorized to offer you a payoff for the contact information, a bundle of money under the table, if you tell me who your contacts are in the States. My boss will give you one hundred grand. I can have the money here to you in two days. No one else here will be any wiser. It's just between the three of us. Then my boss will contact your boss and they'll work out the details. It's a win-win situation for all of us. You get rich, your boss gets a bigger piece of the pie in Boston, and my boss gets some of the pie in other cities where you operate. When I went to school for my MBA, I wrote a paper on this kind of deal," Tom lied. "It's called *Trickle Up Economics*," he said solemnly.

Chris had such a coughing fit, that Rafael had to pound him on the back. It was obvious that Rafael was softening.

"All right. It's a deal. But I'm going to keep ya confined here until I get the money. Besides, Boss will be here eventually. He wants to talk to ya, too," he said.

"It's a deal. So who are your contacts?" Tom asked.

"All of our money is sent to Scarface in our south Atlanta warehouse. He physically handles the cash and arranges to distribute it to our contacts. He's currently dealing with the bosses in San Francisco, Los Angeles, Denver and Dallas. The boss in San Francisco is Cecil, the Greek, Romano in the Hyde Park District. The one in Los Angeles is Franco Belliani. He is working out of Beverly Hills with some movie tycoons. And the one in Dallas is Trevor Clankton. He is operating in the Ft. Worth area."

"That's great! Now all we need to do is to make the call tonight, pass on the contact information and, of course, arrange for your money to get here," Tom said happily.

"But I can't let ya leave here to make some fool call. Boss ordered me to keep ya here until he returns. An' that'll be soon," Rafael said.

"Okay, I guess it's your choice," Chris said, shrugging.

"So you don't want the money … and our boys will be here tomorrow to take over the operation when they don't hear from us tonight. I guess it's gonna be some bloody fight, isn't it?" Tom said.

It was clear that Rafael was caught between a rock and a hard place. Tom could tell he was torn—wanting to believe their story, but still loyal to Boss. He turned away from them and continued operating the press in silence. Tom looked at Chris and grinned when he saw his friend's familiar, mischievous wink. They sat silently for several minutes and waited for Rafael to make a decision.

"So, what's the verdict? Are you gonna release us so we can make that call, or you gonna die in the onslaught tomorrow?" Chris asked.

Rafael ignored Chris and continued setting up the press with new sheets of paper. But, Chris seemed determined to goad an answer from him.

"It's sure gonna be messy around here," Chris chided. "I know for a fact some of the most ruthless hoodlums from Boston will be arriving right here tomorrow afternoon, and they'll be delighted to hack your head off and challenge Boss. They're gonna love taking over this operation. Then you won't have a chance. You had better start thinking about your last rites … your last meal and … your last print job."

Tom saw a muscle in Rafael's cheek jerk. The man wheeled on Chris and grabbed him by the throat. Chris' eyes were huge in his face.

"Shut up! Ya sack o' lies!" Rafael bellowed. "I've heard 'nuf! Boss said to keep ya here, and that's what I'm gonna do!"

Incident at Cat Island

The Centurion carrying Sheila and Boss approached the airstrip 5 miles east of the island at 500 feet. It had been an extremely long day with only three hours sleep for each of them. The only things fueling Sheila's exhausted mind were adrenaline and raw fear. She was almost grateful for the distraction when, with only ten minutes to go before touchdown, Boss rekindled his tirade. At least with him shouting insults at her, she wasn't likely to nod off.

Sheila greased the plane onto the runway. Just before she reached the turnoff onto the taxiway, she blew out a sigh of relief and allowed her heavy eyes to close for a brief moment.

The sting of Boss' hand against the side of her head brought her back to reality, "Hey, stupid, wake up! You're about to crash the plane."

Sheila jerked her head upright just as the plane veered off the runway into the grass. She snapped out of her daze and shoved the left pedal to the floor to steer the plane back onto the runway. Applying the brakes to slow the plane down and regain control, she turned onto the taxiway and rolled the aircraft onto the ramp. No one was around when she brought the plane to a halt outside of the office. Boss opened his door, stiffly crawled out of the passenger seat, slammed the door shut and stalked to the office. After she tied the plane down and removed their personal gear, she joined him inside.

"Boss, I ... I have to get some sleep. I can't go any further. You don't need me to do anything else right now, do you?" she begged.

"No. I think I'm going to do the same. If everything's gone according to plan, I told the guys at Cat Island that I'd be over there tomorrow morning. You be here early tomorrow," Boss demanded.

The two went their separate ways and disappeared as the sun sank toward the western horizon. The island soon became dark and quiet. Only the surf pounding the beach could be heard in the distance. The air that hung over the island felt hot and still.

CHAPTER 22

Rescue

Every muscle in Tom's body hurt after a night spent on a hard stone floor. Even his head ached from the fear of what today was going to bring. Hearing Rafael say that Boss had promised to deal with them personally was very unsettling. He hoped their story about their Boston connection would buy them some time with Boss until they could come up with a real escape plan. In the meantime, Tom struggled to free himself from the chain that was locked around his ankle. Chris' injured ankle had enlarged so much that when he put any pressure on it to stand up, he howled in pain. Tom reached over and gave him a pat on the shoulder.

"Hang in there, kid. I know your ankle is killing you, but we're going to find a way out of here, even if I have to carry you," he whispered. "There's still hope. We came close to escaping last night. If we can tweak our story a bit, maybe we can fool Boss into letting us free long enough to make that return call to the Secret Service."

"Maybe," Chris said.

"Think! You're the idea man," Tom teased. He hated seeing Chris in so much pain. "Man! I'm starving. Don't they have to feed us? Isn't that part of the Geneva Convention?"

He was relieved to hear Chris laugh.

Soon, Rafael entered the cellar carrying a box. "Mornin', boys," he greeted cheerfully. "Brought you some chow."

"What you got? Fresh sausage, buttered grits, fried eggs and cinnamon toast?" Chris asked.

"Sure! And then a pony ride when yur all finished!" Rafael joked.

He placed the box next to them and opened it up. Inside were two biscuits and several slices of papaya.

"Where's the coffee?" Chris quipped. "What kind of restaurant is this?"

"This ain't no restaurant, buddy, but I'll get ya some coffee from my own pot in the back room."

Rafael poured each a hot cup, then turned his attention to mixing up another batch of ink and sorting out his paper stock. After inking the rollers, he cranked the presses and began printing sheets of $100 bills.

Around ten o'clock the cellar door blasted opened, and a middle-aged man in a crisp, white, linen suit stormed in, with Sheila following on his heels. It didn't take a genius to figure out that this must be the infamous Boss that everyone talked about.

Boss strolled over to Chris and Tom, stood a few feet away and looked them over as though he were examining horse flesh.

"Well, well, well. So you are the slippery eels. You have managed to slip through my fingers one too many times. But not again. I'm going to have the distinct pleasure of seeing to it that you never slip through anything ever again. Your little adventure has come to an end, boys."

Boss smiled cruelly and stuck his cigar between his teeth. "But first, I'm going to finish up some work here with Rafael. I believe in work before play. That's how I got to be Boss—taking care of business before pleasure. So, sit." He waved them toward the floor and opened his arms wide as though he was hosting them at his country home. "Be comfortable here at my Barrington Plantation." His smiled faded. "It'll be the last thing you enjoy. Get my drift?" Boss turned his back and ordered, "Sheila, run back to the plane and bring up the box of cash we got from Mussini."

"I can do better than that," Sheila said. "I had one of the boys bring it up. It's right here on the floor next to the press."

"Great," Boss said. "Give it to Rafael to verify the count."

Sheila brought the box of cash to Rafael. He sat down at the table and popped the paper bank band off of the first stack of one hundred dollar bills. He licked his thumb, then started the count. Seconds later, he snatched a bill from the stack and held it up to the light, then a second bill, and a third. He grabbed a magnifying glass, peered through it and exclaimed. "We've been stung! These bills ya got from Mussini—they're fake!"

Boss strode to the table and snatched a bill from his hand. Rafael's finger shook when he pointed out the telltale signs that the bill was counterfeit.

"S … see? The watermark's missing, and the serial number is one digit short."

All the color drained from Boss' sun-wrinkled face. His eyes seemed to lose focus even while they were still locked onto the money. Tom realized that receiving counterfeit cash for counterfeit cash had to be the ultimate insult in the underworld. It was certainly an insult to Boss' intelligence, at the very least. No doubt, heads would roll in the Atlanta operation. Tom tried to remember the name of the contact there—*Scarface*. Undoubtedly, whoever this Scarface was, he was going to pay a big price, probably his life, for letting this happen. He shuddered at the thought. Maybe Renee, who had claimed to be from Atlanta, was also somehow involved in this botched Mussini deal, and would be sharing his fate.

Obviously frustrated, Boss stalked toward the door, throwing over a chair in his way. "I gotta have some fresh air. I can't think in here," he snarled. Boss ran up the steps to the cellar door and threw it open with such violent force that it smashed back against the concrete wall and broke the door handle.

In the wake of Boss' departure, silence rang through the underground room. Nervous glances were exchanged all around, even between captives and captors. Not one word was spoken.

It wasn't very long before Boss came back to the door. He motioned for Rafael and Sheila to join him there. They stood huddled together, talking quietly, occasionally tossing a look toward Chris and Tom, but speaking too softly for their conversation to be overheard.

A few minutes later, Boss, Sheila and Rafael walked toward them, grim-faced, and unlocked the chains from their ankles. They led their prisoners out of the building and down the path to the airstrip. Chris moaned in pain and would have limped along slowly, but Rafael forced him to keep up with the group.

When they reached the dirt parking ramp twenty minutes later, Boss grabbed Tom by the arm and forced him into the burned-out wreckage of his Cessna. Rafael shoved Chris into the smoldering remains behind Tom. They were pushed onto the partially melted pilot and copilot's seats and slammed down on the burnt, twisted springs. Boss tied them tightly to the seat frames with cord he took from his pocket, while Sheila collected small sticks, leaves and tree limbs from the nearby woods. She returned with an armload of kindling and stuffed it neatly under the seats.

Boss lit a match and managed to start a small flame at the bottom of the stick pile under Tom's seat. It flickered and went out. He snatched another match from the book in his hand, struck it and held it to the driest leaves in the pile. A wisp of smoke curled up. Then a tiny flame burst out. Patiently, Boss fed another leaf, then a small stick into the tiny flicker. When the end of the stick caught, he moved it under Chris' seat to start the fire there. Soon the fire was spreading on its own.

Boss stepped back and brushed his hands off. "Ah ... there we go. Won't be long now. Those flames will soon build into a full bonfire and consume the both of you," he smirked. "If you're ever discovered, it will look like you burned up in your plane... just a tragic accident, you see."

Tom and Chris struggled frantically against the bonds that held them as the small fire began to crackle more intensely. They heard Boss' evil laugh while he watched. They were so frightened, that the drone of two approaching aircraft almost didn't register until they were right overhead. When the Beach Queen Air and a Piper Aztec circled over the clearing, Boss, Sheila and Rafael strained their eyes to identify them.

As soon as it became obvious that the airplanes were going to land, the frightened trio fled under the canopy of the jungle and raced up the path toward the old plantation site. The two planes touched down on the grass strip, slammed on their brakes just before reaching the end of the runway, turned around and taxied rapidly to the dirt parking area. The pilots rolled in as close as safely possible to the smoking wreckage, shut down their engines, leaped out the doors and raced toward the Cessna just as the flames were starting to blister the backs of Tom's legs. Each of the pilots sprayed fire extinguishers, they had grabbed from their planes, quickly putting out the fire. Another man pulled out his knife to slash the ropes holding the captives to the hot seat frames.

Three special Secret Service agents and two Bahamian policemen also piled out of the two rescue planes and dashed over to the charred wreckage to help. Tom identified Chris and himself to the team and informed them that he was the one who had called the FAA and the Secret Service. One of the Bahamian policemen, Jackson, agreed to stay with Chris at the airstrip as it was obvious that Chris' ankle was so swollen it was impossible for him to walk any long distance.

Special Agent, Randolph Cramdon, was in charge of the team. Tom led Mr. Cramdon and the rest of the force up the hill toward the plantation site, and along the way he briefed him about Boss, Sheila and Rafael.

Agent Cramdon said, "We'll catch 'em. By the way, we met a friend of yours at the George Town airport. A Roberto Role said he had arranged to meet you at the airport today."

"Oh, that's great! Roberto! Is he still at the airport?" Tom asked.

"I don't know. He's somewhere in George Town. He said to tell you he would wait for you at a friend's house until tomorrow. He left you a telephone number at the airport where he could be reached. He seemed quite anxious to see you," Mr. Cramdon said.

"I'm excited to see him, too. We met as the result of a note in a bottle."

At the agent's quizzical expression, Tom laughed out loud. "It's a long story. I won't bore you with the details. I want you to capture these criminals first," Tom replied.

"That's why we're here," Cramdon said. "My men will take care of them while we talk for a few minutes. Roberto was worried that something might have happened to you. He knew you had arrived earlier in the week, and when he didn't hear from you, he became concerned. He mentioned that you had planned to come to George Town to follow up on some theory that a mysterious piece of driftwood you found in North Carolina might have come from an old plantation on Cat Island—Barrington Plantation," I believe he said.

"Then we ran into a kid, Jeremy, who does little odd jobs around the airport. He seems to know everyone. We identified ourselves as police and asked him if he remembered anything about your arrival or where you might be staying."

Tom reached up and held a branch aside so the agent could pass through.

"I remember Jeremy. He charged me a dollar a chock for my wheels."

The agent laughed. "That's him. A very enterprising young man. He wanted a dollar for each answer to our questions, until we explained that he was required by law to answer them for free."

Tom snorted. "The boy is going to end up a millionaire."

"In the end we convinced him we're the good guys."

Cramdon shook his head. "Poor kid was terrified of his boss. He said the man had been extremely upset about things this week. Jeremy had been curious, so he had secretly listened in on one of their conversations. He said that he heard that the two guys from North Carolina had been captured and were being held as prisoners."

"Then Jeremy gave us the key information that led us here. I asked him if he thought you were taken to Cat Island, and he said he had heard his boss say something about money printing going on at Cat Island, specifically Cutlass Bay. And then he volunteered that he heard his boss tell someone to take you to the plantation. Since your plane was not at the George Town airport, we came to check out Jeremy's story to see if you were here on Cat Island, especially since in your telephone call a few days ago you referred to counterfeiting. He pleaded with us not to tell his boss or anyone about our conversation. We assured him that he would be protected."

Tom felt a rush of affection for the scared, young boy with

the dollar signs in his eyes. "I'm so glad you believed him," he said.

"Well, it's been my experience that, in a true emergency, kids rarely lie. Besides, it was obvious he kind of liked you guys. So, between the information he and Roberto gave us, here we are."

Just before reaching the top of the hill at the Barrington Plantation site, the agents fanned out and approached the foundation cautiously. They crept down the rock stairs to the door. With a quick, violent kick, two of the agents forced the door open and ran into the room with their guns drawn. The room was empty.

They probed the records on the premises and made a rough estimate of the quantity of counterfeit money on the tables and the money obtained from Mussini. They found shipping records and telephone numbers as well as names of ink and paper suppliers, distribution centers and mob contacts in San Francisco, Chicago and Denver. The investigators then destroyed all of the money except for one sheet of freshly printed one-hundred dollar bills from Mussini and all the printing plates which they kept for evidence. In wrapping up their search, they took pictures of the press room, equipment, supplies, and offices.

The Bahamian police agreed to send a team to the site in a few days to destroy the equipment and remove the remaining materials. Meanwhile they quickly turned their attention to tracking down the gang before darkness set in. The agents split up and went in three directions with a plan to meet back at the airstrip in one hour.

At the bottom of the hill, however, Boss, Sheila and Rafael suddenly emerged from the woods making a desperate dash for Sheila's Centurion. Jackson spotted them by the time they were a hundred yards from the plane and shouted as he aimed his gun at Boss' legs, "Stop, or I shoot!"

Instead of stopping, Boss panicked. He wheeled around and started running back toward the woods.

Chris watched helplessly as Officer Jackson had to choose between stopping Boss or going after Rafael and Sheila. He almost cried when Jackson turned his back on the two that were still running for the plane.

"Sir, look! The other two counterfeiters—they're escaping to their plane!" Chris shouted.

"I know. I'll git 'um in a minute," came a calm reply. The policeman called to Boss, "Halt! I won't shoot ya if ya stop right there."

Boss kept running. A shot rang out and he fell to the ground clutching his leg and hollering in pain. Blood oozed between his fingers. The policeman ran up to him, knelt down and looked at the wound. Seemingly satisfied, he took a crisp white handkerchief from his pocket and tied it around Boss' leg to stem the flow of blood.

"Why'd ya run from me? What's yur name?" Jackson asked. Boss refused to answer. After he repeated his questions several times, he asked, "Do ya live here at this settlement?"

Boss muttered incoherently to himself, seemingly incapable of answering. He wrung his hands, and wore a pathetic look on his face. Chris watched it all in horror. He shook his head, amazed that a short time earlier he had been afraid of this miserable old man.

At that moment, Chris heard the propeller on the Centurion begin to turn. The plane started to move forward and head away from the dirt parking ramp. Jackson ran after the plane, took careful aim and fired a shot at the left wing piercing the aileron and breaking the control cable that led to the steering column in the cockpit. The aileron flopped down and became useless. When Sheila realized then she could no longer steer or bank the plane, she slammed on the brakes and shut off the engine. The plane's door opened, and she appeared wild-eyed in the door with Rafael right behind her.

Jackson shouted, "Halt or I'll shoot. Just like I did to yur friend."

Chris saw Sheila waiver. The sight of Boss lying on the ground with blood seeping and staining crimson his white, linen handkerchief must have shocked her into realizing there was no way off the island now. She turned around, resigned to her fate, and raised her hands in the air. Rafael did the same.

Jackson approached them cautiously, handcuffed them and

escorted them back as prisoners to the Cessna. Then he helped Boss limp back to join his accomplices at the burned-out plane.

Jackson sat down on a rock next to Chris and held the three at gunpoint while he waited for the return of his team on the hill. He and Chris talked quietly.

The hour went by quickly. The Secret Service Agents and the Bahamian policemen returned from the woods, and as soon as they spotted Jackson and the three gang members sitting by the Centurion, they ran up and congratulated officer Jackson for his heroic work.

"How did you manage all this alone?" one of the agents said to Jackson.

"I'll tell you later. Important thing is we have 'um in custody," Jackson said.

One of the agents asked the Bahamian policemen, "Do you know these people?"

"Yes, Sir, I do," one of them said, as he pointed to Boss. "That big man, he's the boss of the Conch Harbour Inn, and I've seen him many times at the airport in George Town." Then he looked at Rafael and continued, "But this man ... I see him around George Town. However, I don't know his name or what he does."

"I can tell you what he does," Tom said. "He is the man who runs the printing presses at the top of the hill."

"And what about the girl?" the agent asked.

"I can tell you a few things about her, too," Tom said. "She met us at the Wilmington, North Carolina, airport in the pilot lounge a couple of weeks ago. She introduced herself on the pretext that she was very interested in our trip to the Bahamas. But now I think she must have been sent to Wilmington to head us off after I had called the George Town airport to get some information about Barrington Plantation. I remember mentioning to someone at George Town that we might fly here and also possibly to Cat Island, and he had strongly discouraged me from coming here."

Chris interrupted, "Sheila wanted to know which plane belonged to Tom, and he showed it to her. After that, she was gone. Then outta the blue, a girl named Renee called from Atlanta and wanted to come along with us to George Town. And when we agreed, things started happening to the plane. First, we found wires cut in the engine compartment. Then we found a dynamite pressure bomb set to go off when we reached 5000 feet between Florida and the Bahamas. We should have reported it. I *knew* we should have reported it! Just before that almost disaster, Renee also conveniently disappeared. She's gotta be in with the mob, too!"

Tom nodded. "Oh, Rafael told us where the money is being sent in the United States and the names of some of their suppliers."

"That's great! Between what you've told us and the corroboration we found in the records here at the site, we've got a very strong case," the agent said.

The two planes were loaded with the prisoners, and Chris and Tom got in the Queen Air while one of the agents took pictures of the remains of the charred Cardinal 33223 where it lay in a heap at the end of the parking ramp.

When they arrived in George Town, Tom and Chris hoped to see Jeremy. But he was nowhere in sight. A nurse was waiting inside the terminal to treat Chris' ankle and Boss' injured leg. She handed Tom a note.

"Roberto is still here! He is staying with a friend in town. He said to call him when we return," Tom shouted.

The Bahamian Police insisted that Tom and Chris accompany them to the police station to file the proper reports and complete the investigation.

"We'll do that when we finish here with the police," Chris said. Then he turned to ask the nurse, "Where is our young friend, Jeremy? We want to see him."

"Jeremy isn't here today. I have no idea where he might be," she apologized.

"We have to thank him before we leave. He saved our lives," Tom said.

"If I see him, I'll tell him it's important that he come see you," she assured Tom.

They left the airport and drove to the police station to finish the inquiry. Tom told them his story of how this ordeal began and the names of the gangsters involved. Boss, Sheila and Rafael were all jailed in George Town—in cells well-separated, for their mutual protection from one another. The Secret Service agents reported their findings to U.S. headquarters, as well as to the respective stateside agencies that would be involved in the prosecution of the case. They agreed to fly Tom and Chris home to North Carolina, but advised them they might be called upon to testify later, as the situation might warrant.

When the Bahamian Police questioned Chris and Tom about names connected with the counterfeiting ring, Tom thought for a moment about Cora and Josh Simms. Even though Josh and Cora had turned them in, Tom felt compassion for these simple people, who had agreed to let them live in their home. He realized that they must have been under awful pressure from Boss and his mob. Without asking, Tom knew Chris felt the same. Both kept quiet.

Because the investigation was running late into the night, Tom and Chris were required to remain overnight in George Town. The Bahamian Police offered them accommodations in town until the following morning. Chris suggested to Tom that they return to Miss Pendella's cottage. So the policeman telephoned the Pink Shell Bar and asked for Miss Pendella. He handed the phone to Tom.

"Hello, is this Miss Pendella?" Tom asked.

"Yes," she said.

"This is Tom Hannaford. My friend, Chris, and I rented your cottage last weekend. Remember?"

"Yes, of course," she said.

"Can we stay at the beach cottage tonight, just one more night?" he asked.

"What? You make no sense. You told me you want to rent my house for one week. You pay $500. I agree. Your week is up tomorrow. You need move out by noon tomorrow. Why do you ask to stay one more night when you're already there? You make no sense," she said.

Tom had totally lost all track of their time on the islands. Obviously, Miss Pendella was unaware that they had abandoned her house earlier.

"Oh, yes, you're right. I couldn't even remember which day this was. Great, I'm sorry. I thought today was the day we had to leave," he said.

"You still make no sense. If today was your checkout day, you would've been out by noon, not by 9:00 P.M., as is the time now," she insisted.

"Uh, never mind, I guess I had too much Bahamian Punch tonight. We'll check out tomorrow. Forget that I called. Sorry. You have a good night," he said, preparing to hang up.

"Uh, wait, Mr. Hannaford. My nephew, Roberto—he called today and said he's in town. He's been trying to reach you. Have you seen him?" she asked.

"Roberto? Roberto Role?" Tom said.

"Yes, of course."

"He's your nephew? How interesting! As a matter of fact, I'm planning to call him now."

"He tell me you out somewhere, but he say nothin' else," she hesitated. "And I don't know nothin' else about nothin'. I just a simple, peace-loving woman."

Tom immediately called Roberto and gave him a quick one minute summary of what all had happened and asked him to join them at their cottage right away. He agreed. They left the station and headed down the road to their cottage, and within half an hour, there was a knock on their door.

"Man, I hope that is not the police or the Secret Service again. I've had enough of that," Chris complained.

"I'm sure it's not. It has to be Roberto."

Tom opened the door. "Roberto?" Tom asked.

"Yes. Tom?" he replied.

"Come in! Come in!" Tom cried, throwing the door wide open. They gave each other a hug and Tom introduced him to Chris.

"I can't believe we have known each other for so many years but we've never met. You look great, man. We have got so much to talk about," Tom said.

"Yes, we do. It's great to see you, too," Roberto said.

"First, you and Jeremy saved my life!" Tom exclaimed. "I can't thank you enough. The hunch you and Jeremy had to send the police to Cutlass Bay came just in the nick of time. I mean, we're talking just minutes before Chris and I would literally have been toast! You are incredible! What a friend! You are the very best! I just can't stop thanking you."

"Hey, that's what friends are for," Roberto grinned. "We help each other, right?"

"You got that right," Tom said.

"Who is Jeremy?" Roberto asked.

"Oh, he's a very special kid who works at the airport. He's a line boy, just trying to make a few bucks for spending money. We met him when we arrived in Georgetown a week ago. He's quite a kid. We have to find him before we leave the island."

"Let me tell you why I suspected you might be caught up somehow by counterfeiters at Cat Island," Roberto began. "Clara Pendella, who is my aunt, told me about some gossip she had heard about funny money being printed there...."

"Yes, and one of the Secret Service Agents told me that you had mentioned we might be at Cat Island because of my interest in the flotsam I found at Wrightsville Beach" Tom interrupted.

"Well, when I was looking for you and Chris at the airport and couldn't find you, Aunt Clara told me you rented her cottage for the week."

"Yeah. I just talked to your aunt a little while ago. She mentioned you were looking for us," Tom replied.

Roberto continued, "I called the cottage from the airport, but you weren't here. As soon as I hung up the telephone, two planes pulled up to the ramp at the airport. The passengers jumped out of the plane, and they identified themselves as Secret Service Agents when they approached me and ..."

Tom interrupted again, "Oh, we know all about it. The agents told us the great information you gave them at the airport."

"Okay, well you know how it is living on an island. Women talk. It's almost impossible to keep secrets here."

"Ha! It all fits, doesn't it?" Chris exclaimed.

Incident at Cat Island

"Okay, tell me everything. What happened at Cat Island?" Roberto eagerly asked.

Tom and Chris spent the next two hours relating to Roberto all the harrowing details about their adventure.

"So, Roberto, how is your son, Stephen, doing now?" Tom asked.

"He's doing okay. He's nine now and getting good grades in school. He says he wants to work on boats when he grows up, like his Dad. I told him he could choose whatever job he would like, and I keep encouraging him to study hard to keep those good grades. Hopefully, he'll be able to get a scholarship and go on to college. But that will be his decision. I've told him about you two and he was disappointed his schoolwork kept him from coming with me to George Town this time. But I told him he'll have many chances to meet you in the future. In fact, I promised. So you guys really have to come back."

"We will."

"Of course! We're eager to see him, too," Chris echoed.

"Tell me, Roberto, how are you coping with the loss of your Maria?"

"Oh, I'm doing okay. Of course, I miss her dearly … and it will never be the same without her, as you know. But life moves on, and we have to do the best we can with what we have. We can't feel sorry for ourselves all of our lives," Roberto sighed.

"You have the right attitude. I admire your courage. It's tough, though," Tom admitted. "Sometimes I still feel very sad and angry that Sandra's gone. In the beginning, I used to ask myself if it was really worth it to continue living. But I try to keep my head up and keep going. It's been four years now, and I'm doing okay."

Tom reached out and punched Chris playfully on the arm. "It took this big galoot to remind me that Sandra would have kicked my butt for thinking that way. She would want me to live life to its fullest, so I keep busy, and that keeps my mind off the negative things." He cleared his throat and changed the subject.

"Hey, you wrote recently that you just graduated from the College of the Bahamas with a business degree. Congratulations!

What are you going to do now?"

"As soon as I can get some money saved up, I want to start my own marina," Roberto said proudly.

"Well, I know where you can get some instant cash right now, freshly printed," Tom joked.

"Oh yeah? Too bad I'm not a crook!" Roberto laughed. "I thought of other career opportunities. I like to write, and I met a friend while I was in school who wanted to be a writer. He told me he wanted his writings to make people scream, cry, and howl in pain and anger. But he ended up writing error messages for some computer software manufacturer. I thought that was hilarious, but he is making good money. I told him that job wasn't for me."

"I think the marina business is a great idea," Chris said. "You've had a lot of hands-on experience in that kind of work. But if you need any professional advice, I know about marinas. I'm a sailor at heart. Is it going to be in your home town, Deadman's Cay?" Chris asked.

"Probably not. Our settlement is so small; we don't have much transient traffic. I don't know where yet. Perhaps here in George Town," Roberto said.

The three of them were so excited about their burgeoning friendship they continued talking until 3:00 A.M. before they looked at the clock.

"Whoops! It's late. We've got to get some sleep. Roberto, you're welcome to stay here with us tonight," Tom offered.

"Thanks. Sounds good to me," Roberto said.

"Great. There's an extra bed in my room. You can sleep here tonight, if that's okay with you," Tom said.

"Sure, that's fine."

A few minutes later, the cottage was dark and silent. But Tom lay awake for a long time thinking about how he was going to find Jeremy.

Somehow, before they left the island, he just *had* to find Jeremy.

CHAPTER 23

The Turtles

Off the coast of Florida, some three miles from the entrance channel to the Miami River, Captain Garth signaled the engine room to slow down the freighter to two-thirds speed. It was late afternoon, and the sun was casting a hazy glare ahead making the entrance difficult to spot from a distance. He asked Yan to come to the bridge to help navigate the ship through the field of buoy markers in the bay. The crew, uneasy about their uncertain future, had had little to say on the return trip to the old warehouse. They had avoided contacting Boss because of his explosive anger whenever things went wrong at the Cat Island operation. Their fear was heightened immensely now that the North Carolina boys could bring their empire crumbling down. Captain Garth paced the decks of the ship every moment he was awake. He seemed particularly distressed that Boss had not called to tell him about the fate of the intruders at Cat Island. A pall had fallen over the ship—a distinct, uncomfortable feeling that things had not gone well on the island.

An hour later the freighter entered the Miami River and began its slow movement upstream toward the warehouse dock. As the captain eased the ship against the dock, the Cuban and other deck hands threw the bow and stern lines over the side and onto the dock to be tied to the pilings. Within twenty minutes the crew had secured the ship to its home pier, and the captain signaled the engineer to shut down the boilers.

When the crew lowered the gangplank and walked off the ship, the Miami police ambushed them from inside the warehouse and questioned them about their involvement in the Cat Island operations. At the same time, two policemen went up to the second floor of the warehouse and found Rufus trembling and hiding in a dark back room. After a brief search, they found sufficient incriminating evidence to directly link Rufus to the counterfeiting ring. They slapped handcuffs on the pitiful old man and read him his rights.

Meanwhile, policemen boarded the ship and flushed out Yan, Jones, the engineer, and Captain Garth for questioning. They quickly discovered that Yan lacked papers and that he had entered the United States illegally. As a condition for a plea bargain and promise of immunity from criminal prosecution, he readily volunteered all he knew about the illegal counterfeiting supplies which Captain Garth and his crew had been transporting.

The police searched the cargo holds, crew quarters, and documents on board for further evidence that could link them to the Cat Island operations. But their investigation did not find any other corroborating physical evidence tying them directly to the counterfeiting. Captain Garth was a smart man. He and his remaining crew denied having any knowledge of the counterfeit plot. But based on Yan's preliminary confession, the police ordered the crew quarantined on board pending further investigation.

In George Town, the following morning, Chris, Tom and Roberto met the agents at the police station for more questions. Finally, the investigators agreed they had done all they could in George Town. They authorized the Bahamian police to hold Rafael, Sheila and Boss for indictment and criminal prosecution.

"Well, Roberto, I guess we have to be heading back home to North Carolina with the Secret Service," Tom said. "I wish you could come home for a visit with us, but I know you have a job to do here. Thanks again for all that you have done for us."

"Of course! I'm glad I was here to help. I am so happy we finally had a chance to meet. I do want to come see you guys. Maybe, I can take some time off this Fall. I have a friend who runs a small cargo boat between Long Island, Nassau and Miami. Maybe I could hitch a ride with him and find a way up to North Carolina from there," Roberto said.

"That would be super. I'll hold you to it," Tom said. "Plan to stay with us at least two weeks. Could you?"

"Well, a week anyway," Roberto assured them.

Tom and Chris gave Roberto a pat on the back and a handshake, and Roberto headed back toward town.

"Hey, I'll write you next week and let you know how all this ends," Tom shouted to Roberto before he faded away from view.

Chris and Tom gathered up their personal gear and climbed into the van with the Secret Service Agents to ride to the George Town Airport. As they passed through the center of the village, Tom felt a wave of sadness wash over him at the thought of the loss of his beloved Cessna.

"Man, I feel terrible about us not being able to fly my plane back to North Carolina," he said.

"Cheer up. The insurance company will cover your plane. You can always buy another one," Chris consoled.

"It won't be the same. Even another Cardinal just will not be the same as the one I lost," Tom insisted. "I suppose I'll get some kind of plane. I'm not going to throw away all of the training and experience I have had over the past 10 years. I want to continue flying. When we return home, I'll file a claim with my insurance company, and I'll notify the FAA. But it just won't be the same."

"Don't forget, the most important thing is we survived this awful ordeal," Chris said. "And the odds were really stacked against us that we would ever escape the hands of those murderous thugs! We're extremely lucky just to be alive. And a huge thanks goes to Roberto and Jeremy. Without their help, well … you know what I'm saying. So, my old buddy, old pal, the loss of your plane is really not a big deal compared to what we could have lost."

"You're right, Chris. But it's still depressing," Tom sighed.

It was a short ride to airport. When they arrived at the parking lot, Chris and Tom immediately jumped out of the van and ran inside the terminal to look for Jeremy. Their young friend was sitting in a chair right by the window, looking in the other direction toward the aircraft parking ramp.

"Jeremy!" Tom shouted. Jeremy abruptly turned around in his chair, and before he could stand up, Tom rushed up to him, grabbed him by the arm, stood him up and gave him a tight hug.

"Jeremy, you are a big hero. We owe our lives to you. I'll never ever forget you. Thanks so much for caring about us. You and our other friend, Roberto ... you're the best," Tom exclaimed.

"Oh, Mister, I was so scared, but the police were very kind. I'm afraid my boss gonna hurt me. He's so mean!" Jeremy cried.

"Don't worry about Boss. He's not your boss anymore. He's in jail. You'll be okay." Tom stuck his hand out and grabbed Jeremy's small hand. He shook it vigorously. "Incidentally, my name is Tom Hannaford, and this is my friend, Chris. We've never officially met, I guess."

"Yes, we have, sorta," Jeremy said. "I read your name on the registration card you filled out when you landed."

"Of course. You're such a bright young man. Well, I just wanted to thank you and give you a hug for helping us. You are a brave kid! No reward is enough, but for your help, here is a little gift from us," Tom said as he handed Jeremy four twenty-dollar bills. "I wish it were more, but Chris and I are fresh out of cash at the moment. I hope this will help you."

Jeremy's eyes got a little watery, and he looked in silence at the money in his hands, not knowing what to say next, but he blinked hard and gave each of his new friends a big hug in return.

"Keep up the good work, and we'll be back someday. We'd sort of like to watch you grow up," Chris added.

Tom and Chris boarded the Queen Air with a couple of the agents while the others boarded the Piper Aztec. The pilot and his copilot had filed a flight plan straight to Miami to meet with the Miami police to follow up on the investigation of the coastal freighter crew. They took off from George Town, turned west-northwest and climbed to 8000 feet. About thirty minutes later, the pilot contacted Nassau Approach Control and received an instrument clearance direct to Miami.

Incident at Cat Island

"Tom, we highly suspect that a small coastal freighter and a warehouse in Atlanta were involved with the Cat Island operation," Mr. Cramdon said. "The Miami police have boarded the freighter on the Miami River and have requested we fly you back to see if you can identify any of the crew before we go on to North Carolina. The police found a few pallets of ink and paper in the warehouse where the freighter was docked.

"The Harbor Police carried out a surprise inspection on this very freighter when it was leaving the harbor recently, but at that time, they had thought it was clean.

"So far, we haven't been able to prove that the freighter actually transported the supplies from there to Cat Island. Captain Garth probably destroyed all evidence on board. But during our interrogation of the crew, the ship's navigator, Yan, who was in this country illegally, readily accepted a plea bargain and confessed that they were indeed transporting supplies to the Cat Island counterfeiting operation. We are busy checking out his confession now."

Soon, the pilots had the Florida coast line in sight, and they were given clearance to land at the Tamiami airport on the outskirts of Miami. The crew in the other plane, the Piper Aztec, continued up the coast to Atlanta. When Tom, Chris and the investigators landed, the agents from Miami picked them up and drove them to the warehouse and freighter on the Miami River. There they briefly inspected the dock offices and then boarded the ship. Mr. Cramdon ordered Captain Garth to have all of his crew members gather in his quarters. With everyone assembled, Chris and Tom were asked whether they had seen any of these crew members on Cat Island. They had to admit they recognized no one. But Mr. Cramdon told Tom and Chris later that documents seized from the print shop at Barrington Plantation further implicated the freighter's involvement, tightening the criminal noose around the crew's neck.

Tom Hudgin

In Atlanta, the Aztec circled around the city to the north and landed at Dekalb-Peachtree airport. Waiting at the airport parking ramp was another van to take the agents to the south side of Atlanta in the abandoned warehouse district where they hoped to find and arrest the gang members involved in the distribution of the counterfeit money. The van stopped two blocks away from a deteriorated warehouse in a deserted alley, for a rendezvous with the Atlanta police. After a brief strategy session, the team moved in for the raid. The van and police cruisers parked outside the building and blocked the entrance door, while three agents and two policemen cautiously maneuvered through a small door and entered the dark, vast interior. With flashlights in hand, they walked in single file along the sidewall, climbed the wooden staircase in the back of the building and paused when they reached a closed door at the top. The signal was given to move forward, and one of the agents violently kicked the door, breaking loose the lock. When the door slammed against the wall, a startled Scarface jumped up out of his chair and stood frozen in shock.

With guns pointed at Scarface, one agent ordered, "Hands in the air! We won't shoot if you do what we tell you. We're Secret Service Agents." Another agent searched Scarface's pockets for any identification and weapons. The police found several million dollars in counterfeit bills, as well as distribution records. Digging further, they found correspondence with Boss and other gang leaders in Chicago, San Francisco and Denver. Handcuffs were tightened around Scarface's wrists, and he was read his rights. He was informed he was being charged with being an accomplice to the counterfeit money operations in the Bahamas. Head hung down, he was escorted out of the office and down the stairs, while the Atlanta police took more pictures and confiscated incriminating evidence.

They had reached the bottom of the staircase and were walking along the wall halfway across the warehouse, when they suddenly heard the hiss and whir of a large, garage-like door opening. The agents clicked off their lights and melted into the deep shadows. When the door was fully open, a Ferrari shot through the entrance into the warehouse. The car's wheels squealed as the car did a 180-degree donut on the concrete floor and came to an abrupt screeching halt at the bottom of the stairs. With the engine still running, the driver gracefully leaped from the front seat and hurried toward the stairs.

At the sudden call of "Freeze! Hands up! This is the police," the driver panicked, dashed back to the car, ducked inside and accelerated toward the street. One carefully aimed bullet grazed the driver's arm through the open window, and the car slammed into the front wall of the warehouse. It took two agents to pull the desperate, frightened, blond culprit from the fancy car. She fought like a tigress—kicking, biting, even spitting—before they handcuffed her and searched her for identification.

It was Renee Wilshire. She and Scarface, both stunned by the sudden turn of events and seething at one another, were taken by squad car to the police station for interrogation and arraignment.

After two more hours of tiring investigation in Miami, the agents finally returned with Tom and Chris to the Tamiami Airport and departed for North Carolina. Tom fought the desire to sleep. It wasn't easy with the hypnotic drone of the twin engines humming as they passed over Cape Canaveral. He forced himself to sit up straight and decided to write Roberto a note before they reached home.

Dear Roberto,

I feel like I'm on a roller coaster. One minute I am thrilled to have had the chance to meet you for the first time after all these years that we have written to each other. The next minute I am saddened by the events that happened on Cat Island. I am happy that Chris and I had the chance to spend a few precious hours with you and with some of the local folks like the Simms. But I am confused as to why Josh and Cora betrayed us—Josh's fear of harm to Cora, I suppose. I still have a special place in my heart for them, because I appreciate their taking two strangers in and giving us a chance to learn more about rural life in the Bahamas. That's why I didn't mention their names to the police. And I hope you'll keep this to yourself. Somehow, I just can't bring myself to believe they had anything to do with the Cat Island operation. I am shocked to find out that Boss was head of the counterfeit printing gang.

But there were many good encounters. Certainly, the best was meeting a very dear friend—you. Miss Pendella and the clerk at the general store were very nice to us, as well. And I'll never forget Jeremy. What a kid! I am sure if we had had a chance to spend more time in George Town, as we originally planned, we would have met many more wonderful people. If only we had more time.

Tom paused and handed the unfinished letter to Chris to look over and add anything he wished. Chris wrote:

Hi. This is Chris writing now. I ditto Tom's remarks. Thanks for all you did for us. I'm counting on you visiting with us later this year. As I mentioned last night at the cottage, I have a sailboat and would love to take you and Tom on a sailing cruise along the coast of North Carolina. The water is not as spectacular as the central Bahamas, but there are some neat places to sail on our coast. I promise to stay in touch, too. Good luck in your marina business venture. I hope it happens soon.

Chris handed the pad back to Tom, but Tom was too tired to think of anything more to add at the moment, so he put the pad down in his lap and looked out the window. He began thinking about his job at Carter Pharmaceuticals. No one would believe his adventure, unless perhaps an account of it appeared in the newspaper. But he had another pressing thought. He wasn't ready to go back to work. He had left his job a week ago, partly because he was burned out. He'd reached a peak of exhaustion from meeting unreasonable deadlines and tensions created by his boss and coworkers.

Incident at Cat Island

He'd been desperate to get away and relax and do nothing but sit on the beach of a remote island or on the deck of a sailboat over a beautiful reef in the peacefulness of a tropical paradise. Instead he had spent his cherished vacation week under even more extreme stress, fighting for his life. He wondered if he could ask his boss to give him another week off and not count the past seven days as vacation. He wondered whether or not his boss would understand. He just knew he still needed more time to relax.

"Chris, what would you think if I told you I might quit my job when we get back?" Tom said.

"Are you kidding? What are you talking about? You have a great job. What's wrong with your job?"

"Well, nothing particularly. It's just I needed a week off for fun and relaxation in the tropics, and that didn't happen. And I know my boss won't give me another week off to make up for it," Tom said. "So, I feel cheated, in a way."

"Ask him anyway," Chris insisted. "I'll be your witness. And besides, I'll bet this fiasco will be in all the newspapers. That will prove that we not only discovered but also helped destroy that treacherous counterfeiting ring. If you don't ask your boss, I'll call him myself, and I'll make an appointment to discuss your bravery."

"You can't do that. He'll fire me for sure then, if you get involved," Tom said.

"No he won't," Chris insisted. "Tell you what. To make this easier for you, tell your boss that you and I want to meet with him, say over lunch. Together you and I can pack a powerful but true, convincing story about our adventure. Then we can make a plea for you to have some additional time off. If he's compassionate, he'll understand and give you the time off. Since you were thinking of quiting anyway, what have you got to lose?"

"I guess you have a point. Okay. I'll give it a try," Tom said.

The Queen Air continued its flight along the coastline of Florida, Georgia and on to North Carolina. Tom continued to stare out the window, reflecting over last week's events in the central Bahamas again and again. Due to exhaustion and brief amount of sleep the night before, Chris and Tom had little to say to each other the remainder of the trip. A little over an hour later, they spotted the Cape Fear River near Wilmington. As the plane started its initial descent to the airport, they fastened their seat belts for the final leg of their journey. When their plane flew directly over Wrightsville Beach on its approach to the runway at Wilmington, Tom looked out the window and saw his house, and then the surf spreading rhythmically across the sandy beach near where he had found the floating piece of driftwood. They were almost home.

The voice came from far away, then closer.

"Tom! Tom! Wake up. The turtles are hatching!" Chris exclaimed, dropping down beside him on the beach. "You fell asleep sitting here on the sand dunes. I could see you twitching. That must have been some dream!"

Rubbing his eyes and yawning, Tom shook the mental haze away. "Yeah, I guess you could say that," he said.

They sat on the warm sand and watched the dozens of hatchling turtles dig their way out and race toward the surf. It was an incredible sight—one that Tom would remember for a long time.

Finally, they stood up to walk back along the beach toward Tom's small house. Just below the steps that led up from the beach trail, Chris placed his hand on Tom's arm, pointed toward the water's edge, and said, "Hey! What's that in the surf? Is that a ...? It looks like some kind of ...."

Tom took Chris by the shoulders and turned him back toward the house.

"Never mind," Tom said. "Never mind!"

Chris' laughter rang across the water.

Incident at Cat Island

Grateful appreciation is extended for:

Cover illustrations by Kathy Fields-Pate
Text editing by Lisa Kay Hauser
Sea turtle sketch by Jean Kelleher

Tom Hudgin

Other books by Hickory Tales Publishing

High adventure story for adults and young adults
Quicksilver Deep

Fantasy-adventure stories for fans of
*Harry Potter, The Chronicles of Narnia
and A Series of Unfortunate Events*
Prince Albert in a Can
Prince Albert, Book Two: The Beast School
Prince Albert, Book 3: The Realm Pirates

Inspiring Stories for young People
The Promise
Hoot Owl Shares the Dawn
**Chalmette: The Battle for New Orleans and
How the British Nearly Stole the Loiuisiana Territory**

Children's rhyming color picture book
The Circus
(recommended by Ringling Brothers
and Barnum and Bailey Circus
at their online web site)

We take pride that all our books are healthy reading with no foul
language and have some moral or inspiring message to deliver.

Please view and purchase our books at
www.hickorytales.com, amazon.com, barnesandnoble.com,
borders.com, waldenbooks.com, daltonbooks.com and most
online book sites.

Books may also be ordered 24 hr./day
securely with your credit card
at **www.hickorytales.com**

Incident at Cat Island

Tom Hudgin is a native North Carolinian from the Wilmington area. Upon earning a Bachelor of Science degree in chemistry at Muskingum College in 1964, he obtained a commission in the US Navy and served 5 years active duty on board ships in the Pacific, 15 years in the reserves and retired as a Navy Commander in the 1980's.

Following active duty in the Navy, he held key management positions in manufacturing, quality assurance, regulatory affairs and business development in the pharmaceutical industry with such companies as Hoechst-Roussel, Glaxo and Adria Laboratories.

During this period he earned his MBA from Xavier University in marketing and traveled to plants throughout the United States and Europe negotiating and developing product introductions for the United States.

In 1990, after working 29 years in the phamaceutical industry, he formed his own company, Wilmington Quality Associates, a business management consulting firm that focuses on helping individuals and companies improve their performance.

Tom is now a sought-after motivational speaker, delivering his own unique style of humorous, entertaining presentations to audiences at national trade shows, conventions, dinner engagements, and corporations. His speaking engagements have been well received by his audiences and he is frequently invited back.

Tom has been the Chairman of the Board for the Cape Fear Credit Union in Wilmington, North Carolina for many years.

On the personal side, Tom is a licensed pilot with 2000 hours of flight time and has made numerous air excursions throughout the Bahamas. He is the author of *Winning At Packaging* (a book on people skills that work) and has published many articles for trade magazines such as *Striving For Excellence: Motivating Your Data Center Staff* for the Data Center Management Periodical in Nov. 2003. He is a skilled blue-water sailor, and in 1996 he and two other venturous souls sailed a 38-ft. ketch from the Caribbean Islands across the Atlantic to Europe. Tom and his wife are accomplished recorder players. They currently live on a farm along the southern coast of North Carolina where they raise llamas... just for fun.

Tom would welcome your email at tomhudgin@earthlink.net